WILD CARD

NORTH RIDGE

BOOK I

KARINA HALLE

CONTENT WARNING

Wild Card is the first book in the USA Today Bestselling North Ridge Series (first published in 2017), though it can be read as a standalone. If you've read it before, do note that in addition to the new covers, an extra chapter has been added halfway through the book.

Wild Card contains graphic language and sexual content, a loved one with cancer, physical abuse by parent (on page), sexual abuse by a parent (off page), and grief (loss of parent, past). Please take these warnings seriously if any of the above is triggering to you. Your mental health is important.

For my wild card

"There's always this kind of nostalgia for a place, a place where you can reckon with yourself"
   – Sam Shepard

PROLOGUE
RACHEL

The word *love* never sounded so wild as it did when it came from the lips of Shane Nelson.

That one simple word that would set my heart loose, like a horse galloping across the plains, free and real and pure. And yet my heart would always return.

My heart would always return to him.

"I love you, Raven," he'd say, and I wouldn't just hear it. I'd feel it. I'd live it. The love he had for me, the love I had for him—it was in my every breath. It hitched the moon in my sky.

Raven was my nickname, partly because it sounded like Rachel, partly because he grew up on Ravenswood Ranch, partly because it was at that ranch, nestled at the foot of Cherry Peak where the forested slopes yield to rolling hills of yellow grass and sagebrush, that I fell in love with the clever birds.

It's where I fell in love with him.

Shane and I would spend hours on horseback, riding side by side, pretending to help out his father and grandpa by checking on the cattle while the birds called to each other from the tops of the ponderosa pines. The reality is, we just wanted to spend every second we could together. We were nothing if not inseparable.

It's like we knew that time was running out. Even as a teenager, there was a sense of urgency, like a ticking clock that was counting the long minutes until a bomb went off. I so desperately wanted to run away from North Ridge and never come back. I so desperately wanted, needed, Shane to come with me.

But even though he told me he would, I knew he wouldn't. His home, his heart, was here. Not with me. And as time continued to wreak havoc on us, as we made wild love like we were dying, afraid of the distance when we weren't skin to skin, the more Shane continued to pull away. I didn't see it at the time but then again, you never do.

Loss of love is the most terrifying feeling in the world. It's the feeling of your heart emptying, slowly being drained. Because that's the thing about love. It's free to give. It's never free to receive. We all know the cost of loving someone, of being open-hearted, open-souled. We know that at any moment it could all end. The world is filled with worst-case scenarios. People die. People cheat. People fall out of love. People lose sight of who they are, or what they want. People...they grow apart.

I'm still not sure what happened on that fateful night—which of the above it was that made everything crash and burn around us. What led Shane to do the things he did, what made him smash my bleeding heart into smithereens.

All I knew was that the love we shared was over.

Years of being full.

Heartful, soulful, wonderful.

All gone.

And he finally gave me the will, the drive, to leave North Ridge behind.

Never to look back.

Never to return.

Until now.

CHAPTER 1

SHANE

"I heard that Rachel Waters is back in town."

It takes a moment for the words to properly sink in. I slowly raise my head and look at Delilah as she cracks open a beer for another customer.

"Come again?" I ask her, ignoring the stillness in my chest.

A flash of something comes over her green eyes, maybe pity, maybe trepidation. I hadn't heard Rachel's name uttered in ages and yet Del's treating it like we just broke up yesterday.

It wasn't yesterday. It's been six years since Rachel Waters left the town of North Ridge, British Columbia, six years since I last saw her. I haven't even been able to stalk her on social media. She's had that shit locked down since the day she left, as if she wanted to forget every single thing, every single person that had something to do with this little mountain town.

Most of all, she wanted to forget me.

So to hear that she's back, well, it's more than a surprise.

"She's back," Delilah says with a shrug, heading down the

bar to slide the pale ales toward Jeremy and Finn, sitting where they're always sitting.

"I heard that too," Jer says, scratching at his scraggly grey beard. "Don't know why, but I have a feeling it has to do with Vernalee. Beth down at the hospital says she's been in a few times. Don't know what for."

Vernalee Waters is Rachel's mother, and she's tough as nails. She's not the type to go to the hospital for anything, not if she can help it.

"I saw her today," a voice from the corner booth says.

I turn on my stool to see Joe sitting there, palming a beer, cigarette smoke billowing from the corner of his mouth.

"What in God's name do you think you're you doing?" Delilah says, and in a flash she's swinging herself over the bar instead of walking around it, stalking over to Joe's table. She rips the cigarette from his mouth before stamping it out with the heel of her boot. "Damn it, Joe."

Joe just laughs like he always does. I wouldn't say he's the town drunk as we have quite a few of those, but he's definitely *this* bar's drunk. And nearly every night here at the Bear Trap, the same song and dance plays out. Delilah, the bartender/owner and a girl who is pretty much a sister to me, dukes it out with Old Joe over smoking. If it's not smoking, it's that he's snuck in a bottle of liquor, adding it to his drinks or just "forgetting" to bring money.

But their nightly routine is the least of my concern right now.

"You saw her, Joe?" I ask the old-timer.

He flashes Del a sweet smile and then nods at me. "Sure did. In Safeway. Almost didn't recognize her. She looks good, though. Put on some weight, but she always was too skinny."

I swallow, shifting in my seat. I want to ask more but I shouldn't. Everyone in this room knows how it ended between us. Very dramatically, very publicly. Something neither of us would like to think of again. I pushed her away in a storm of lies, broke both our damn hearts, and the only good thing to come out of it is the fact that she left, far away from the demons in this town.

So, the fact that Rachel is here of all places and her mother was in the hospital, the two have to be connected.

This is throwing me for a fucking loop.

Somewhere, deep in my chest, a raw hope is starting to stir.

Delilah sighs, wiping her hands on her jeans, and jerks her chin at me. "Want another beer, cowboy?"

I fight the urge to roll my eyes. I hate that nickname. Cowboy. Granted, I do work on the family ranch as my full-time job but even so, it's not like I wear a cowboy hat and boots on the street. Even now I'm dressed in black jeans, a battered old baseball cap with the ranch's faded logo, a white tee under a red flannel. Tattoos under my clothes. Vans on my feet. Even though it's the middle of summer here in North Ridge, the nights can be chilly.

"Would you run away with me?"

Rachel's voice echoes in my head, a voice that I shouldn't hear. Her face looms large yet vague, a passing phantasm in my mind, that look in her eyes. It took so long to realize what she was running away from, took so long to see the depths of her pain. I should have known from the start.

Shit, I hope this isn't the start of old memories getting dredged up, memories I've spent six years trying to bury.

"I probably shouldn't," I tell Del.

She's surprised. I don't blame her. I'm usually drinking on Saturday night, pretty much the only time off I get from the ranch. "Early start tomorrow?" she asks.

"Not really," I tell her. "Might have to go out on the range, move some cows." And at my lack of argument, I pick up my empty beer bottle and wave it at her with a nod.

"Pushover," she says with a smile as she reaches into the fridge and pulls out another cold one, passing it over to me.

Del's mother, Jeanine, was my nanny growing up. After my mother died when I was six months old, my father needed as much help as he could to raise me and my brothers, Maverick and Fox, while he and my grandpa ran Ravenswood Ranch. Jeanine and Del lived in the guest cottage on the property for as long as I could remember. She was six when I was born and she's felt like my big sister ever since.

And she *is* big, too, as in tall. Delilah is five foot eleven and in great shape. It's probably why she does such a good job at running the Bear Trap. She's usually as sweet as can be and her face is girl-next-door cute, but she's got a lot of sass and I've seen her throw a few punches to unruly patrons more than a few times. Most of the guys don't think the tall pretty girl has it in her so it's often a moment worth putting on YouTube, if you're into that kind of thing.

But North Ridge is a small town. Population of 10,000 in the off-season. Word travels fast. If you're going to be an asshole and pick fights, the Bear Trap isn't the place to do it, social media videos of a girl handing you your ass aside.

Not that many tourists come here anyway. It's dimly lit, the walls dark wood, and there's a layer of peanut shells on the floor with bowls of peanuts at each table. The neon signs, advertising beer companies that are no longer in business, buzz and flicker half-heartedly. Delilah keeps the bar stocked with only the basics, and if you come in here ordering a drink that has more than three ingredients, she'll look at you like you're hard of hearing.

Outside, thunder rumbles, drawing our attention over to the windows. Cherry Peak rises in the distance across the river, a mass of dark clouds approaching from the north. That's home to me. Ravenswood Ranch lies in the foothills, the perfect place to raise beef cattle. There's the Queen's

River running past, then the open plains and rolling hills that run alongside it, the elevation toward the peak slow and gradual, going from tall grass to pine and eventually to alpine. All seven hundred acres belong to the Nelson family. Hopefully they always will.

"Could be lightning strikes," Del says, and when I look at her, there's worry on her brow. My brother Fox is a smoke jumper and the two of them are close. Del doesn't seem to worry about much but she's always worrying about Fox.

"Could be," I tell her, taking a swig of the beer. "But you know better by now than to worry about him, don't you?"

She stares out the window for a few beats until she comes back to earth and realizes what I've said. She gives me a sheepish grin while straightening her shoulders a moment later. "I know. But you know it's my job to worry about you boys."

No. It's your job to worry about Fox. You don't give me half as much hell.

Not that it bothers me. Like I said, Del is like a sister to my family. But I've been noticing over the years that her attention is a bit lopsided when it comes to my brothers.

"And it's my job to worry about the herd. I better go back to the ranch, make sure I'm around in case there are problems." I pound back the rest of the bottle and place a twenty-dollar bill on the bar before waving goodbye to the others.

The air outside has changed dramatically since I've been in the bar. Earlier it was hot as sin with the kind of humidity that makes your clothes stick to your skin. Now with the coming storm and the evening settling in, the air pressure has transformed. There's a freshness to it, like it's crawling with life and electricity. The dark clouds are starting to crowd over the ranch, and long sheets of grey rain are skirting across the river. The skies above the town have an eerie golden glow from the setting sun. In minutes, the deluge will be here.

I used to love summer storms as a kid. I'd be the first to run out into them with my arms out, feeling that charge in the air, calling on the lightning until Jeanine would pull me back into the house, where I would watch with Mav and Fox from the windows. Once a strike of lightning lit our old shed on fire and we had to call on a lot of help to put it out. I'm pretty sure that's what triggered Fox's fascination with flames.

Now, though, storms just cause nothing but problems for me. Because of North Ridge's placement, settled at the southern end of British Columbia, with dry, rolling hills on one side, the start of the Selkirk Mountain range and the Kokanee Glacier on the other, a long, deep lake in the middle, it's the perfect breeding ground for storms. In the winter, they can bury the town in drifts or kill your cattle if it comes in too early. That's when Maverick has his work cut out for him as head of the local search and rescue team.

In the summer, the lightning brings a constant threat of wildfires, which Fox fights, and if not that, flash flooding. Last year we had a hell of a time when a mudslide took out a few of our cows. Three of them didn't make it. I know by now you shouldn't get emotionally attached to beef cattle, but every loss like that hurts.

As I head toward my dusty, beat-up Tacoma, I feel a tug in my brain. It wants to reflect on the past. Not last year, not the year before.

It wants to think about Rachel.

It wants to think about Rachel and that time we were caught in a thunderstorm.

The first time I ever saw her with new eyes.

The first time I kissed her.

I pause at my truck and hold down my baseball cap as a gust of wind comes through. Part of me probably should have stayed behind in that bar, just to be around company. I know I would have put pint after pint into my system trying to poison the feelings out of me. It would have ended as it usually does, me passing out on a cot in the back room, Del laying out Advil and Gatorade beside me for the morning. In fact, it was my father who earlier today encouraged me to take the night off, head down to the pub and let loose.

The other part, the older, smarter part, knows that I have work to do and a head I need to keep on straight. It's the braver part, to be honest. Knowing when I get back to the ranch, that my dad and grandpa will probably be out, that I'll be alone. With the worker's cottage empty for now—our old ranch hand David just left for university last week—the place is deserted and there's something about the open sky and the towering peaks that make your brain go into overdrive. When you're alone on a ranch, you have a lot of time to think. A lot of time to dwell on what could have been, on everything you should have done differently. Thank God I have the dogs and the horses for company.

That said, it's not uncommon to have Mav drop by. Even though he shares a swanky alpine-style chalet with Fox on the opposite end of town, something compels him to come by every other night, either to have dinner with us or to lend a hand. Especially in the summer, when search and rescue isn't in as high demand, reduced to a few hikers going off into the mountains and getting lost.

I get in the truck and hold my breath until the engine turns over. She's been giving me trouble lately and I'm too stubborn to trade her in for a newer vehicle. She gets the job done and, well, there's definitely a lot of sentiment at play.

It was in the back of this truck where I first told Rachel I loved her.

"Fuck," I mutter after a moment, sitting in the parking lot just as the skies open up and the rain starts to pour down, a drumbeat on the roof that builds and builds but the crescendo never comes. It's almost maddening.

Hearing that Rachel is in town has put me in a mental time machine. Six years ago I pushed her away because I had to, because I was stupid and immature and full of blind rage and the kind of naivety only young love can grant you. I pushed her away, brutally, irreparably, because of my own selfish choice. Six years ago I blasted my own heart to smithereens because I thought I had no other option, and even though I've tried every day to put it past me, tried to move on, the truth lingers. It's kindling for future flames.

I never told Rachel the truth about what happened that night. Why my knuckles were raw and bleeding. Everything was a lie, right down to me telling her, yelling at her, that I didn't love her anymore.

It's a lie that's been trailing me ever since, like my shadow, except darker and deeper.

And it's far too late to come clean.

What good would it do?

The rain doesn't seem to be letting up. I shake my head, trying to bring myself back to the present. But what use is the present right now when the past has its nails in it, firmly holding on. How can I go on and shove this all aside, how can I step forward with my life knowing she's here?

She's here.

It's enough to make me go crazy.

I put the truck in drive and peel out of the parking lot, faster than I mean to, the wheels skidding in the rain before I straighten out and pull out onto Main Street. The cracked stone façade of the library, the yellow, red, and peach colors of the historic storefronts, Sam's grocery store that the locals still shop at even with a new giant Safeway around the block —they all blur past me as I hit the gas, getting luck with the lights, green leading the way until I'm on the highway heading toward the ranch. Rain splatters on the windshield and my wipers can barely keep up.

Up ahead there's a car pulled to the side of the road, a figure hovering beside it.

Even though I just want to get back to the ranch and don't feel like dealing with anybody, I'll never drive past someone who might need my help. That's the first rule of thumb out here—help others as you'd like to be helped. It's a wild, unforgiving land and people need to stick together.

Without thinking, I pull the truck over to the side of the road and assess the situation.

There's something strangely familiar about all of this. I don't know if it's the force of the downpour, Cherry Peak and the ranch completely hidden by thick mist, the look of the old car, or the way the figure moves in the distance. But it's enough to make me stay an extra second inside, grappling with the feeling of déjà vu as it smokes through my veins.

I take in a deep breath and step out.

I'm soaked in seconds and I pull my cap down against the lashings as I walk along the side of the road toward the figure.

But it's not just any figure.

"Having some trouble?" I ask.

There's a change in the air, like there's a lightning storm concentrated right between us, building, swirling until I look up.

And meet her eyes.

Rachel.

Right here. Right now.

Standing before me like a rain-soaked ghost, an angel dragged from the river, long dark hair framing her white skin.

It's like the lightning strikes me.

Right in the heart.

CHAPTER 2
RACHEL

"Goddamn it!" my mother swears, raising her fist to slam it into the steering wheel.

Without thinking, I reach out and grab her wrist, just tight enough to hold her back.

Shit. Her bones feel like a bird's under my grasp. It's only hitting me now at how much weight she's lost. My stomach sinks and I quickly release her, awkwardly taking my hand back.

"Your doctor said you need to take it easy," I tell her, trying to sound as firm as possible.

She laughs. "Easy? First you almost wouldn't let me drive, now you're telling me I can't get mad when the damn car breaks down?"

"It's not broken down," I tell her, reaching over to tap on the fuel gauge. "You're out of gas. I'm not going to ask how long that light has been on."

The good thing about our car being broken down on the outskirts of North Ridge while a thunderstorm is brewing is that this might mean our dinner plans are off. And even though Hank Nelson mentioned it would just be my mother and me and his father, Ravenswood Ranch is the last place in the world I would want to be. Hell, North Ridge comes a close second.

Two weeks ago I got a phone call that changed everything.

It wasn't from my mother, though it should have been.

No, my mother and I haven't spoken too often throughout the years. We've both made a half-hearted attempt to have a mother-daughter relationship, but the truth is, I've still got resentment that even years of counseling and medication hasn't gotten rid of, and she's as fucking stubborn as ever. Even diagnosed with stage 1A lung cancer, she's acting like there's nothing wrong. If it hadn't been for the brief phone call from Hank Nelson, of all people, I'm pretty sure I would have never found out. Maybe not until it was too late.

"Besides," my mother says, flashing her sharp eyes toward me, "Doctor Cooper is a quack. He's just being overly cautious about it all because there's nothing else to do in this godforsaken town. I might just head over to Kelowna, or even Vancouver, and get a second opinion. I mean, I feel fine."

I find myself nodding, even though she doesn't look fine. It might be the cancer, it might just be because she's gotten so much older. When you haven't seen your mother in the flesh for a long time, the experience can be jarring. "You know I'll take you, but I have to drive. And we'll have to actually put gas in the car."

She gives me an odd look. "You've changed, you know that? What happened to my baby girl?" And then she tries the key again, huffing and puffing at how it won't turn over.

I sigh and take out my cell phone. I didn't have service five minutes ago and I don't have service now. Godforsaken town is right.

When I left North Ridge six years ago, I made it a point

to never return. I thought maybe if my mother begged for me to come back, if she said she missed me, needed me, I would have. But that never happened. It never happened because she never missed me. I did see her in Alberta for my cousin's wedding four years ago, but that's been the extent of it.

As for me missing her, well...Toronto is my home now. The life I have built there has become my whole world. My advertising career, my boyfriend Samuel, my friends, my condo. Everything that means something to me is in that city.

I honestly hoped I'd never see this place again.

And I especially didn't think I'd have to put my life on hold. When I told my boss Ed that I'd be going down to help my mother, he graciously gave me permission to take off as much time as I needed. My account would be transferred to Pete, who works below me. I wouldn't have to worry.

But I do worry. I worry that this isn't going to be a quick trip at all, that my mother will need me even though that's the last thing she wants. I mean, she might have to get part of her lung removed and she has no one here, not really. My father has been in prison for the last four years, *thank God*, which leaves her all alone.

Besides, in the last three days I've been back in town, I haven't heard her talking to any of her friends. When I asked about them, she just waved me away and told me to get her a cigarette.

Which I won't, of course. The number one thing she's complained about since I've been here is that I've put on weight (which I have, so sue me), followed by that I've "changed," and that she has to quit smoking. It doesn't seem to matter that she has lung cancer, she still doesn't think she needs to quit. That, or she doesn't care.

The only thing she does seem to care about is Hank, though it's in a total roundabout way. She's been acting like she's going to this dinner tonight out of charity, but I can tell she's looking forward to it.

Me, on the other hand, well, as long as the Ford Tempo is out of gas and we're stranded here on the side of the highway, I'm not complaining. It's embarrassing, for sure, to have this happen in your old town where anyone you know can see you as you're parked awkwardly on the side of the road, but the sooner we get help, the sooner we can return to her shitty apartment and hopefully I can whip up a simple pasta for us.

I ignore the fact that Hank Nelson is nothing if not persistent and will hold you to a rain check.

Speaking of rain, the ominous clouds are now above us and in minutes I know we're going to get drenched. The weather in this area is predictably unpredictable as always.

"Stay here, I'll flag someone," I tell my mother before opening up the door and carefully stepping outside.

Even though it's the height of summer, this highway is more or less a dead end. After it crosses the Queens River toward Ravenswood Ranch, it continues on toward a provincial campground and then just ends. As such, there's only been a few cars passing by, most of them packed to the roof with camping equipment, none of them local. One thing about this place that some people find charming is that if you're in any sort of trouble, the locals are first to help you out.

Which is why I don't expect to stand by the side of the road for too long. Not even when a loud, thunderous boom sounds from above and the clouds seem to crack open with rain.

"Shit," I swear, getting drenched in seconds as the rain pours down, hard enough to bounce off the pavement. I move to get back inside the car when I spot headlights coming toward us. I peer through the hair plastered against my face and stick out my thumb before I decide to start frantically waving.

I can barely see through the rain now, but as the car gets closer, I see that it's a truck.

A forest green Toyota Tacoma.

A car that's far too familiar to me.

I remember the day that Shane Nelson finally saved up enough money to buy it.

Oh God, please let him have sold that beast to someone else.

But before it even starts to pull to the side of the road, my heart is already sinking.

No, it's not just sinking.

It's twisting and turning over on itself, a hard, tangled knot in my chest.

I know it's him.

My ex-love. The reason I stayed in North Ridge for longer than I should have.

I need to get back in the car. Lock the doors. Do something totally irrational and foolish like run down the highway in a thunderstorm in the opposite direction.

But I don't. Because my mother is right. I have changed. I'm no longer that girl that ran away. I might not be here by choice but I'm going to stand my ground, no matter what he did to me.

Even if there's a hurricane in my chest, matching the storm outside, equally as vicious.

Shane steps out of the vehicle in that easy way of his, as if the rain isn't pelting him in the face. His ball cap is pulled down and he walks toward us in a hurried half lope.

Every single memory of him is slamming into the front of my brain, no longer buried in the back. They morph and change, from us together as children, to dating as teens, to every wild and real and beautiful thing in between, and suddenly the memories fade and it's just the here and now.

"Having some trouble?" he asks, just a few feet away now. My breath hitches at the sound of his voice. It's deeper somehow, more gravelly. More everything.

I'm tongue-tied. Dumb on my feet.

Then he tips his cap back and his eyes meet mine. I was expecting the look of shock on his face, because I know I'm the last person he'd expect to see. There's just a small spark, a flash, and then it's buried behind that cold, handsome face.

Fuck me.

"Rachel?" he asks gently, but his voice is flat.

God, his voice. It slithers into my bones.

I swallow and nod. "The car is out of gas," I say feebly, as if he's a stranger.

He *is* a stranger.

He's been a stranger in my own damn memories.

"Okay," he says, blinking.

This is awkward. It's painful. I don't even feel the rain anymore, just this burning in my chest.

I can't believe this is happening.

"Shane Nelson!" My mother exclaims as she leans across the passenger seat and rolls down the window, staring up at him. "Jesus Murphy, what are you doing here?"

Now he grins at her, looking relieved at the distraction. I hate how beautiful his smile still is. "I live here, Mrs. Waters, just like you do."

"*Ms.* Waters," she reminds him, her voice going cold for a second. Then she smiles. "You know I never see you anymore."

"I'm a busy boy," he says.

"A busy man." I don't think I like her light tone, like she's welcoming this whole interaction. She was always the one to tell me that leaving him and North Ridge was the best decision I ever made. It had practically become her mantra.

Shane's eyes flit to mine briefly, but it's enough for the fire in my chest to strengthen. "I only heard you were back today."

I nod. "Just came to deal with family business."

"Apparently I have lung cancer." My mother drops the words like a loaded bomb.

Shane barely flinches. "I'm so sorry to hear that."

"It doesn't matter. I'm not sure I believe the doctors in this town anyway." And at that, she coughs, looking momentarily embarrassed. "Lucky we happen to be headed your way."

Now he looks stunned. "You are?"

She nods. "You didn't know?"

He's avoiding my eyes now, but yeah, no way in hell did he know. He finally looks as uncomfortable as I feel. I take a bit of petty pride in that.

He shakes his head. "Know what?"

My mother sighs dramatically. "I used to think word spread quickly in this town. Well, I suppose I should come get in your truck and you can drive us to the ranch, unless you happen to have a gas can in your back and like standing in the rain like a damn fool."

I'm already soaked to the bone, but I've barely noticed even though the rain isn't letting up anytime soon. I can't notice anything but *him*.

"Of course," Shane says quickly, opening the door to help my mother out of the car. He still has his manners, something Hank ingrained into all of the Nelson brothers. That makes this all worse.

I grab both our purses from the car and follow Shane and my mother, my eyes briefly trailing over his tall body, his wide shoulders that only a lifetime of ranch work can bring, his firm butt in those jeans.

Jesus. What is wrong with me?

I close my eyes briefly, trying to get a hold of myself. I

immediately think about Samuel, my boyfriend back in Toronto. Smart, ambitious, determined Samuel. A million ways different from Shane, a million times better. Sure, we've only been dating for about eight months but it's really going somewhere, I know it is, it has to.

Focusing on Samuel makes me feel better. For a while there I was starting to think I didn't miss him as much as I should.

But then I'm getting in the truck, and it brings back so many memories that I half expect to find my bra behind the seat.

Luckily, my mother sits shotgun beside Shane, leaving me in the back seat, wishing I could shrink away. I'm good at that, pretending I'm not somewhere, trying not to take up space.

The truck rolls off down the highway while my mother talks nonstop. It doesn't matter with Shane—he's always been the silent type—but my mother isn't normally this chatty either. My heart winces a bit as I'm hit with the realization that my mother is really lonely.

Ever since I landed at our tiny regional airport a few days ago and she met me there (again, she shouldn't have been driving), she's been talking to me like we are old friends. Because we've never been close, I was taken aback by it and just listened. But with her excitement over the dinner and the way she's now blabbering on to Shane about the weather, I know for sure she's literally all alone.

My mother doesn't work. I thought she had a job at the library but she acts like she hasn't had that for some time. Her apartment is in a state of disarray, dirty and messy and littered with cigarette butts. She honestly doesn't have a soul except for me, and now she's battling cancer. She's acting like she's fine and it's no big deal, but of course it's a big deal. It's a fucking huge deal, no matter the stage of it.

My heart clenches. I can only hope Hank still loves his wine and whisky because I'm going to need a lot of it to get through all of these competing feelings that are bashing me on the side of the head. Even though we've never been close and my mother has burned me in so many ways, I still feel like shit that I haven't been the best daughter.

And then of course there's Shane, someone else who lit me on fire and left me high and dry. Two people who have had the biggest impact on my life and they're both sitting right in front of me.

The rain doesn't let up until we've crossed the bridge over the river and pulled into Ravenswood Ranch, the truck sloshing over mud-filled potholes as we head up the long drive.

It's just as I remembered, and the nostalgia is getting more punishing by the second. To the right is the stable where I learned to ride, to the left is the big red barn where I watched Shane tattoo heifers and weigh bulls, where I spent many summers touching it up with coats of paint.

At the base of Cherry Peak, where the long, gradual slope of yellow grass and sagebrush turns to pine, is the main house, a sprawling old thing that always had a great deal of charm. Behind that, even though I can't see them clearly from this angle and through the rain, should be the worker's cottage and the guest house. Beyond that, in the folding fields and hills, are more ancient log barns and hay sheds and hidden places that contain a million memories.

It doesn't look like a single thing has changed. I don't know why I expected everything to be different, to look different and feel different. Maybe because in six years, everything about my own life has changed. But here...at Ravenswood Ranch, it's like going back in a time machine.

And I'm not sure I like the results.

"We're here," Shane says, his voice jolting through me,

and for a moment I have to wrestle with what year it is, who I am now. So many things aren't jiving, especially being back here with him.

I find myself cursing my mother for not putting gas in the car, but in her condition who can blame her. Besides, it's not her fault Shane is here. If anything, Hank was the one who assured me that Shane wouldn't be here for dinner.

While my mother opens the door and starts to climb out, Shane briefly catches my eyes in the rearview mirror.

Beautiful golden brown, the color of strong tea, and brimming with intensity. Those eyes used to know me better than anyone.

He doesn't know you anymore, I remind myself as I look away.

I climb out of the truck, the rain having stopped in the last few moments, and hear the loud, gruff voice of Hank as he opens the front door. "Well, looky here," he says with a big smile. All my years here and I hadn't known Hank to smile very often, so the fact that he genuinely looks pleased to see us throws me off. Hell, what isn't throwing me off right now?

His smile only falters when he looks over at Shane and quickly puts it all together.

"I didn't think you were coming home until late," he tells Shane. "Saturday night and all."

I have to wonder what he does on Saturday nights and then I stop myself. He used to spend them with me, but the last thing I need to do is focus on how he's spending his time now.

Shane just nods. "I know. Change of heart. Gotta get up early to start on the silaging."

"Good point. And we'll probably have to move them heifers over to a better range." Hank smiles at me through his bushy mustache. "I bet this brings back all the boring memories, doesn't it, Rachel? My, you're looking mighty pretty."

"Thanks, Hank," I tell him, clearing my throat and flashing him a smile.

"City life agrees with you," he says, and I swear I see a hint of sadness in his eyes.

"So," my mother says quickly, "Shane is staying for dinner now. Hope you made enough. If I remember correctly, the boy had quite the appetite."

We all look at Shane. If he got back in that truck I wouldn't be upset.

He rubs the back of his neck. "I should probably go back to your car, put some gas in it."

I'm momentarily relieved that he wants to leave as much as I want him to.

"Oh, hell no," my mother says. "You let us worry about that, okay? You're staying for dinner. Right, Hank?"

"Of course," Hank says, his eyes meeting mine for a moment. *I'm sorry*, they say, because he knows the only reason I even came here is because Shane was supposed to be elsewhere. I give him a slight smile in response. I can be the adult here. Sure, Shane was the catalyst that made me leave this place and build a better life elsewhere, but that was a good thing, right? I'm finally happy. Even though Shane broke me, he made me stronger. Better.

And because I'm stronger, I can survive this dinner.

I can survive the next few weeks as I figure out how to help my mother.

"Let's get inside then before the rain picks back up," Hank says, briefly placing his hand on my mother's shoulder and ushering her into the house. "We haven't had rain for twenty days and we need it, but you never know what's going to happen out here."

You can say that again.

I quickly hurry after them, not wanting to be stuck close to Shane, not even for a moment. But just as I step on the porch, about to go through the door, he clears his throat from behind me.

"Rachel," he says, his voice both soft and hoarse, knifing through me.

Damn it. I want to keep walking and ignore it but I know I'm better than that.

I take in a deep breath and turn around.

He takes off his cap and runs a hand through his hair, still light brown and thick. I know exactly what that hair feels like between my fingers, the nights I spent in his arms stroking it until he fell asleep. He said it always relaxed him, like a massage. I loved watching him sleep, how at peace he finally looked. The same went for those moments after we made love.

My heart clinches at the memories and I do what I can to move past it.

"How are you?" he asks.

I swallow. "Good. You?"

"Good." He pauses, sighs, and looks at me earnestly. "Hey, I know this is weird."

Weird? That's putting it mildly. But I manage to press my lips together, keeping the words inside.

"You were the last person I expected to see today," he goes on, looking behind him at the storm as it fades into the distance. "I'd heard earlier that you were in town. Honestly, I'm surprised."

"Well, that makes two of us," I admit.

I'm surprised at how well I'm handling this. Even though "handling this" really just means I'm keeping my cool and haven't thrown anything at him yet. I eye a pair of shears sitting on the rocking chair on the porch. There's still time.

"I'm really sorry about your mother," he says. "And I'm even more sorry I haven't been there for her."

I scrunch up my nose. "Why would you have to be there for her? She's my mother, not yours."

As I say that, I wonder if he's taking it personally. That was always one of Shane's deepest, darkest demons, the fact that his mother died when he was so young. He's had mother figures, his nanny Jeanine mostly, sometimes my own mother, but even so I wonder if it's something he's been able to come to terms with. It certainly tormented him back in the day.

"I know she's not my mother," he says, intensity flaring in his eyes. "I just had no idea she was sick. I wish I'd known."

"Well, I'm surprised you didn't. It was your father that told me in the first place."

"My dad?"

I nod. "Yup. He called me two weeks ago and said my mother had been diagnosed with lung cancer. Early stages and something she can totally fight, but he told me she needs me and I should probably come down for a bit and see how things go."

Shane looks beyond confused and I can tell it's news to him. He's been kept in the dark almost as much as I have. "He never told me."

"Maybe he didn't think it was your business. Honestly, I didn't even know our parents were close." I want to add that especially since he broke my heart and practically sent me away from this town.

"I didn't either," he says. "Fuck. Well, then, I'm sorry you're here under these circumstances."

"I'm sorry I'm here at all," I say, and instantly regret it. So much for playing it cool.

"Look," he says. "I know I deserve that…"

And here it comes.

Foot, meet mouth.

"This isn't all about you, Shane. It's been six years. There was a good reason why I left, and you know what it is, but it's not all you. You just gave me the push. And I'm grateful for it, I really am. Because now I finally have a career I love—I work in advertising, and it's challenging and the money is good and I have friends. I have a boyfriend." I watch to see if that affects him but his expression doesn't change. "I have a life. And I love it. This is the last place I want to be and the last thing my mother needs is to have fucking cancer."

He watches me for a few moments. My heart is racing in my chest at all the word vomit I just spat out. "I'm really happy for you, you know," he says softly. "You deserve all those wonderful things you have now. You were smart to leave. You're too good, too smart for this place."

I can't tell if he means that or not, but he probably does. Shane is nothing if not sincere.

But then he turns and heads toward his truck.

"Where are you going?" I ask.

"Going to get out of your hair," he says, pausing to look at me over the door as he opens it. "Your mom's car needs gas. I'll fill her up now, so all my dad needs to do later is drop you off and you're good to go. Tell them to save some food for me."

And then he's in the truck and pulling away, bouncing along the dirt road and potholes.

I know I wanted him gone, but as relieved as I feel that the confrontation is over, it's left me feeling curiously unmoored. Adrift. I'd always wondered what I'd say to him if I ever saw him again, but I have a feeling that wasn't it. How can it be? How can a few hasty words exonerate years of pain and turmoil?

I exhale slowly, pushing all the air out of my lungs, my nerves still dancing.

So that was my first meeting with Shane. Well, the first meeting with the new Shane, with the new me.

Then why do I feel like the old bricks of my life are sliding back into place?

CHAPTER 3

SHANE

PAST – 9 YEARS OLD

The thunder rumbles, shaking nearly the whole house.

I immediately run out of my bedroom and head for the windows in the living room and dining room that face the river. Fox is already there, scanning the skies.

"Did I miss it?" I ask him.

He nods. "It was fucking awesome."

"Fox!" Jeanine yells from the kitchen. "You know the rules. No swearing in front of your brother."

"Whatever," Fox mutters under his breath, eyes trained to the dark clouds.

"And Shane, don't go outside. It's dangerous!" she quickly adds, knowing what I was going to do.

"I can't hear you!" I yell back at her, and after I throw a smile at Fox, I run out of the house before either of them can stop me. Fox is fourteen and thinks he's some kind of god now just because he can pick me up and throw me over his shoulder or put me in a headlock. I'm only nine years old, but give me a year or two and I'll probably be taller than him. At least that's what Delilah says to me when she's trying to cheer me up.

The wind is picking up, blasting me right in the face.

I laugh into it. It's such an odd sound that I laugh louder.

I can't remember the last time I laughed.

That's funny in itself so I laugh even more.

The rain is starting to pour over town, heading for us.

Come get me, I think.

That's when the world cracks open with a flash of white gold light, fork lightning hitting the river.

"Wow!" I cry out just as the air goes *BOOM*.

This is so freaking cool! October storms are the absolute best. Too bad Halloween is still a few weeks away or it would be extra spooky.

"Shane!" Jeanine appears at the door, a mixing bowl in her arms, her red hair blowing around her face. "Get back inside before you get hurt."

"The lightning won't hurt me!" I tell her. I know it won't. I feel like the lightning and I are one and the same. I can feel it in my bones.

"No, but you're going to get rained on. Don't forget, you want to make a good impression in front of the new police chief and his daughter." She watches me for a moment before she turns back into the house. She put extra emphasis on the word daughter. I'm sure Delilah told her everything.

I grumble to myself, wishing I could stand outside and watch the storm get larger and fiercer, even though I know the horses in the barn are hating this right now. If I was nervous before, I'm more embarrassed now that she knows about my crush.

With a big sigh, I turn around and kick a stone. I watch it hop across the dry earth just as a drop of rain darkens the spot beside it.

"Shane!" Fox is now yelling from inside the house and I know if I don't hurry he's going to come out and drag me in.

I run inside before I make things worse. After all, I don't want to ruin anyone's Thanksgiving.

"THEY'RE HERE!" DELILAH SAYS EXCITEDLY, AND WE WATCH as headlights come down through the darkness toward the house. Even in the pitch black I can tell when they're going over the bridge that skirts over Cherry Creek (just a trickle of water these days), then around the crop of ponderosa pine that my grandpa refuses to cut down.

"Is your father ready?" Jeanine asks. She looks us all in the eyes so it's hard to know who she's talking to.

There's me, sitting beside Del by the windows. Then there's Fox, arms crossed in the middle of the room like he's some hotshot. Maverick is hovering by the door like he's ready to leave.

But since no one moves or says a word, Jeanine yells up the stairs of the big house. "Hank. Your guests are here!"

A pause. Then, "My guests?" he yells back from somewhere upstairs.

"Yes, your guests," she says, wiping the back of her hand across her forehead and looking worn out despite having put on some makeup and a dress. "It wasn't my idea to invite the new chief constable and his family over."

"It's the right thing to do," my father shouts back. "It's Thanksgiving. This is what the holiday means. And yes, I'm ready, everyone hold your horses."

"Cool your jets," Del adds.

"Calm your tits," Maverick says with a smirk.

Jeanine seems too tired to even be mad at him. "Okay everyone, stand up straight and be on your best behavior."

"Yes, all that too," my father says, walking down the stairs.

Fox whistles. I always wished I could whistle.

"You're looking dapper, Dad," he says.

I'm not really sure what dapper means but I don't think my dad is it. He's wearing dark jeans and a jean shirt. The Canadian tuxedo, as Fox calls it. His belt has a huge shiny buckle—I think it's one he won back from his rodeo days. His hair is slicked back off his face like some mobster in the Godfather movie we watched the other night.

My dad doesn't seem to believe it either. "This is just what I look like when I'm not covered in cow shit."

"Hank," Jeanine warns.

He waves her off. "The boys have heard worse. Where's your grandpa?"

We hear the toilet down the hall flush and I burst into giggles. "He's been in there for like an hour."

"Hey, Shane boy, constipation is no joke," my father says sternly.

Which only makes me laugh more.

I'm so nervous.

And I shouldn't be, right? Rachel Waters is the daughter of the town's new cop. She's sitting inside the car that's just pulling up outside the house, next to our row of dusty trucks. She sits next to me in class, and she's so quiet and so pretty. I really like her, even though she barely says anything. But she does speak to me and not to the other boys, so that counts for something.

My father told us a week ago that we were going to have them all over for dinner, I guess cuz they don't know anyone in town yet. My dad has a reputation as a grump but my grandpa is like the town's patriarch, whatever that means, and he said that it's the right thing to do, to invite them over for

Thanksgiving dinner. It must make no difference to Jeanine since she's cooking for so many of us anyway. Plus, this way, we get to have ham *and* a turkey.

"Stand up straight, Shane," my father says to me, patting me on the shoulder. I immediately put my shoulders back. He acts like posture is the end of the world. I mean, it's not like having great posture makes you smart or rich.

By the time grandpa finally trundles out of the washroom, running his hands through his thin grey hair and pushing it back against his head like he's trying to be in some Godfather movie too, there's a knock at the door.

Maverick opens it. "Merry Christmas!" he exclaims.

Except it's October, it's Thanksgiving, and now Mav just looks like a big dork.

The man on the other side of the door pretends to find my brother funny but I know he's lying because no one finds Mav funny.

I've seen the constable pick Rachel up from school once before in his car. He's tall and balding with a moustache that looks like a caterpillar. He's got a big smile and white teeth, but his eyes don't seem to blink.

I don't trust him. I don't like him.

Rachel's mom is behind him, short with a face that's kinda pretty but also small, like a mouse.

Then there's Rachel herself.

Rachel looks like an angel, especially tonight. Her hair is long and dark and super shiny. It reminds me of raven's wings. But she looks totally nervous and I don't blame her. There's a lot of us here, and we're all just staring at her like a bunch of turds.

The introductions are made quickly by my grandpa. He can be quick when he wants to be. Pretty soon all my brothers, my dad, Jeanine and Del know Rachel, her mom, and her dad.

Our dining room table is a big wooden thing, something my grandpa says was made from a huge oak tree when he was a young boy, but it's not big enough for everyone so Jeanine takes out a folding table from the closet and sets it up in the corner of the room.

I know this is the "kids" table, she doesn't even have to say it, but I don't mind being the kid for once because there's only one other kid here: Rachel.

"Shane, Rachel, you'll have to sit here," she says as she quickly puts down a red plastic tablecloth that we usually use on the picnic table. She glances at me briefly and gives me a small smile. I know what she's doing, like she's trying to put Rachel and I together on purpose, and my cheeks go red.

When the table is ready and set, Rachel and I sit down across from each other. She's so pretty that my tongue feels like dirt in my mouth. I can't speak. And she doesn't speak either, so we just stare at each other. Funny that it feels like enough.

We should invent a secret language.

I try and convey this with my eyes but Rachel just looks at me like I'm weird. Okay, maybe I am being a bit weird right now. But how cool would that be? My brothers ignore me so I've never been able to do this with them.

The food is passed around, the adults start to talk, then my grandpa insists we say grace. He's funny like that. He's the only one of us who mentions God or prayer, but it's important to him so we all do it.

As I'm saying grace, I open one eye to peek at Rachel.

She's watching me, and when I catch her, she smiles.

Gosh, she's pretty. I should be saying grace for her.

When it's over, the adults go back to talking to each other. Sometimes Rachel's mother will ask Fox or Mav what they like to do but the police chief doesn't seem to care. In fact, he doesn't seem to like it when she talks.

I'm not sure what to say to Rachel at first so I stuff my mouth with turkey and observe the room. I like to do that. Jeanine says I'm the strong, silent type, though I still don't think I'll get as strong as my brothers. But I like to watch people. Sometimes I pretend I'm watching a play and I narrate it all in my head.

There's Maverick, always trying to make someone laugh even though his jokes are dumb. Fox just thinks he's too cool for school, flexing his stupid muscles, trying to impress Del.

"So when did you two meet?" Rachel's mom says to my dad and Jeanine.

My face goes red for no reason. I see my brothers stiffen. None of us like this question even though we're not ashamed of it.

The chief clears his throat. "Vernalee," he says sharply, and the look that he gives her is like he's trying to fry her alive on the spot. He's kind of scary.

But Vernalee just looks at Jeanine in surprise. Because she doesn't know.

"I'm actually the nanny," Jeanine says calmly with a nice smile on her face. "Hank's wife, Emily, died when Shane was just six months old."

"Oh, I'm so sorry," Vernalee exclaims loudly, hand at her throat.

"Okay, enough," the police chief says. "They clearly don't want to talk about it and you made a fool of yourself bringing it up."

I look over at Rachel and she seems to shrink before my eyes, her shoulders curling in, staring down at her plate like she wants to disappear.

"It's quite alright," my father says quickly. "Honestly. It's been a long time. We're just all so lucky that Jeanine was here for us and still is."

Jeanine and him exchange a pleasant look.

My father has had to say that so many times. So have I. But living in a small town, unless someone is new, everyone knows so we don't have to say it often anymore.

It's weird for me because to me Jeanine feels like a mother, my mother, but I also know she's not. Even when I was really young, I called her Jeanine because that's what my father would call her. I don't know what it's like to have a real mother. I think if there is a God, like the one that grandpa believes in, he thinks I don't deserve one.

The truth is, I'm the reason my mother is dead. I've heard it put that way more than once.

"So," Rachel says in a small voice.

I look at her in surprise. The adults have gone back to talking about other things. My grandpa was quick to change the subject to the ranch.

But then Rachel doesn't say anything else so I say, "Do you like the food?"

She smiles, nodding. "It's very good. We usually have ham, but I like turkey better because of the gravy. Did you know, in America they do Thanksgiving at the end of November? That's so close to Christmas. I'd hate to be a turkey there in the winter."

"We used to have turkeys," I tell her. "But we ate them."

Rachel scrunches up her nose.

"I'm not sure where this turkey came from." I point at the plate, talking fast. "But we just have chickens now, out in the coop. We only eat their eggs."

"Do you have any dogs?" she asks.

"We do. All my brothers have one. Me too. Mine's called Blue cuz he's a Blue Heeler. But Fox's is called Red and Maverick's is Yellow. So maybe that's not why he's called Blue." I stop talking because I sound like a moron.

"I'd love to meet them all," she says. "Especially your Blue."

I smile at her. Suddenly I don't feel so dumb anymore.

"They're all in the barn right now, maybe sleeping in the hay. Or out and about. Jeanine wanted the dogs out of the house for dinner." I suck in a breath and summon courage. "Maybe you could come over one day after school. We have lots of horses too. Do you like horses?"

"I love horses," she says, eyes bright. They're so blue, bluer than the summer sky. "I'll ask my parents later." Her eyes dart to them and she watches for a moment, almost fearfully.

I try to give her a smile of encouragement but just like that, her eyes stop shining and she grows quiet again. I decide to make it my mission to get her over riding one day. Maybe Jeanine or my dad or grandpa can call up Rachel's parents and ask. After this, they'd *have* to let us be friends.

After dinner is over and dessert is served (homemade pumpkin pie, my favorite!), Jeanine comes back over to our little table and crouches down between us. She holds out a wishbone.

"This is the turkey's wishbone," she says. "I dried it in the oven while we were eating so it's easier to break. Have you done this before, Rachel?"

Rachel shakes her head, staring at the wishbone curiously. I've done it a few times, but usually my brothers fight for it first and I've never had the bigger part, which means my wishes have never come true.

"The wishbone," Jeanine explains kindly, "is magic. What happens is you think of a wish in your head, something your heart really, really wants, then you both grasp one end of the bone and pull toward yourself until it breaks. Whoever has the bigger piece, their wish will come true. If it breaks evenly, both your wishes will come true. But you must never tell anyone your wish until after it comes true. Okay?"

We both nod and Jeanine leaves, squeezing my shoulder as she goes.

Rachel and I both take one end of the bone.

I close my eyes briefly and I listen to my heart and what it's saying and I hope and pray and wish with all my might.

I pull.

She pulls.

I open my eyes.

I have the bigger half.

For a second I feel like laughing with joy, then I see how sad and disappointed Rachel looks. She was really counting on that wish.

I want to tell her that it's her wish that counts more than anything, that if I could give her mine and still have it come true, I would.

But the thing is...my wish would help us both.

I just have to wait for it to come true.

CHAPTER 4

RACHEL

"Did you scare Shane off already?" Hank asks me as I step inside the Nelson's home. He and my mother are sitting at the kitchen table, both having a glass of wine. I can hear someone puttering around in the kitchen. It looks the same as it always did, warm wooden floors, faded floral yellow wallpaper, horseshoes and steer horns and a slew of pictures hanging in tiny brass frames, a tattered rocking horse in the corner.

"He said he's going to fill the car up with gas," I say as casually as I can muster. "And for you to save him dinner."

My mother smiles at Hank. "He's such a good boy."

My eyes narrow briefly. It seems like my mother forgot what happened between us. I guess for some people, six years is long enough to erase all the ugly bits. I can only hope that hasn't applied to the way she feels about my father.

"He is good," Hank says gruffly, as if he doesn't want to admit it. Hank has always meant well and has a good heart, but I've seen how he is with his sons. There's some real tough love going on, but it seems to work since all his boys were raised well.

But if Shane is so good, why did he leave you like that?
Why did he tell you that he never loved you?

I remember that night like it was yesterday, the night where my heart bled out. I took that wishbone necklace he got me for my sixteenth birthday and threw it in his face in front of everyone. I stared into the eyes of my love as they became the eyes of a stranger.

Shane didn't just break up with me, he pushed me away and tried to *destroy* me.

I'll never forget that, even if everyone else here already has.

God, I almost wish I could go back outside and do that scene with him over again to really try and hit him where it hurts.

"Raven!" Dick Nelson, Hank's father, appears in the kitchen doorway, throwing his hands out. The man is so adorable and happy to see me that I let it slide that he called me by Shane's old nickname for me.

"Hey, Dick," I tell him, feeling shy all of a sudden.

"Well, come on over here and give me a hug, eh!" Most people in North Ridge don't have a discernible accent, but Dick's is full-on Canadian. Sometimes I think he puts it on.

Even though Dick has always been a grandpa to me—I never knew my own because they died, and spending so much time here as I did, it was hard not to think of him as anything but—it's still surprising to see he hasn't changed much. He's a bit skinnier, but he's not frail in the slightest. His skin is weathered and tanned like old cowboy boots, eyes a twinkling blue beneath white bushy brows.

He pulls me into a fierce hug, smelling like pipe tobacco. Like Hank, Dick is a straight shooter but seems to do it with a gallon of joy. I've missed this man.

"You've put on some weight," he says to me as he pulls back.

"Thanks," I say dryly, feeling myself cringe.

"It suits you," he says. "When you were a teenager you were too thin. Body of a boy, I used to say."

I frown, almost letting out a laugh. "Thanks again." It wasn't that bad, actually, though I was terribly self-conscious about my flat chest and knock knees. I honestly didn't eat very much, for various reasons. The last six years, though, my body has decided that stress demands food and since advertising is one of the most stressful careers you can have, I've been stuffing my face. Hence, the weight gain. At least I have breasts now, though I don't think my body has gotten the memo to stop expanding.

"Want a drink? Seems your mother and Hank have already dipped into the wine, but I've always got whisky and that's never treated us wrong, has it?"

Whisky? Why the fuck not?

"Make it a double," I tell him with a smile.

"Ooh, you've gotten sassier," he says and leans forward. "I like that." He winks and heads back into the kitchen with an extra spring in his step. "Vernalee, you better keep an eye on that girl. She might go around breaking some hearts in this town."

I clear my throat before anyone can say anything. "The only heart I'm breaking is my boyfriend's, back in Toronto. He misses me." I think.

But the moment I say that, I regret it. My mother stiffens, going on the defensive like I knew she would. "You didn't have to come here, Rachel," she says. "I can manage perfectly fine without you."

"You need her," Hank says, pressing his fingers into the table as he gives her a levelling stare. "It's been too long. It's not right for you to have to suffer without your daughter here to help you."

"You don't get to decide that, Hank," she says, and now

my eyes are volleying between the both of them. Even though I'm involved in this, it feels primarily between the two of them. "I'm fine. I keep telling you that."

"If Beth at the hospital wasn't such a blabbermouth, you would have told no one."

"And that's my choice. Because there's nothing to worry about."

His brow furrows and that intense Nelson look comes through. "You have stage one lung cancer. It's not nothing. You have to go in for surgery to have part of your lung removed and that's if you're lucky."

"I'm fine." She's practically grinding her teeth.

"Vernalee."

"Henry," she challenges, calling him by his full name.

"No fighting at the dinner table. That's always been the rule, and since Jeanine isn't here to enforce it, I am," Dick says from the kitchen, plopping ice cubes in our drinks.

"Where is Jeanine anyway?" I ask.

"Still at the house on Maple Street," Hank says. "Del lives with her now. She was living with an ex, engaged and all that, but they broke up so she's back home with her ma. Jeanine's arthritis is pretty bad so Del helps a lot. And she's still running the Bear Trap. Actually, she owns it now."

While I'm here I should probably go to the bar and say hello. Del's always been one of my favorite people here. I'm just a bit scared of running into the whole town while I'm there. From the day I turned nineteen, the legal drinking age, I practically lived there.

Dick walks past me, handing me my drink before gesturing to the table. "Sit down, Rachel, make yourself at home. After all, this will be your home for a little bit. Or at least Vernalee's."

Normally I wouldn't think much of that since I've heard North Ridge will always be my home, but there's something about the room and how the air in it changes that makes my skin prickle.

"What do you mean?" I ask carefully.

Dick sits down and then looks at me in surprise, as if he's not quite sure he said something. "What?"

"What you just said…about it being my mother's home…"

Dick chews on his lip for a moment, his eyes going blank, but Hank and my mother, well they could be sending telepathic telegrams for all I know.

"Rachel, honey, sit down," my mother says, patting the seat next to her. She doesn't normally call me honey, so I know something is wrong.

I feel like standing right where I am, staring down at them, but honestly, I'm tired. I take a seat and prepare myself for the next crazy awful thing in my day.

But she doesn't say anything. Her eyes fill with shame, deeper than I've ever seen on her, almost as deep as the day I left, and she looks away.

Hank sighs as he watches her. There's such an alarming tenderness in his gaze that something in me warms. His eyes aren't golden, like his son's, but there is so much of him in Shane. The kind of sincerity that you can't fake.

He looks at me. "Your mother is in a tough situation. She's going to move out of her apartment in a few days and move in here. With our last worker gone, the worker's cottage is completely empty right now."

I look at everyone. "I don't understand. What tough situation?"

My first thought, the one that grips my heart, is that my father is out of jail somehow and she's here in hiding.

"She hasn't worked for a year," Hank says. "She lost her job at the library."

"And who else would hire me?" She lifts up her hands as if in offering.

"Plenty would have loved to help you out, Vernalee," he scolds her. "But you were too damn stubborn."

"No need for fighting," Dick says calmly as he sips his whisky.

"Anyway," Hank continues, "it's too late now. You have to concentrate on getting healthy, getting better. You've been treating yourself like garbage and you know it. Drinking, smoking, barely eating. Some days I came by and you wouldn't even get out of bed."

God. With every word Hank speaks, my heart sinks lower and lower. I know we're not close, but I still should have been there for her. Our phone calls had been so brief, so shallow.

"Henry, please," she says softly, folding her frail hands in front of her, the age spots starting to leap off her skin. She looks so ashamed.

I don't know what it is about being a daughter, but I find it nearly impossible to shut my heart off from her. It doesn't matter that years ago, when I needed her most, when I trusted her with my deepest, most shameful secrets, she turned her back on me. Didn't believe me. It doesn't matter that she left me feeling like I had no one else in the world, no one but Shane. Because seeing her in pain, seeing how alone she is, how bad she's actually gotten...it's breaking me inside. A daughter can't just shut out her mother's pain like a switch, even if she wishes she could.

"Your daughter needs the truth and you know it. She's always deserved better. Rachel was the one who always had to suffer," he says.

I look at him sharply, and when he nods, I know he knows far more than I ever wanted him to.

"It's just temporary," my mother finally says in a small voice. She looks at me. "It's for the best. I'm being evicted, Rachel."

"What?"

"I tried to hide it from you for as long as I could, but..."

"Evicted?" I put my hands out, nearly knocking over the whisky glass. "Mom. Come on. This is an easy problem to fix. I have money."

"No, Rachel—"

"I have a good job!"

"You just bought yourself a condo that costs far more than even your good job can afford."

How does she know that? "That's the price of real estate in Toronto. I can manage my mortgage, no problem."

"But are you saving?" Hank asks. I jerk my chin back, wondering why it's his business. He goes on with a shrug, "If you're not saving, you're not doing well. And you definitely can't afford to pay for your mother's rent. Not when I have a perfectly nice house for her here. You remember the worker's cottage, don't you? Three bedrooms, two baths, a kitchen. It's not new and can use some repairs but it's got everything she needs and everything you need while you stay here."

"I'm not staying here."

"Rachel," my mother warns. "You really want to stay in a hotel?"

"Why on God's green earth would this Raven girl stay in a hotel?" Dick says as he shakes his head. "We're like her second family. You're staying here, sweetheart."

I don't have the heart to tell Dick that there's nothing wrong with this wonderful place, just one of the men who inhabits it.

"I'm sorry," my mother says. "I was going to tell you..."

"When? When someone showed up at your door and physically kicked you out?" I'm trying hard not to be angry because I know how stubborn she can be, but God.

"Our plan was to tell you tonight," Hank says. "I just wanted you to know your mother is in good hands. In fact, things couldn't be better. When you go back to Toronto, we'll be taking care of her."

"Oh, come on," she says, taking a sip of wine. "You know I can take care of myself."

But taking care of yourself apparently means not eating or working. Just drinking and smoking until you die, I think to myself. I know before my father went to jail that he at least had the foresight to have money in a savings account, but there's no way it would have been enough to keep her afloat for more than a year.

Oh, Mom. My heart is so heavy.

"It looks like you'll be living with us until your mother gets better," Dick says cheerfully. "It sure will be nice to have a woman on this ranch. The good lord knows Shane isn't bringing anyone home from church or anywhere else."

I raise my brows. Both at the mention of church, and the fact that, at least according to Dick, he hasn't been dating anyone. I'm not sure why I feel pleased at that, like it would make any difference whether he has a girlfriend or a fiancée or a wife or not. I mean, I have Samuel.

Speaking of which, I'm sure if he knew I was going to be pretty much living with my ex-boyfriend while I'm here, he wouldn't be too happy. Then again, by the amount of time he takes to respond to my texts in annoying one-word answers like "K" (is there anything worse?), he might not care that much.

I exhale loudly, reaching for my glass. I'm not only going to be living in North Ridge for an unknown amount of time, I'm going to be living here of all places.

Right next door to the boy that broke my heart.

CHAPTER 5

SHANE

"I'm guessing you heard the news," Grandpa says to me over a steaming cup of coffee.

I nod, not wanting to talk about it, and gesture to his bowl of cut up berries, the only part of his breakfast he hasn't touched. "You know you have to finish those. That's the trade-off. You can have bacon and eggs but you have to eat your fruit."

He scowls at me, even though his eyes are still twinkling. "This is horseshit. I'm full. And I've gone all my damn life not eating fruit, and look at me, I'm fit as a fiddle."

I know none of that is true. We have a small orchard behind the worker's cottage, old fruit trees bearing sweet apples, yellow cherries, and perfect plums. I never knew much about my grandmother because she died when I was three, but I knew that she was a supreme baker. She would win pie contests all across the province, back in the day when pie contests were a big deal and all that. I have no doubt he at least got his fruit that way for years.

"And don't switch the subject," he says, pushing the

47

berries toward me. I hesitate, then take them. I can never pass up strawberries.

"I'm not switching anything. Vernalee is moving into the worker's cottage. That's great. She needs people right now, good people."

"Damn right she needs good people. Poor woman having to put up with that man." He points his coffee cup at me. "You know, the minute I saw Constable Waters I knew he was trouble. I've seen a few men like him in my day and it's always worse when they get into positions of power. The cops we had before, they were good men. They liked being in North Ridge. They raised families here. Not saying that we don't welcome outsiders, but there's a way about this town that we'd like to keep. Keep it honest, keep it kind, keep it humble. That's what we stand for. And that damn man...he stood for none of those things. He came into this town and he ruined more than a few lives. He was a liar, and frankly, pure evil. And that's the truth."

Any mention of that man makes my blood boil. I'm not short-tempered except when it comes to him, and I've spent the last six years thinking about all the things I should have done. "You talk about him as if he's dead," I eventually say. "He's still out there."

"Well, he's rotting in prison where he belongs. I can only hope our court system keeps him there. You have to wonder how many people he hurt before he got caught."

I can tell from the way my grandpa is saying this that he doesn't know the full extent of what Chief Constable Errol Waters was capable of. Sometimes I don't think I do either. But what he does know is that one day he beat someone to death. A native boy, out on his reserve, shooting cans drunk. Things got out of hand, but instead of arresting him, he beat the boy until he was dead, then tried to cover it up by saying he was defending his life. There were witnesses. Maybe he didn't even see them, maybe he didn't care. Thought they were beneath him, that he was above the law, that he could get away with murder. But they recorded it all, and because of that, Errol Waters was sent to jail.

I've been in his shoes before. I know what it feels like to have anger and revenge take control of your body. But I had reasons for my actions, a sense of justice. All Errol had was hate. Hate for his wife, his daughter, for everyone.

The thing is, that boy's life could have been saved if I'd only had the guts to say something all those years ago.

"I suppose it's not the best thing to be talking about before we start our day," he tells me before he slurps back the rest of his coffee. "How's your headache?"

I give him a steady look. "I don't have a headache."

"You came back late last night."

My grandfather is in his eighties but he has the ears of a hawk. It caused a lot of problems back when we were teenagers and I was sneaking out to see Rachel or sneaking her in to my room late at night.

Last night, after I took a jerry can and filled up their car with gas, I went right back to the Bear Trap. It was busy and full of people I didn't feel like talking to, but I managed to keep to myself, drinking beer after beer until I was able to sleep some of it off in the back room. I guess old habits do die hard.

"I feel fine," I tell him. "Let's get going."

Summer on the ranch keeps us pretty good and busy. At the moment we're short-staffed, though we're trying to rope Maverick into helping us on his days off. One of the tasks is to move cattle from one range to the next to prevent over-grazing. Though we own seven hundred acres, we have a tenure on 10,000 acres on bordering Crown Land that goes all the way around Cherry Peak, which means there's a lot of ground to cover.

Luckily today we're moving some cows from an area about an hour's ride from here to the next available grazing spot. This group isn't large, and with just me and my grandfather, plus the dogs, Fletcher, Duke, and Darling, we should get the herd moved with ease.

There's nothing like being out on the open range to cure what ails you. But the fresh air, the rolling clouds in the distance, the way the golden grass makes the hills look like they're cloaked in velvet, none of it is managing to clear my head.

All I can think about is Rachel.

Last night nearly killed me.

I honestly thought that if I saw Rachel again, I would be okay. That I could handle it. That it wouldn't hurt more than a mere scratch, that I wouldn't drown in the memories and the way I used to feel about her.

But none of that was true. It wasn't a scratch—it was a knife to my heart. I wasn't drowning in the memories—I was dying in them. And every single thing I felt about her came rushing back, a flash flood of desire and pain that nearly blindsided me.

The worst part of all of this is, when it comes down to it... I don't think I ever stopped missing her. The days turned to weeks, the weeks to months, seasons came and went, the years followed, and yet deep in the darkest parts of me, I've missed her. More than I would ever let myself admit.

A pair of ravens fly overhead, their large wings making that distinguished whooshing sound, stirring up air like a storm, and my grandfather looks up. "Do you still believe in good luck, Shane?"

I glance at him curiously. We've been riding for just over an hour now and are just about to the crest of a hill, the dogs at our heels. I watch as the ravens swoop down over the other side, disappearing from sight. The sky is tinged with red, deepening in the corners, haze from the wildfires that are raging in the province this time of year, caused usually by lightning strikes, sometimes by careless humans. I know for a fact that Fox is out there right now, fighting them, though it's something I don't tend to dwell on.

My attention is brought to my grandpa. "Luck? What do you mean?"

"Nothing," he says, leaning forward in his saddle for the last push to the top, taking the weight off the back of his horse, Manuel. "But I remember you kept that half a wishbone in a glass jar for many years."

It's still in the glass. Tucked away in the closet since I can't bear to look at it, because in the end, it was just another wish that didn't come true. But it's still there. I guess that says something.

"It had sentimental value," I finally say, and my grandpa nods, mulling it over before clucking to Manuel.

We reach the crest and look down at the land below us. It takes my breath away. The golden grass is tinged orange from the light, sweeping into forests of pine. In the distance, the always snow-capped peaks of the glaciers sit. In front of everything are the cows, all twenty-three of them. A fraction of our herd, but it's enough to keep us busy.

They raise their heads from the grass. This isn't even Crown Land anymore, at least not the parcel of acres we're allowed to use until mid-October, and the cows are looking at us as if they know they've gone out of bounds.

Fletcher, my dog, a descendent of Blue, whines impatiently, ready to get herding. The dogs live for this life, thrive in having a job and a purpose. Sometimes, if I feel I've lost my way a bit, I look to them and try and find my path all over again. The passion for the every day, for what you're born to do.

But I wait for grandpa, because in the end it's still his ranch and he doesn't seem too quick to move.

"You worry about your brother?" he asks me, staring at that mean red sun.

"Fox?"

"I would say John too, but he doesn't need anyone's worry. You want to talk about luck, he's got that in spades." John is Maverick's real name. My father said the nickname stuck when he was five. Apparently he fell in love with *Top Gun*.

"Sometimes," I admit. "But Fox seems to know what he's doing." And that's the truth. I know the ins and outs of his job, but I couldn't do it. I don't have the stamina and I'm not a thrill seeker. I'm content to invite danger and adventure but not court it for long periods of time. What Fox does, it puts his life at risk every day. I mean, the man jumps out of an airplane into a forest fire. I don't know what sane person does that.

But in some ways, I don't really know Fox. We haven't had the easiest relationship. Maybe it's something to do with him being the oldest, therefore there's the most distance between us. Sometimes I think it's something deeper, like resentment that worked its way into his bones, the fact that our mother died because of me, but that might just be my own complex.

"It's good to worry though," he goes on, resting his hands on the saddle horn. Manuel dips his head, content, smart enough not to try for the dry grass. "Just remember that life is out of our hands."

I wait patiently, sensing he's going to continue. He always does. Grandpa will talk your ear off for hours if you're not careful.

"Fox was always troublesome, the minute he was born. I saw him in your mother's arms and I knew it. There's always a troublesome Nelson in the family. Little did I know that your father would have three of them."

How am I troublesome? I want to ask, but Grandpa goes on. "Fox was climbing out of his crib before he could walk. When he could walk, he was climbing up the couch. I swear he jumped in the lake and taught himself to swim. Whatever adventure he could find, he would find it. Your mother did what she could to protect him, but in the end, she couldn't. Because beyond the best that she could do, it was out of her hands."

He looks at me and grins. It makes him look positively young. "Then came John, and it was the same thing all over again. He wasn't as bold as Fox. Fox possesses a strange absence of fear. But John had the confidence. He always believed he could do something and he did it. Just like that. If he ever failed, he brushed himself off and smiled, as if it was the fella's plan all along. It gave your mother a heart attack, I swear, just trying to keep up with those two. But she let life play out as it needed to."

I swallow. I don't want him to go on. I can listen for hours about the way my mother was with Mav and Fox. But once it comes to me, I don't want to hear it.

"Then she had you," he says after a long pause. "As you know, she didn't know she could have any more children. We'd been told that John was the last. But you popped up. A surprise. And God, did your mother ever love you. She thought she was the luckiest woman in the world. You were a gift, Shane. A blessing." He lets out a long sigh, his eyes drifting over the cattle and the blood-red sun. "And you were just like the other two, only quieter. You never cried. You were always so calm, like you were already lost in your thoughts. And though you weren't climbing out of your crib, you weren't afraid, either. You were the most serious baby I'd ever met and we all loved you for it. You looked at fear, weighed it carefully, and then faced it."

I'm clenching my jaw. I don't want him to continue. I

want to get the cows and go. Sensing my impatience and change of vibe, my mare, Polly, shifts underneath me, alert.

"I know you don't believe it," he says. "I don't know how to make you believe it. None of us do. But when your mother took her life, it had nothing to do with you, Shane. You were just a baby. And she was a sick woman. Lost to society, to the doctors, to us. We knew but we didn't really know. But we were the adults. We should have realized how serious her depression was. And we didn't. We failed her, not you. Never you, Shane. She loved you."

It takes me a moment to clear my throat, to find the words. "What does this have to do with luck?"

"It does or it doesn't," he says after watching me for a moment. "But luck is something we latch onto because we believe in hope. And hope exists because we believe in something better." He pauses. "The fault of man is that we never live long enough to be the person we want to be." He looks at me. "Who do you want to be, Shane? The man who makes wishes on broken bones? Or the man who makes things happen?"

"I don't know what you mean," I say quietly. He's talked circles around me.

"You do," he says with a dry laugh. "Oh, of course you do, boy. You always know what everyone means. Nothing slips past you, even when you want it to. I know what you and Rachel had was special, is special. And I've seen special. I've seen it with your father and mother. I've lived it between me and Anne. Cynics might tell you that young love isn't real love, but when love is real, it's real, and time and age don't have a damn thing to do with it."

"Rachel and I broke up a long time ago," I remind him.

"And now she's living next door to you."

"Temporarily."

"The amount of time doesn't matter. What matters is

she's here. And whatever you both had, it was never settled. With any luck, you'll finally settle it. I know that you've been dealing with demons your whole life, Shane. I see them on you, trailing like shadows. I know it makes you think you're not worthy of love. But you are. And the minute you believe it, the minute things will change. You trust me, don't you?"

I give him a quick smile as an answer. I had a feeling today's ride wouldn't be like the others.

But after we ride down the slope toward the herd and the dogs gather them up with ease, driving them home, the red sun at our backs, I see the ravens again.

Omens of luck.

I'm a man who wishes on broken bones.

I'm a man who has a second chance to make things right.

CHAPTER 6

RACHEL

I stare at the three dots on my phone's messaging system. I swear, this feature was invented for torture purposes, so the person on the other end gets all the time in the world to wonder what the other is saying.

And just like before, the dots disappear and I'm left in suspense. I squeeze the phone in my hand like a stress-reliever ball, taking a deep breath.

Today is moving day, and as if that's not stressful enough, I'm trying to talk to Samuel and my boss at the same time, and both of them keep typing their messages then erasing them.

"They'll be here any minute," my mother yells from the kitchen. "Are you done in there? Stomach problems?"

I've locked myself in the bathroom because it's the only place I've been able to get any privacy. I've asked my boss if it's okay that I stay a bit longer on account of my mother—I know she's going to be in good hands living at the Nelson's but I'm not leaving her anytime soon—and he has yet to reply.

I did the same with Samuel, and at first I got a *Sure* in response, which, I have to admit, didn't sit well with me. Then I texted back, *Are you really okay with it? I might be gone for another two or three weeks, at least until my mother has her surgery.*

And now, those three flashing dots.

Finally, his text pops up.

Do what you gotta do.

That's it.

I text back: *I miss you.*

Three flashing dots.

Fucking hell.

Then my boss, Ed, answers: *Ideally, this isn't the best situation and you're going to be out of vacation pay within a week. But I understand you have to be there.*

Ugh. I've been working my way up at Campbell and Brown for two years now, lucky enough to score a job as receptionist straight out of university, and I've sacrificed my vacations out of the sheer fear that someone would swoop in and take over my job. That's pretty much what it's like in advertising; it's as cutthroat as people make it out to be, and I think it's taken a few years off my life.

I don't want to ask how Pete is handling my account because Pete is a go-getter who has always been clamoring for my job and he's probably going above and beyond. Not that I haven't, but when you've been busting your ass for two years with no vacations and late nights and as much overtime as you can handle, you can't keep giving one hundred and ten percent.

"Rachel," my mother says again, and I sigh, checking my phone before slipping it into the pocket of my jean shorts. No three dots from Samuel, no reply. Whatever his response was, which should have been, *I miss you too*, has been erased.

I have to admit, that stings.

I step out of the bathroom. My mom is standing in the middle of the living room, looking especially small with all the boxes piled high around her. She gives me a tepid smile, and I realize that she looks close to crying. My mother never cried, not even when I left North Ridge, so to see her so vulnerable like this really hits me hard.

"It's going to be okay, Mom," I tell her softly, walking toward her like I'm approaching a wild animal. It reminds me of the time Shane and I found an injured baby badger in the woods and took it in. It took a few weeks until the little guy's leg healed, but Shane doted on that thing around the clock.

I wonder if that's how my mother will emerge from all of this. When she beats the cancer—which she will—and gets back on her feet with the help of Hank and Dick, will she come out of Ravenswood Ranch stronger than ever? I hope so. My mother was often harsh, so strong and determined, and while I like having her soft, it's this perpetual sadness that she carries with her that I can't deal with. I just want to erase it.

As if she can feel my pity, she straightens up, trying to be tough. "I know it will be okay. Moving is just such a pain in the ass."

"You must have liked this place," I say, gesturing to it. She had a lot of photos, knickknacks and random things cluttering up every shelf and windowsill, a sign that she had made it her home as much as she could. Though I wasn't here when my father went to jail, I know that it would have been hard on her to sell the house and move in here, to one of the few apartment buildings in town. But at least it was a fresh start.

"It's a dump and you know it," she says to me, and when I meet her eyes, she smirks.

There's a knock at the door, and I hold my breath as I go to open it. Hank had said someone would come by to help us with the boxes and I'm really hoping that he knows better than to send Shane.

When I open it, I break into a smile. It's Maverick.

"Rachel," he says in his deep voice, looking me up and down, his grin growing wider. "I can hardly believe it. Come here."

Maverick leans over and pulls me into a big bear hug.

Holy shit. Maverick has always been very active and in shape, but now he feels like he's made of pure muscle. It's like being embraced by a warm brick wall.

I pull back and try to get a look at him. His dark hair is short, like it's growing out of a buzz cut, his face rough with stubble with a smear of dirt on his cheek. He's wearing a white t-shirt that stretches across his wide chest, the dark tattoos on his arms on full display. The man is sex on a stick and he knows it, especially judging by his cocky smile and the way his vibrant green eyes shine as he looks at me. A toothpick hangs from his full lips, just as I remembered them.

"You're such a man now, Mav," I tell him, my hands holding onto his biceps firmly. "I mean, the last time I saw you..." I trail off. The last time I saw him I was crying my eyes out and he was staring at Shane in complete confusion. "You're looking good."

"You know, I don't think you've ever paid me a compliment before," he says, leaning against the doorway and crossing his arms so his muscles pop out even more.

"That's because you've never needed it," I tell him. "Are you still pissing off the women in town?"

His grin deepens. "You know I am. Running out of options, though. A lot of the ladies leave and it seems only men are taking their place."

"Well, hey, you're flexible, right?"

He rolls his eyes and looks over my head at my mother. "Vernalee. You're looking gorgeous."

My mother erupts into giggles. I look over at her and she's actually blushing. Even my mother isn't immune to Maverick's charms, though when I was younger she would complain about his tattoos. Shane even has a few, including his mother's name on his arm, and my mother didn't approve of that one either.

"And you're a sight for sore eyes," she says when she recovers.

"I'm definitely better looking than these boxes," he says and strolls on in to pick up the first one, which he does with ease. He looks around him. "We're just taking the boxes, eh?"

"Yeah," I tell him as I pick up one that's moderately heavy. "Shouldn't take too long. There are movers coming by later to take the big furniture and put it in the storage facility. Since the worker's cottage is fully furnished, there's no point in adding to the clutter."

"And it's just temporary, anyway," my mother adds. It's been almost a week since we had dinner at Ravenswood and I learned of the move, and since then my mother has brought up the fact that it's temporary every chance she can get. I'm not sure if she's trying to convince me or herself.

With Maverick's muscles and speed, it doesn't take long before the back of his shiny truck is piled high with boxes and we're all dripping with sweat. This is the time of year that I don't miss much. The temperatures in North Ridge start to soar until it's far worse than Toronto's summer heat. The only advantage here is the low humidity, but there's still a red haze in the air from the wildfires that sticks to your lungs. I made sure my mother spent most of the move supervising and not lifting a finger.

Now she's closing the door to the apartment building, staring at it wistfully before joining us in the truck.

"It's the start of a new era," I tell her as she climbs into the front seat.

She just nods. "New truck, Maverick?"

"Yup. This baby is the new pride and joy of the North Ridge Search and Rescue Team. Unfortunately, it's not really mine. Next week the decals come in with the company logo, but until then, I can dream." For extra emphasis, he guns the truck down the street, the roar of the hemi engine echoing off the buildings.

"I heard you're the head honcho now," I tell him.

Another cocky grin graces his lips as he flicks his toothpick. "You got that right, darling. I'm pretty much the boss of the whole operation, though sometimes I wish I was still a new punk on the job. I got away with a lot more stuff back then."

"Like what?"

"Well, I'm not going to go into too much detail but we briefly had a woman on the team a few years ago, and let's just say that what I did with her then I couldn't get away with now."

I roll my eyes. "Of course it has something to do with sex."

My mother shakes her head. "Maverick, you're a Nelson. You have a reputation to uphold."

"What?" he asks.

"Being a gentleman," she says. "Dick, Hank, Shane, Fox, you...you're the pride of this town. I wouldn't be surprised if young boys looked up to you."

"Mom, the only reputation Maverick has is being a man whore."

"Hey," he says, brow furrowed in mock hurt.

"Watch your language, young lady," my mother says. "In my day, they were called playboys."

"Same difference," I say. "Hey, someone needs to give Maverick a hard time."

Mav laughs. He's always had such a loud, boisterous laugh

that you can't help but laugh too. "You're probably right about that. You know what, Rachel, I've missed your sass. You've always kept me on my toes. You shouldn't have waited so long to come visit."

My mother and I grow quiet, the truck filling with tension. Mav glances at her and then eyes me in the rearview mirror, apologetic.

After a beat I say, "I know. I should have come earlier."

"It took your mother having cancer to finally convince you," my mother says quietly.

I could argue back. Could tell her that she's never once invited me, never once told me to come. But I don't. It's time to start putting those grievances behind me and try to repair the sketchy relationship we have. "I know. And that wasn't right. I'm sorry."

"Well," Maverick says, trying to make the conversation light again, "the good thing is that you're here. That's all that matters. And more than that, you'll be staying at the ranch, which is pretty much your second home anyway. You'll be all caught up with everyone's lives and bullshit in no time, and it'll be like you never left at all."

Oh, joy.

By the time we get to the ranch, the sun has amped up its intensity, trying desperately to burn though the hazy sky. It creates a greenhouse effect and it feels like we're all bugs being held in a jar with a tiny airhole, the consequence of a young child gone mad with power. I'm soaked in sweat when I step out of the truck, my bare legs leaving gross marks on the leather seats.

"It's a scorcher," my mother says, wiping her brow.

"And that's why all you're going to do is walk into that house and have some iced tea with Dick," I tell her, just as Hank steps out of the door and onto the porch.

"Listen to your daughter, Vernalee," Hank tells her gruffly.

"This heat is no one's friend. I'll supervise these two." He smiles at me. "Don't worry, Del's here to help too. She's already in the cottage making sure everything is clean as can be."

Then he comes over and takes my mother tenderly by the arm, leading her into the house and ushering her inside like a stubborn dog.

Speaking of dogs, just then Fletcher comes loping in from around the corner of the house. He was just a puppy when I left town, and now he's a big cattle dog with the kindest eyes I've ever seen.

Fletcher barks at me excitedly, then darts over to Maverick, running circles around him.

"Hey, boy," Mav says to him, bending down to scratch him behind the ears.

"Do you still have a dog?" I ask him. Growing up, he had a cattle dog, as all the boys did, but he was never the best at taking care of him. I think Jeanine had to feed him on more than one occasion. Maverick definitely had something close to ADHD as a teenager.

"I do," he says. "Believe me, I know, I'm the last person that should have one. But my cousin, I'm not sure if you remember him, he runs a rescue shelter off of Vancouver Island and asked if I wanted to foster a dog that was in the area. And then I met her and it was love at first sight. She's a pitbull mix, though, so herding cattle is not one of her interests. Lying around in the sun like a sack of potatoes is."

The look on Maverick's face is adorable. He's so handsome and rugged and manly, and yet talking about his dog, you'd think he was completely in love.

"What's her name?"

"Chewie."

I laugh. "Because she chews on things or she sounds like Chewbacca?"

"Both."

"Rachel!"

I look over to see Delilah coming toward us from around the house, waving her hand in the air at me.

If Maverick has grown into an even more powerful man, Del has become quite the stunning woman. Even though she was always tall and athletic, she now carries herself with a sense of grace, like she's gliding across a dance floor and not wiping her hands on dirty ripped jeans as she walks through dusty brown grass and white wildflowers.

"Hey you," I tell her, giving her a hug. I'm only five foot five and she's at least five inches taller than me. "Did you grow even more?"

In the past she was always self-conscious about her height so the moment I say that, I regret it.

But she just smiles and shrugs. "If I have, it's needed to keep the drunks on their toes. How have you been? You look great!"

"Thanks," I tell her. "Sorry I haven't kept in touch."

"That's fine. I know you've been busy. You don't even have a Facebook account, do you?"

"No, I erased that shit when I left. Started over."

"I don't blame you."

Maverick is watching us curiously. I know I can be real about things with Del, because even though she's almost like a sister to the Nelson brothers, she's still a girl and she understands. Maverick, on the other hand, is pretty protective over Shane and probably doesn't want to hear me slamming him, even if it's totally understandable.

"Come on, girls," he says to us, heading to the back of the truck and picking up a box. "You can chat and work at the same time."

Except that's a lie. While the three of us move the boxes into the worker's cottage in no time, the air makes it hard to chat and breathe and move heavy shit at once. Luckily, Del made some lemonade, so when we're done, we take a seat on the rocking chairs on the small porch of the worker's cottage and relax. Since this will be my mother's house, I don't want to put any of her stuff away without her input.

Maverick leaves to take his dog for a walk, and as he disappears around the main house, Del turns to me and says, "On a scale of one to ten, how much do you hate being here?"

I can't help but smile. She has these dimples that throw you off while she never hesitates to ask the hard questions.

"Actually, it's not so bad," I admit slowly. "Well, the view is nice." I raise my glass to the scene in front of us, the gentle sloping hills, the barns, the river and the town and mountains behind it. "It costs a fortune for a view in Toronto, and even the best ones over Lake Ontario can't compare to this." I give her a sheepish look. "When I first stepped foot here a week ago, I would have said ten. There's no place I hate more. But since then...I don't know. The town isn't so bad. Neither are the people. It's just..."

She nods, giving me a quick smile. "I know. It's just one person."

I sigh. "Honestly, I don't want to hate him anymore. And I really thought I let go of it over the years. That's why I started over. I wanted to erase this life from my memory because he *was* my life. But seeing him again...I just don't know if I can get past it. You know? I should. I really should. We were young and he broke my heart, and so what? Life went on. I went on. I'm happy now, really I am, and I have a boyfriend who's great and what Shane did shouldn't matter."

"But it does," she says, her eyes kind. She sips her lemonade, the ice cubes rattling in the glass, and leans back against the chair. "I think the real problem is that you never got closure. You just...left."

"I know. But I had to. You know how badly I wanted to

leave—I was always begging Shane to run away with me. But he could never leave this place, even though he said he would. And now, well, I have to wonder if it was all a lie. If he never intended to leave, if it was just something he said to shut me up. He broke me, Del. How do you go from telling someone you want to grow old with them to telling them that you never loved them? I still don't understand."

"You need to talk to him."

I make a growling noise. "That's the last thing I want. I tried the other day, but...I just yelled at him."

"You have a right to yell. And Shane's a good man, despite what he did. He knows he deserves your wrath, so let him have it. Tell him how you really feel. Get it off your shoulders and then you'll find your closure. You'll move on."

"I thought I had moved on."

Her lips quirk up into a wan smile. "No, honey. You never did. You can tell yourself that a million times, but if you had, this wouldn't matter so much. And I know it matters because I can see it in your eyes and hear it in your voice. Time may have changed you in some ways, Rachel, but you're still the same girl I know, and I knew you pretty damn well. You've done what you could to move on, but you'll never be free until you confront him."

That sounds terrifying. It shouldn't be, but it is. And Del is totally right, of course. I've done the things that look good on paper all in an attempt to move on, but the fact is, I haven't. Shane still dominates my heart. I need to get it all out so he no longer has that hold on me.

There was something pained in Del's tone, though, that has me studying her curiously. Like she knows exactly what I've gone through. "How are you? I heard you got engaged."

She rolls her eyes. "Nothing is a secret here. Yeah, I did. Remember Bobby Barrett? Well, we started dating and everything was going great and we got engaged and I said yes, because, well, when you have a nice guy that you love, that's what you do, right? But then the closer we got to wedding plans, the more I started to get cold feet. And he's smart, so he picked up on it. We called it off. It was pretty much as mutual of a breakup as you can get, but...I don't know, it still smarts."

"And how is Fox?"

I knew it was a loaded question and I swear her cheeks are turning pink. "He's fine. He's been out fighting the fires, the usual. I haven't seen him for a few weeks since there was a big blaze up north near 100 Mile House where almost everyone was called in."

The reason I asked about Fox is that I'm pretty sure he's the reason Del got cold feet when it came to her engagement. Though no one has ever publicly acknowledged it and she's never admitted as such, I think Del has secretly been in love with him for a long time.

I want to press the issue, but I'm not sure it would be welcome, so I say, "And has Fox been seeing anyone? I have a hard time believing that any of these boys are single."

Another small smile. "They are, believe it or not. Fox was dating a girl while I was with Bobby, but they broke it off a few months ago. Mav is Mav. Always getting in trouble, but I haven't seen him stay with a girl longer than a few weeks, though he's not getting any younger and should probably grow up at some point. And Shane..." She drifts off and bites her lip while looking at dust rising in the distance, probably from Mav's truck. "He actually had been seeing someone for a year or so."

This is the first I'd heard of this. "Who? Do I know her?"

She nods. "Kristin McGee."

It's funny how when you talk about people you went to school with and grew up with you always use their full names. I frown, remembering vaguely that Kristin used to be the lifeguard at the community pool and Willow Lake during the summer. She was tall, tanned, hot, like a less done-up Pamela Anderson, complete with the giant rack. I also remember her because she was Fox's girlfriend throughout high school.

"Shane dated his brother's ex?" I ask.

Del laughs. "Yeah. Fox didn't care since it was so long ago, but we were all surprised."

I know I have absolutely no right to feel jealous over this, especially since I dated a few guys here and there in university before I met Samuel, but even so, I feel it.

"Is she still?" I gesture to my boobs.

"Yeah. Totally fake now too," Del says. "I don't know why she got implants because it just doesn't fit in this town and people talk like crazy. Man, I used to hate her, but she's okay now. They were an odd couple but it was nice to see Shane happy for once."

I swallow hard.

I don't have too much time to dwell on it because soon after my mother and Hank come by to start unpacking. After Del heads back to the bar to start her shift, the three of us work until around nine and then call it quits. With the setting sun burning red in the hazy sky and shining in through the windows, it gives the cottage an apocalyptic glow as we quickly munch down some simple sandwiches that Dick prepared.

My mother seems happy with it. Even though the cottage is small and old, with her stuff and personal touches, the place looks like it could be featured on HGTV, all reclaimed wood and folksy details.

By eleven, I'm exhausted. I head into my new—temporary —bedroom and crawl into bed, kicking off the thick covers and pulling the sheets over me. I rest my head back on the pillow and watch the gauzy white curtains dance as a hot breeze blows in through the open window. Craning my neck back, I can see a slice of the sky. It's the color of the deepest ink, crowded with a million shining stars.

I see a flash of a shooting one but I'm too afraid to make a wish, too scared to look deep inside and find out what my heart really wants.

I've only made one wish before and it never came true.

CHAPTER 7

RACHEL

PAST – 13 YEARS OLD

"**R**achel, sweetie, it's past your bedtime."

My mother is hovering behind me while I sit on the couch, the TV on at low volume.

"I'll go to bed in a minute," I tell her, my eyes glued to Conan O' Brien on the screen. I love Conan, but I'm not really watching him, not paying attention. It only looks that way.

"Rachel," my mother warns, pressing her hands on the back of the couch. For a moment I imagine her hands coming down and strangling me. Sometimes I wonder if that's what both my parents want to do with me. My mother, because she's afraid of me, my father for the same reasons but different causes. Very different.

"In a minute," I tell her, and I know how I sound. Bratty. Like a teenager. And I am a teenager now. I passed twelve a few months back.

For so long I wanted to be older. But now I realize what being older brings. What being older means.

It's shameful.

I am so ashamed.

I'm tense, bracing for the argument to follow. That's all we do now, my mother and me. We yell and argue and it goes back and forth until she has to drag my father into it.

And then I shut up, because that's what I know how to do. That's how I am to grow. In the corner, a hidden weed. I can't take up too much space, I can't be known. I can only slink back and be quiet and let them forget I exist.

Only he doesn't forget. I wish he did. More than anything I truly wish I didn't exist to him.

But my mother sighs. She's tired. She leaves me and goes out on the porch to light a cigarette, waiting for my father to get home. I don't know why she does that, why she doesn't go to sleep until he gets home. She can't fear him too. She loves him too much. Or maybe I don't know the difference. Maybe I'm too young to know and too old to ignore it.

I don't feel like arguing today. There's too much I should be thinking about. My homework that I didn't do, that's due tomorrow. The fact that Angela Chase is having a birthday party this weekend and I wasn't invited (and really why should I be—I barely talk to her, I barely talk to anyone). I'm looking forward to seeing Shane tomorrow in first period.

The thought of him is really the only reason I can smile these days. At first, I thought it was silly but I'm starting to understand that Shane isn't just my friend anymore. He's more than that. I don't think he knows it, but it's true.

But I could never have the nerve to tell him. That's not what girls are supposed to do anyway. They're supposed to wait for the guy to tell them.

I sigh, feeling my heart do this fluttering thing, like I've got hummingbirds in my chest. It's so freaking weird how I can alternate between feeling so alive and wishing I was dead at the same time.

I go to my bedroom and close the door. I don't know why I bother, but I do because maybe today it will stay closed.

I get dressed even though I know there's no point, but it's all I have. I put on my pajama pants, my tank top, a flannel shirt, and I crawl under the covers.

I pull them almost up over my head and I face the wall.

The lights are all off.

I try to sleep.

I breathe in and breathe out.

I pray to dream, to be taken away.

But time speeds up, maybe hours pass, and then the door creaks open.

I don't have to open my eyes to know a narrow path of light is shining at my back.

He comes in the room. Shuts the door behind him.

I pretend to sleep.

I shrink in my mind, invisible.

I am not here.

I never will be here.

I cease to exist.

"ARE YOU STILL COMING OVER?" SHANE ASKS ME, HOOKING his thumbs under his backpack as we leave Mrs. Robson's class. School is done for the day.

"Of course I am," I tell him, giving him a smile.

He watches me carefully. He's always watching me. I don't mind. It makes me feel good to know I'm interesting to him, that I'm something he thinks about, cares about. Sometimes that feeling, the one in my chest, the one I get from looking deep into his eyes, erases all the bad stuff in my life. It makes me forget.

Sometimes, in the morning, when all I feel is shame and disgust, when I look at myself in the mirror and hate everything I see, I remember that Shane likes who I am, likes what he sees when he looks at me. And if he can feel that way about me, I can't be that bad.

"You've just been quiet lately," he says as we walk outside to his school bus. We live on opposite sides of town so when I'm not on my school bus, I'm on his. My mother works as a librarian so she's always working after school, and my dad, well, I'm glad he's usually working too. The funny thing is, neither of them care where I am. I guess because I'm always with Shane and they trust him and the Nelsons. They always know where to find me.

"I don't know," I tell him. "I'm just..." How do I even explain to him what's been going on? I couldn't. I can't. "I guess I'm not sleeping well. It's fine. So, what do you want to do today?"

He stares at me for a few moments as if he doesn't believe me or something. But as we get on the bus, he lets it go.

"We could go for a ride," he says.

"It looks like it might storm." I glance out the window at the dark clouds moving in from the west.

"You love storms."

"So do you."

"Okay, well maybe we can borrow some dusters in case it rains."

"I don't care about the rain," I tell him. Honestly, I don't care about much except for him. We can do whatever, muck the stalls, collect chicken poop for Jeanine's compost, paint the barn—as long as I'm with him, it doesn't matter. We'll have fun.

"Okay, we'll go for a ride then. Maybe check out that old barn, the spooky one by the pond."

I shiver. That barn is like a hundred years old and I think Shane's dad said it used to be a shelter during the gold rush days. I think it's haunted.

"Maybe," Shane says with a cheeky smile, "we can have a sleepover there one night. Do you dare?"

I let out a nervous laugh at the thought of sleeping next to him. Of course, that could never happen. My parents would never allow it. Our hours together after school and on the weekends are all I'll ever get.

I love being around Shane. I love being around his brothers, his grandpa, even his grumpy father. I love the horses, the ranch, the wide open spaces. It's across town but it feels like it's a world away. The river separates my life at home from a life with Shane and when we cross over it, all my troubles melt away.

The bus drops us off at the foot of the long, dusty drive, and though it's early June, it's already super hot and we're both sweaty and gross by the time we get to the house.

Jeanine opens the front door, wiping her hands on a dish towel.

"Are you guys hungry?" she asks us. "I can whip up some snacks."

Shane looks to me in question.

"I'm fine," I tell her. Jeanine is always trying to get me to eat, says I'm just skin and bones.

"We're going for a ride," Shane tells her as we toss our backpacks onto the porch, our heavy books thudding against the floorboards, nearly knocking over the stack of cowboy and rubber boots lined up against the wall.

Jeanine purses her lips at the sight. "Okay, but be careful. It might storm later. And be back in two hours."

"Yes, ma'am," we tell her in unison before turning around and running down to the stable.

The stables are my favorite place to be in the whole world. I wish I could bottle the scent of manure and hay and wood and smell it every time I was feeling down. Shane kind of smells the same way, but combined with fresh air and sunshine. I would never tell him that I like the way he smells —he'd probably think that's weird or creepy, but it's true.

The stalls are empty because it's summer and the horses are out to pasture, so we grab their halters off the hooks and run out into the field. I usually ride Teddy, a short and stocky quarter horse that's this funky red roan color, like he's been dipped in rust and sprinkled with icing sugar, while Shane has this gorgeous Arabian called Moonshine. He's completely black except for a star at his nose and looks exactly like the horse in that old movie *The Black Stallion*.

Sometimes getting the horses is easy. Today it's hard. They're keeping their distance and acting all spazzy.

"Maybe it's the weather," Shane says as he tries to approach Moonshine before the horse starts trotting in the opposite direction. "I heard horses can sense all kinds of shit."

Luckily it doesn't take me long before I round up Teddy. He's old and what Hank would call "bomb proof." Then Shane eventually corners Moonshine, talking to the horse in calm, easy tones like he's some kind of horse whisperer. But it works and I'm impressed. Is there anything he can't do?

It's not long before we've got them saddled up and are heading out to the right of Cherry Peak, riding down along the river for a bit before we take them up through a forest that skirts along the side of a ridge.

We don't normally go this way because the ground is all rocky, and there's not a lot of open space to gallop and really let the horses fly, but this is where the old homesteader's barn is located. Even the trail there is somewhat spooky, with lots of undergrowth in the forest and low hanging trees.

Finally, we come to a clearing on the crest of a hill. The trees have tapered off and right below us are the remains of the old barn, vines overtaking the dark, splintered wood, knee-high grass surrounding it. Beyond the barn you can see the river far below, like an icy blue thread as it joins an arm of Kootenay Lake. I grew up in a town north of Edmonton in Alberta and we never had anything as beautiful as this.

And we never had a boy as beautiful as Shane.

"So, are you feeling brave?" Shane asks me, leaning against the horn of his saddle and looking like a cowboy. He flashes me a smile and somehow that makes me feel more afraid.

Afraid of my feelings for him.

"You really want to go inside?" I ask warily.

He shrugs. "Only if you want to."

But it feels like a challenge and I've never been one to back away from one.

"Let's check it out."

We ride the horses down to the barn and hop off, tying them loosely to a rotted post just as two ravens sail out of the barn.

I let out a yelp as they fly above us, their wings making this incredible whooshing sound. We watch as they disappear over the ridge, calling to each other as they go with deep, rumbling *caws*.

"My grandpa says ravens are good luck," Shane says. He reaches for me and brushes my long black hair over my shoulder. I nearly freeze at his touch even as shivers cascade down my spine. "You have hair like raven wings. I should call you Raven."

I smile. I like that. I don't want to be Rachel Waters when I'm around him, daughter of the police chief, a girl that should be invisible. I want to be Raven and fly. I want Shane to keep staring at me like he's doing right now, as if I'm some wondrous mystical creature.

"Okay," I say. I think my voice is shaking.

He starts to move toward me, leaning in, and for a moment I think he's going to kiss me.

Holy...

But then he just tugs playfully at the ends of my hair and says, "Let's go inside."

He leads the way, and I follow close behind. I'm not even sure this place is safe to be in.

He pokes his head in through the crooked doorway and peers inside. The whole building is at a slant, looking like it could collapse at any moment. This is the farthest we've ever gone before. We've never gone inside.

I wait at his back, watching his breath rise and fall. He's nervous too. It just seems so dark and scary.

But then he breathes in deep and steps inside.

I watch as he disappears around the corner.

"Shane?" I whisper.

"This is so cool," he says, unseen. "Come on in here. Careful, the floorboards are weak."

"Are there any spiders?"

"Oh come on, ravens aren't afraid of spiders. They aren't afraid of anything."

I wish that were true. But I go inside anyway.

It's dark at first, but then as I walk into the barn, I can see the details more. There's an old rusted stove in the corner, and a three-legged chair. A stack of rotting crates. A bale of hay covered in rat poo and mold. An old lantern hangs from the rafters, the glass cracked. In the far corner of the building, where a bunch of beams have fallen to the ground, Shane disappears.

"Be careful," I cry out after him.

He doesn't respond.

"Shane?"

No response. He has disappeared and become one with the shadows.

"Shane?" I call out, my voice getting sucked up with the dust.

Slowly I creep past the fallen beams. My whole body feels

like it's being poked by needles, I'm so afraid. It's so dark here, with only a little bit of grey light punching through a hole in the sagging ceiling. I think I see a shape moving in the corner, or maybe it's my eyes. There's a sound of something scurrying.

I'm about to call for him again when a hand touches my shoulder.

I scream, whirling around, and start punching wildly.

I strike something.

"Ow!' Shane cries out, his figure appearing in front of me.

"Oh my god!" I put my hand to my chest, as if it can keep my heart from leaping out. "I'm so sorry!"

"It's fine, it's fine," he says, and in the dimness, I can see him grabbing the side of his jaw.

I reach out and touch his face, expecting him to flinch and move away, but he doesn't.

This is the first time I've ever touched his face.

It's softer than I thought it would be.

My fingers linger at his jaw, not sure where to go or what to do but I know I don't want to take my hand away. "You're a jerk. You tried to scare me," I whisper.

"I know, I thought it would be funny," he says. He puts his hand on top of my fingers and holds them there. "I thought you'd laugh. I'm sorry."

His hand drops away but he takes my fingers with it, holding on to them tight.

I feel like I can't breathe. Waves of electricity travel up my arm to my heart, making it feel light and fizzy.

"It's okay," I say, but I'm not even sure the words come out. There's something happening in this space between us— it's like the world is turning around us faster and faster and we're staying still.

Shane leans in and my breath catches in my lungs.

He squeezes my hand with one hand as the other goes to my face, cupping my chin.

Then his lips press against mine.

And my world spins and melts and my heart flies out of my chest on raven wings.

He's kissing me.

My first kiss.

Shane is my first kiss.

I'm so in love with this boy.

Oh my god...I'm actually in love.

The way I feel about him...it now has a name.

I don't even know how to move my lips back, and for a moment I am completely still on the outside even though I'm a whirlwind on the inside. Then I find the strength, the will to kiss him back, our mouths open just enough that I can taste the orange juice he had earlier.

Finally, we both pull away from each other and it's only then that I feel like I can breathe.

But I no longer feel like the same person I was five minutes ago.

In the dark reaches of my heart, I feel an impossible hope.

A seedling that Shane planted with his lips.

We stare at each other in the darkness. He's still holding on to my hand. I think he's smiling. I'm smiling.

Then there's a flash of light and the air explodes with a loud BOOM that shakes the whole building, causing something to fall over in the corner.

Thunder.

"Holy shit that was close," Shane swears. "We have to get out of here."

He pulls me around the fallen beams toward the door just as it sounds like the building is being pelted with rocks. Hail!

We peek outside as round, white hail, the size of dice, comes raining down, bouncing on the grass. Lightning slices across the sky, making me yelp again. I sound like a silly girl, but I can't help it.

Moonshine is scared too, even more than me. Spooked, he rears up, the reins attached to the post snapping in half.

"Moonshine!" Shane yells, about to run after the horse but I pull him back into the doorway and we watch as Moonshine gallops into the pines the way we came. Thankfully Teddy is totally unfazed by all of this and remains where he is, even as the hail bounces off of him.

Another lightning strike happens down by the river, the boom of thunder making me cover my ears.

"It's okay," Shane says, grabbing my hand again and squeezing it hard. "It will pass."

"What if it hits the building?"

"We'll be fine, I promise," he says. "Don't worry, I'll protect you."

And I believe him. Because it's Shane.

Just like he says, the lightning and thunder move on and the hail stops.

"Wow," he says, looking around at the white studded landscape. "That was kind of cool."

I nod. I'm not sure what I'm still hung up on—the storm or the fact that he kissed me.

He *kissed* me.

"Come on," he says. "We'll ride Teddy back." He unties Teddy and climbs on, holding his arm out for me. "I'll pull you up."

Teddy isn't a tall horse, but even so I'm wary about trying to get on this way. I take Shane's hand and he pulls me up. It's awkward, but I manage to sit right behind him in the saddle, my legs pressed against his, my chest against his back. I know we just kissed but this feels even more intimate.

"So much for ravens being good luck," I say as we start to

ride into the trees and back down the mountain. I tighten my arms around his flat stomach.

"You don't think so?" he asks.

I stare at the golden hairs on the back of his neck, wondering if my breath is tickling them. I wonder what would happen if I put my lips there. I wonder if these kinds of thoughts will ever go away or if I'm destined to think of Shane like this forever.

You love him. You love him, you love him.

I swallow. It feels like I have sawdust in my mouth. "Moonshine ran away on you. What if you never get him back?"

"Moonshine went right back to the stable. I promise," Shane says confidently. Then he lowers his voice. "And maybe if we hadn't seen the ravens, I would have never had the courage to kiss you."

"Oh," I say softly, my fingers pressing harder into him.

"And maybe you never would have kissed me back," he adds. "And I don't think I could have ever truly lived without knowing what your lips felt like."

Oh my god. He's being so romantic. My lips are starting to tingle just from his words.

"Shane," I say to him, resting my head against the back of his shoulder.

"What?"

"What does this mean?"

He doesn't say anything for a moment. "That I kissed you?"

"Yeah. Are we still friends?"

"We'll always be friends, Rachel," he says, and his voice is deep and serious. "Always. But now, I hope we're more. I like you. I like you a lot."

"I like you a lot, too."

"More than a friend?"

"Way more than a friend."

It feels good to actually say it. So good. We ride in silence for a few moments and I close my eyes, breathing him in, feeling his heart beating through his back. I don't ever want this ride to end.

"Shane?"

"Yeah?"

"What did you wish for on that wishbone? Remember?"

"I remember," he says, and I can hear the smile in his voice. "But I can't tell you."

"That means it hasn't come true yet."

"No, it hasn't." He pauses. "But it will. One day, it will."

CHAPTER 8

RACHEL

"Is there a Miss Rachel Waters in the house?" A low, gruff voice calls out.

I jump, totally startled, and finish soaking a hand towel in cold water before I turn off the kitchen tap and turn around to see an imposing silhouette standing in the doorway, holding a handful of Queen Anne's lace.

"Fox?" I ask, pressing the cold compress against my forehead, trying to cool down. "Is that you or am I dreaming?" I walk toward him, more than surprised to see him.

"In the flesh," he says, handing me the flowers. "Welcome back."

I take the flowers with a big smile and find myself enveloped in a big bear hug. Like his brothers, Fox is tall and strong with muscles like a beast. I'm practically crushed against him.

"My god, you've turned into the Hulk," I tell him. "Sweaty like him, too."

He pulls back and looks down at himself, casually dressed in cargo shorts and a thin grey shirt that's clinging to his sticky skin. "Actually, I've lost about twenty pounds this month. It's been a fucking nightmare."

"I can imagine. I don't know how you do what you do."

He shrugs. The man has one of the most dangerous jobs and yet never lets it go to his head. "This is the worst year for wildfires since the fifties or something. It's getting so bad, we have firefighters from Mexico coming up to help us. New Zealand, even. I'm lucky I even got a couple days off to come home. Just enough time to rest and eat before I'm sent out again."

"Well, I'm glad you're here," I tell him shyly. Fox was always the most intimidating of his brothers and the relationship between him and Shane was strained at times for a few reasons, but I've always liked the guy. He can be really unpredictable and has a temper that sometimes gets the best of him, but he's honest and intuitive and genuinely cares about people. I guess you'd have to if you're willing to risk your life for them day in and day out.

"The moment I heard you were in town, I had to come see it with my own eyes. You're looking good. Really good. I can't believe it's been that long."

"At first it felt like I'd been gone for a million years, but now that I'm here..."

"It's like you never left."

"Exactly. Except it's way hotter than I remember."

I pick up the wet dish towel and press it against the back of my neck, my hair piled high on top of my head. It's already warm to touch.

"You really need an air conditioner in this old place," Fox says, looking around. "I'll tell Dad it's a worthy investment. I'm sure Shane could set it up pretty quick."

"I'm sure he has enough to do," I tell him, taking the flowers into the kitchen and filling up a vase with water.

Fox lingers by the door. "Have you talked to him?"

"Shane?" I place the flowers in the vase and put it on the middle of the kitchen table. Pretty.

"Yeah."

"Yeah, we've exchanged some words," I tell him. Other than the first day I came to Ravenswood, I actually haven't seen him. Either I've gotten really good at avoiding him or he's gotten really good at avoiding me.

"But have you really talked?"

I frown as I glance at him. "About what?"

"About what happened." I don't say anything and wait for him to go on. "Look, I know it was a long time ago and you're probably over it but...I don't think Shane is."

I let out a dry laugh. "I doubt that. I think Shane was over it, over me, way before it happened. Besides, I know he went out with Kristen McGee."

Fox scratches at his dark beard and grins. "I'm pretty sure he did that just to try and get under my skin. Didn't work, of course." He clears his throat, his features growing serious. "I don't want to get involved with Shane's life, nor yours, but honestly...there's a lot more to this than you think."

His words stab at me and I look at him sharply. "What do you mean?"

He opens his mouth to say something but stops and turns around, listening.

I peer around him. Speak of the devil. Shane is coming up from the house, heading toward us, dressed in jeans, cowboy boots, a black t-shirt with the White Zombie logo on it, and a cowboy hat. His skin is dark and golden from long hours in the sun, his eyes trained on the ground. When he's hanging around in town, Shane wears stuff straight out of the 90's grunge era but when he's on the ranch and working, he's in full-on cowboy mode.

Fox gives me a look that says me he'll tell me later. Or maybe that look doesn't mean that at all.

"Hey," Shane says as he approaches us, stopping a few feet from the porch. I look at him briefly, the swipe of dirt across his cheekbone, the trickle of sweat at his throat. My stomach feels fuzzy and light just from looking at him.

This isn't good.

"Hey," Fox says. "How are you?"

"Not too bad." Shane looks over at me and nods, then looks back to Fox. "Dad told me you wanted the shoes off?"

"I think it would help."

"Shoes off?" I ask, coming over to them.

"Horseshoes," Fox explains to me. "It's not so bad right now, but if it doesn't rain again soon, it's going to get worse, and if you're out riding on the range and the horseshoe strikes a rock, it can create a spark. That's all it takes sometimes to set this place ablaze."

"It won't be a problem," Shane says, taking off his hat and wiping his brow. "We'll have to go out and move some cattle later in the week but Polly and the other horses are fine without their shoes. Are you staying for dinner?"

I can't help but pick up on the tone in Shane's voice. Both wary and hopeful all at once.

"I need to get home and just take a load off," Fox says. He grins at me. "Just wanted to come here first and see Rachel while I had the chance."

"I'll see you before you go, right?" I ask him, not wanting him to leave.

"Hopefully."

He then turns and walks past Shane, giving him a quick punch on the shoulder as he goes. That's pretty much the extent of their relationship.

I expect Shane to follow behind him—when we were growing up, sometimes Shane followed Fox around like a dog looking for scraps—but instead he walks up the steps and hovers on the porch, staring at me.

"How did you sleep last night?"

His expression is honest and open. Shane has a face that makes you want to tell him a million secrets. I swear somewhere in my chest a little piece of my heart is breaking off.

"Fine." I clear my throat, twisting the towel in my hands.

"You moved in okay?"

I nod. "No problems. We had a lot of help."

"Sorry I couldn't be there. I had to fix some of the irrigation pipes."

"No worries."

We both lapse into silence as Shane continues to stand there.

I think about what Del said yesterday about closure.

Face it. Face it, face him, and move on.

I gesture to the rocking chairs on the porch. "Want to come in and put your feet up? I made some lemonade earlier. You look like you could use it."

"Are you sure?"

I nod. "It's fucking hot as balls."

That makes his mouth quirk up into a half-smile. Shane never smiled very much; he was always so serious, but when he does, it's like the sun bursting through the clouds. When I was younger, I did whatever I could to make him smile, just because it made my heart feel like it could fly away.

"All right then," he says, stepping onto the porch and sitting down on one of the chairs.

I turn and head to the kitchen, taking in deep breaths, trying to calm my nerves. I feel hotter now than ever so I splash cold water on my face and the back of my neck before I pour us each a mason jar of lemonade.

Talk to him. Get it all out.

I step back outside and give him a small smile as I pass

him his drink. I catch a whiff of him as I do, and that fuzzy feeling in my stomach intensifies. He smells like I remembered. Dry grass and sunshine and sage. He smells like the very earth itself. Home.

You can do this, I tell myself, ignoring all those stupid feelings fluttering up, the fact that my heart is starting to race.

"Thank you," he says, and he stares at me so intensely that I feel my skin ignite, an inferno growing within me.

A memory takes over—us making love in the hayloft, him so deep inside me in body, heart, and mind that I could swear the whole barn was going to go up in flames.

Run away with me, I'd whispered to him.

I'll go wherever your heart is, he replied.

"I know this must be quite the change," Shane says as he sits down in the rocking chair, bringing my attention back to him, to this Shane in the present. He rests his elbows on his thighs and stares out at the view. His forearms are large, tanned and sculpted, and I know they're strong enough to throw a two-hundred-pound calf over his shoulders. "No skyscrapers here."

I'm so focused on his body that it takes me a moment to respond. "No. But it's a nice change of pace."

"How long do you think you're going to stay?"

I shrug, hating how up in the air all of this is. "I went with my mom to the hospital the other day. The doctors are trying to get her an appointment for her surgery in either Kelowna or somewhere near Vancouver. Even though it's, like, fucking cancer, there's still a waiting list. And of course, I can't even pay her way since there are no private clinics here. Still, they said it shouldn't be more than a few weeks. Fingers crossed."

"That's a lot longer than I thought. Is your job okay with that? All your time off?"

I exhale, the stress from earlier creeping back. "They say they are. It's coming out of my vacation pay now, which sucks because I never take vacations and really wanted to keep that."

"Why don't you take vacations?"

I give him a steady look. "Do *you* ever take vacations?"

"Fair enough. It's rare that I even get an evening off. And anyway, what would I do? For me, all I need to do to have a break is go down to the river or the lake or the hot springs and sort myself out. Maybe go fishing with Maverick. Otherwise, it's a pretty good life. I can't ask for much more."

I have to admit, I'm both envious and happy for him. Envious because growing up, this is all Shane wanted to do and he's doing it and it makes him happy.

He also said he wanted to marry you one day, to have lots of babies, a voice inside me says, forever dredging up the past.

"Well," I say, "it's not like I wouldn't want to jet off to Cuba for a week or spend some time traveling across Europe, but the moment I go, the moment my job becomes vulnerable. There are too many people at the agency dying to have my spot and I've worked too hard to let it go."

He frowns, shaking his head, has a sip of his lemonade, licks his lips. God, those lips. They gave me my first kiss, whispered secrets, promised me the world. "That doesn't sound like a fun career to me."

I look away, feeling slighted. "It *is* a fun career. I mean, it's exciting and challenging and there's always something new to learn." I don't add that I think it's giving me an ulcer, nor the fact that my doctor has prescribed me medication for anxiety which started flaring up again when I started this job.

"I have to say, when I heard that's what you were doing, I was surprised. All that time together and I never once heard you mention any interest in advertising. When we were growing up, all you wanted to do was breed horses and have a garden."

"I have a garden," I say stubbornly, thinking of my potted

plants on my balcony which are probably all dead now because I forgot to get someone to water them. "And I just kind of discovered advertising in university. I was going to do communications but advertising pulled me in."

"Too many episodes of *Mad Men*?" he asks.

I smile. "Shane Nelson, I am shocked you know of a TV show. How else have you changed? Are you doing Netflix binges like the rest of the world?"

"I'll have you know I'm not as ass backwards as you remember."

"Oh really? Tell me one thing that proves otherwise."

"I'll have you know that I have my own Instagram account."

My mouth drops open. "Oh, you do not." I start reaching into my pocket for my phone, ready to call him on his bluff.

"Actually, it's Polly's," he says. "Or it was until I realized horses can be pretty damn boring. And then it became Fletcher's, because, you know, it's Fletcher and that dog is a ham. And the chickens started making an appearance. Sometimes a few calves and heifers. So really, now it's the account for all the animals here."

I glance at my phone, not surprised that Samuel still hasn't texted back to my *I miss you*, and then open Instagram. I have my own account, too, but it's private and I rarely post. I mainly use it to follow our clients or other ad agencies to see what they're doing.

"Look up Ravenswood Ranch," he tells me, and I type it in.

Sure enough, there's an account composed of artfully taken photos of the animals with "punny" captions. He posts every couple days or so, and there's already over 1,000 followers which is a lot for someone who obviously isn't trying very hard.

"You almost look impressed," he says.

"The key word is almost."

He grins at me, and for a moment I'm shocked at how damn easy our banter is. For a second, it's like nothing has changed at all. For a second I feel like I'm home.

And for once, I don't push the feeling away.

But as we're staring at each other, smiling, his grin begins to falter. He slams back the rest of his lemonade and gets up. "Thanks for the drink. Cooled me right down."

He hands the jar to me and I'm so taken aback at how abrupt he's being that I almost don't feel that tiny spark when his fingers brush against mine. And let's be honest, it's not a tiny spark but a surprising jolt of electricity.

"Where are you going?" I ask as he starts down the steps.

He raises his brows, probably as surprised as I am that I asked that, and puts on his hat. "I've got a lot of work to do."

"Oh," I say, and I'm surprised at how disappointed I feel. It's not that I didn't get a chance to properly talk to him, it's just that it was so easy just now. It felt like old times and it felt good.

"See you around, Rachel," he says, tipping his hat to me like a goddamn old-fashioned cowboy, then saunters off toward the ranch house. Naturally, my eyes are trained on his ass as he goes.

I watch until he disappears and then exhale so harshly, it's like I've been holding my breath this entire time.

A FEW DAYS PASS AND IT'S FUNNY HOW I ACTUALLY DON'T see Shane around. My mother and I have eaten dinner at Hank's twice and Shane was off somewhere, doing something or other. I get that the man is busy, but now I know for sure he's avoiding me.

What's most aggravating is the fact that the less I see him, the more I want to see him. It shouldn't be that way, but it is. Maybe it's because I've got it set in my mind now that I have to talk to him, I don't know. But even so, I'm not seeking him out. I'm just not that brave, even though both Fox and Del's words keep running through my head.

I'm bored out of my mind. I'm so used to working, to being busy every single moment of every single day that I'm having a hard time adjusting to the fact that I've got nothing to do. I do what I can to help my mother, but she seems to be doing okay and brushes me off every chance she gets. I still cook and clean for her but that doesn't take up too much of my time. I've tried reading but I just can't get into any books right now. My mind just wants to think about two things. And when I say think, I mean worry.

It wants to worry about work. The reception here isn't that great and the wifi is pretty shitty, so emails take forever to send and load. Even though I've asked to be CCed on every single email that's going to Pete or that Pete sends out, I'm getting less and less of them, and when I finally do get them, it's old news. So, of course, it looks like I don't really care about the clients when I do.

And then I want to worry about Shane. Maybe worry isn't the right word, but more often than not, my mind keeps being drawn back to him. It's probably because I have too much time to think.

But then the opportunity presents itself. Hank sees me moping about on the porch, all hot and irritated and bored, and asks if I wouldn't mind lending a helping hand.

"Of course," I say, grateful for something to do, to feel useful. I lift myself off the rocking chair, wiping my sweaty palms on my shorts. "What do you need?"

"Well," Hank says cautiously, rubbing at his moustache.

"Shane's in the stable and I know there are some repairs to be done. Maybe see if he needs some help."

Oh, I see.

"That's not a problem, is it?" he asks.

I paste a smile on my lips. I don't want to get into this with Hank, not while I'm living on his property. "Not at all. I'd be glad to help."

I head down the sloping grass to the stable, feeling my heart start to kick up with each step I take. When I get to the stable, it's dark and empty, the familiar smell of grain, hay, and manure reaching a happy place inside of me.

I hear the sound of rushing water, so I go around the corner to where the tap is.

And my mouth drops open.

Shane is shirtless and rinsing himself off with the hose. Beside him is his buckskin mare, Polly, but I barely see her. All I can see is the river of water as it runs down the hard, tanned planes of arms, chest, and torso.

Fuck me. When Shane was younger he was in fine shape, albeit a little on the thin side. Now he's filled out completely. He might not be a hulk or a beast like Mav or Fox, but he's fucking fit as hell and absolutely ripped. He even has those sharp V muscles on his hips, something he's never had before.

"Jesus," Shane swears, finally noticing I'm there. I guess I have been standing here silently and gawking at him like an idiot.

I immediately try and play it cool, lifting my chin. "Hey. Sorry to interrupt your shower."

He gives me a small smile and pushes his wet hair off his face.

My god, he's so fucking gorgeous.

Everything inside me is churning, and I'm on fire, inside and out.

"Only way to cool off," he says and gestures to Polly tied

up to the post beside him, who I now realize is also wet. "Figured I'd take care of the both of us."

"Your jeans are all wet," I point out. How observant of me.

"They'll dry in a second," he says, turning the hose over in his hands. "I could take them off if you want."

Don't fall into the trap, Rachel. Keep your cool.

I ignore the comment. "Your dad said you probably needed my help."

He cocks a brow. "Did he now?"

I shrug. "Yeah. And honestly, I need something to do. I'm going crazy with boredom."

He studies my face for a moment, his golden eyes so intense that I fight the urge to look away. "That doesn't sound like the Rachel I know."

Good.

"The Rachel I knew," he goes on, "could lie in a field for hours and be entertained by the clouds."

"Yeah, well that Rachel didn't have a job to worry about and bills to pay."

"That Rachel was a lot more fun."

I give him the stink-eye. "Hey, I'm still fun."

"I doubt it," he says, turning his back to me to pay attention to Polly.

"Hey," I say again, really annoyed now. "Don't pretend like you know me. You don't. I may have changed but it doesn't mean I'm some fussy city bitch now."

He looks over his shoulder at me, frowning. "I would never think that of you."

My throat feels thick as I swallow. "Oh."

"I'm just saying...when you were young, the word bored wasn't in your vocabulary. And believe me, you had a lot to worry about then. I know."

And just like that, all our history hits me square in the

chest. Everything I'd gone through in the past, it was something I'd only told a handful of people throughout my whole life. There was Shane. My mother. And a few shrinks and counselors. Samuel doesn't know. None of my boyfriends did. None of my friends either.

I'm looking at one of the few people, if not the only person, who knows the deepest, darkest parts of me. The pull I feel toward him is indescribable.

He knew them all and he left you, the voice inside me says. *What does that say about him? About you?*

"Hey," he says gently, taking steps toward me until he's just a foot away. He peers down at me and I can't help but stare up at him. He runs the tip of his finger between my brows. "No frowning. Those are the ranch rules."

I close my eyes at his touch, trying desperately to feel grounded. One simple touch and I feel like I just might float away.

He takes his hand away but doesn't step back. I can feel the heat coming off of him. He smells like hay and cold water, and everything inside me is slowly coming alive.

"You really want to help?" he asks, his voice bringing me back.

I nod, opening my eyes to meet his.

"You can start by laughing again."

"Laughing?" I repeat.

"Yeah. Laughing. You have the most beautiful laugh, Rachel. Why do you think I spent so many years trying to make you laugh?"

"I thought I was always trying to make *you* laugh."

"Maybe," he says. "But I think it would do you good."

I give him a wry look. "I'm not about to laugh on cue. Besides, I don't have a lot to laugh about right now."

"With your mom? I get it. But she's going to be okay. And she'll be even better than okay if she knows you're okay."

"But I'm not okay."

There. I said it.

I'm not okay.

Shane watches me and gradually nods, looking off into the distance, squinting at the sun. "I know all of this is hard on you. It's hard on me too."

"How?"

He licks his lips. "I won't pretend I know what it's like to be in your shoes right now. I lost my mother before I even had the chance to know her." He glances at me thoughtfully. "Or maybe that's the same thing for you. That you never really had a chance to know your mother until now."

I sigh, running my hand down my face. I've been dying to talk about this with someone, I just can't believe that it's Shane.

Or maybe I can believe it. Because it feels more than right.

"It's okay if you don't want to talk about it," he says.

"No, no. It's fine. I just...I don't know where to start. When I told my boss that I was coming here, you know what he said? He said, if it's just stage one cancer, then why do you have to go? And for a split second I almost agreed with him. Because that's what I've trained myself to do. To pretend that she doesn't exist, that we have nothing between us that counts." I pause, cringing at how callous those thoughts were. "And then I thought, wait a minute. Why does my mother have to be on her fucking deathbed before I go? Why do people have to die or almost die before we decide we need to make things right? So that's why I came. Because I should have come sooner and I wasn't going to wait until later."

"And how has it been?"

"I don't know. She's different. And maybe it's because I'm different and I'm seeing her through new eyes, or maybe I'm the same and she's changed, I don't know. But it's...both hopeful and scary at the same time. Hopeful because I think maybe we can move past it. Maybe I can forgive her, even if she doesn't ask for forgiveness. And scary because, well... what if she hurts me again? What if she isn't the mother I hope she can be? And what if I'm just...worthless all over again?"

Over those last words, I start choking up. Tears spring to my eyes, burning at the corners.

"Hey," Shane says softly, dropping the hose and wrapping his arms around me. He does this without asking, without offering, holding me like it's second nature.

And though I'm stiff at first because it feels like my heart is breaking for a million different reasons, it's not long before I relax and let myself completely melt into him. It doesn't matter that he's wet, or that I haven't been in his arms since before my life was turned upside down, or that he's the one who tore it all up. None of that matters right now.

Somehow, though, I manage not to cry buckets and have a small bit of control. And it's through that control that I realize that being in Shane's arms is the absolute last place I need to be.

I pull back, putting space between us, and give him an awkward smile. "Sorry. I just...I guess I needed to talk."

He's still watching me, brimming with intensity. "Is that all you need to talk about?"

I breathe in deeply through my nose, trying to summon the courage. "No. I need to talk to you."

He nods. "And I need to talk to you."

I take another step back. "But honestly, I...I don't want to get into it right now. I can't." Even just talking about my mom has put me in this extremely vulnerable state. I don't want to rock the boat.

"I understand," he says. "I just..." He runs his hand through his hair. "There are so many things I need to tell you.

So many things I need you to know. And I know it probably doesn't matter to you, but it matters to me."

Suddenly, I'm afraid. Terrified to the core. Not of him. Of what he might say and how I might feel about it.

The last thing I want is to look at Shane with new eyes. I need to hold on to the anger and bitterness because I think that's the only thing keeping my heart safe right now. It's the only thing keeping my current life on course.

"Maybe some other time," I tell him. "I only wanted to see if you needed help."

He sighs, nodding. "Of course," he says, looking around him before picking up the hose. "Honestly, today I've pretty much got things under control. I'd suggest we go for a ride but since I just washed Polly, maybe we should save that for another time. If you're interested, of course."

"Every time I was stressed out or sad, you'd always get me on a horse," I say quietly, smiling at the memories.

"And it always worked," he says. "You were laughing in no time."

Images of the two of us riding across the range fill my head, both of us double bareback, my arms wrapped around his waist, laughing into the wind as the hooves flew beneath us. We were young, we were free, we didn't care about anything but each other.

What the fuck happened?

But before I can dwell on that, Shane is pointing the hose at me and saying, "Still, I know of another way to make you laugh."

He squeezes the trigger and the water comes on full blast, hitting me right in the chest.

And of course, I'm in a white tank top.

"You asshole!" I yell at him, spinning around, trying to get out of the way, but he keeps that water right on me until I'm soaked to the bone and running away from him, yelling, and yes, laughing. I'm laughing my ass off.

"I told you," he says, grinning from ear to ear.

I shake my head, water flying onto the side of the barn. "I'll get you back for this," I point at him, making sure he knows my threat is real.

Then I stalk away from him, all the way back to the cottage.

I'm smiling the entire time.

CHAPTER 9

SHANE

PAST – 16 YEARS OLD

I'm in trouble.

The front door slams shut, shaking the whole house, and I know it's Fox even before he yells, "Where is that little shit?!"

"Go easy on him," Maverick's muffled voice says from somewhere in the kitchen. These walls are damn thin. At least I have time to prepare myself.

I stand up, put my book away, and move into the middle of my bedroom. Shoulders back, hands curled into fists, feet grounded.

I fucked up. I knew this was coming.

Loud steps come up the staircase, thumping down the hall to my room at the end.

The door slams open, the framed picture of me and Rachel on the wall rattling.

Fox steps inside, his face red, pointing his finger at me. "You have ten seconds to tell me how the fuck you're going to fix this."

I open my mouth to speak.

Fox punches me squarely in the jaw.

Stars fly behind my eyes, and I stumble backward until I hit my desk.

He swings at me again.

I duck and go for his waist, wrapping my arms around him and pushing him back until he's slammed against the opposite wall.

"Hey, cut it out!" Maverick yells at us, appearing at the doorway, but Fox is intent on killing me and I'm intent on trying to save my own hide. Somehow Maverick wrangles himself between us, pushing us apart. All of us are breathing hard, and Fox's eyes show no mercy as he stares at me.

"You fucking piece of shit," Fox yells at me, spit flying. "Who the fuck said you could borrow my truck?"

"It was just for a few hours," I tell him, yelling right back.

"And in that few hours you fucking wrecked it!"

"I didn't wreck it! It's just a dent. It will come out."

"You fuck, you knew I was selling that thing!"

"I didn't know that. I knew you got a Jeep, I didn't think you'd care."

"Guys!" Maverick yells, head volleying between us both. "Grandpa is trying to have a nap."

"Like hell I am," Grandpa says. Oh great, now he's here. "Just what on earth is going on here? It's almost Christmas. Can't you boys show a bit of respect to the Lord?"

"This fuckhead stole my truck!" Fox says, huffing and puffing. "He doesn't even have his full license. And then he totals it."

"It was a dent! And I'm sorry."

"Shane," my grandfather says, sounding beyond disappointed. Shit. I hate that. "Is this true? Did you take his truck?"

My nostrils flare as I try and keep my anger under control.

Perhaps it's unjustified anger, but it's anger all the same. "I wanted to take Rachel to the hot springs."

"Fucking Rachel," Fox swears. "You'll do anything for pussy, won't you?"

"Fox, watch your damn mouth," Grandpa says, stepping into the room. "Rachel is a good girl and has nothing to do with this. Show some respect."

At least Fox has the decency to look chagrined.

"Shane." Grandpa turns his discerning gaze to me. "You know better than this. I'm disappointed in you. You're supposed to be the level-headed one here."

I sigh and look away, rubbing at my jaw. There's going to be a bruise later. "I didn't think anyone would care. Fox said he got a new Jeep down in Idaho. I thought he wouldn't care about the truck." And that's partly the truth. Fox is attending school for firefighting down in the States because it's less expensive to attend and he's only around during holidays. I thought he'd care, but I didn't think he'd care that much. I also didn't think he'd notice. I wasn't supposed to back up into that tree stump. It just happened.

"Well, how am I supposed to sell the truck? That thing was practically brand new and flawless. I was going to get almost all my money back. Now I have to spend extra money or take a loss, and it's a loss either way."

Maverick folds his arms and steps back, satisfied that we've stopped going after each other and wary that we might start up again.

Grandpa looks at me. "Well, boy, how are you going to fix this? Because, in your case, sorry doesn't cut it. You should just be glad that this isn't getting written on your record. If anyone found out that you drove a truck without a full license and then damaged it, you would be in huge horseshit."

"I don't know," I say. I wanted an after-school job but my

dad needs me on the ranch, and I don't get paid for that. "Somehow."

"With what money?" Fox counters.

"You know I don't have any." I glare at him. The last bit of cash I had from doing some odds and ends work went to buying Rachel's Christmas present. "I'd buy the truck off of you if I could."

"Or pay for the repairs," Fox says.

"How would you buy the truck?" Grandpa asks.

"I don't know. But I need a truck, don't I? If I'm going to continue working on the ranch, doing the job of a hired hand, I should at least have a vehicle, and you and Dad are always using yours."

Grandpa nods. "You have a point."

I hate to admit it to them, but there's another reason why I want that truck. It was in that truck, last night at the hot springs under a brilliant full moon, where I finally told Rachel I loved her.

I'd been sitting on that for a long time, holding it close, so afraid that even after dating for three years, that it wouldn't ring true, wouldn't be enough. I've been in love with Rachel from the day I first laid eyes on her, even before I knew what it all meant, and I've let it build and boil and rage inside me. It raged beautifully for years. I think that's the basis for real love. Letting it burn you up from the inside out until you can no longer contain it.

And Rachel returned the favor. Told me she loved me. Said she loved me since forever and for forever.

So, no matter what happens with the truck, if I'm lucky enough to have it or not, that punch in the face was certainly worth taking.

"Listen," Grandpa says, putting his hand on Fox's shoulder. "You're twenty-two years old. Shane is sixteen. He may be a bit of a wild card sometimes, but you're the oldest and you need to take the high road here and set an example. Let Shane have the truck."

"What?" Fox erupts, and when he looks at me I swear I'm dead to him. Then again, I always thought I was. "Why the fuck do you let him get away with everything!"

"He doesn't get away with everything," Grandpa says calmly. "I just think, maybe this time, it's for the best. You'll get your money for the truck, I'll see to that. Your father will pay for it. And then Shane will work that off. The kid oughta be getting paid for his work anyway. I've told your father that many times."

It sounds fair to me, but I know Fox hates it. And while I would sometimes do anything to get him to pay attention to me, including stealing his truck, I don't want him to hate me any more than he does. I know he resents the fact I was born, that it was because of me that our mother killed herself.

And I know he's right too. It's a truth I can't escape from.

"You think you can just float through life without any punishment for the things you've done," Fox says, poking his finger hard into my chest. "Stay the fuck away from my stuff."

Maverick steps forward, ready to push Fox off but Fox shrugs him away and storms out of the room.

I exhale, giving them both a sheepish look. "I'm sorry."

Maverick shakes his head at me. "You need to be more careful with him. You know he's a loose cannon. He could have killed you."

I shrug. "He always wants to kill me."

Grandpa sighs and puts his hand on my shoulder. "You need to keep your head on straight, boy. I know you love Rachel. We all do. But next time you need something, just ask. I know you and Fox have it rough sometimes, and I can only hope that gets better as you both get older, but one of you has to be the bigger person, and it's always better if you both are. Try and play nice for the rest of the holiday, okay? It's Christmas for crying out loud."

And with that, the two of them leave my room, closing the door behind them. When they're gone, I take out my phone and text Rachel.

Hey, baby. Bad news. Fox found out about the truck. I won't be able to take it again. Good news is I might be able to save up and buy it off him. I'll have to see what my father says.

She texts back: *Shitty. How mad was he?*

I text back: *He punched me in the face and I had to tackle him. That mad.*

She texts back: *Oh no! Are you okay? I'm so sorry.*

I'm smiling as I send: *The punch was worth it.*

So no movie tonight?

I had planned to try and get the truck again and take Rachel to the movies. I wanted it to be a real date. Then I wanted to give her her Christmas present early.

Then I wanted to tell her I loved her, over and over and over again.

Then I wanted to...well...I'm getting ahead of myself here. Still, I'll be prepared.

I can have Mav drop me off at the theatre. Or maybe you could just come here and we can do the movie another night?

She waits a few seconds before responding. *I'd love to but I won't be able to get a ride.*

This is probably for several reasons. Her mother is often drunk and can't drive. Her father is usually on duty, and if he's not...well...he wouldn't do it. He doesn't like me, doesn't like Rachel seeing me. And even though she doesn't talk about him much, she's absolutely terrified of him. The less that they interact, the better.

I'll have Mav come get you, I tell her. *Be ready in an hour, okay?*
K.

Poor Mav doesn't even realize he's volunteered for this

and I know I have to tell him now before he starts tucking into his nightly beers. Thankfully, when I tell him, he just rolls his eyes and agrees. Maverick is girl crazy so he's usually willing to help me out when it comes to Rachel. Says he understands though I don't think Mav has even felt a fraction for anyone of what I feel for my raven girl.

It's not long before Maverick's beat-up truck is pulling up to the house, sliding in the snow until it comes to a stop. I can see Maverick laughing behind the steering wheel at his fancy driving skills. He's such a show-off.

Rachel seems immune to his charms and is rolling her eyes as she steps out of the truck and into the snow. She glances at me in the window and smiles.

My chest glows with heat. That smile of hers has the ability to rewrite all my bad days.

She comes inside, and I immediately pull her toward me, kissing her. I don't care if my grandfather is sitting on the couch watching or if Maverick is behind her, making slurping noises.

"I missed you," I whisper to her as I pull away, still cupping her face in my hands.

She gives me a shy smile, obviously too embarrassed to say anything in front of my family. She waves hello at my grandpa, and I take her hand, leading her to my bedroom.

My dad is out at the bar with some friends and if he were home he certainly wouldn't let me take her to my room, but grandpa has never cared.

"Where's Fox?" she asks in a hush after I've closed my bedroom door behind her.

"Sulking somewhere," I tell her. I slip my hands around the small of her waist and nestle my mouth into her neck. She tastes like vanilla.

She lets out a breathy sigh as I suck at her skin, relishing the feel of her, the need for her burning inside me. I'm hard in seconds and press myself against her hips, making sure she knows it.

"Shane," she says softly, her hands sinking into my hair. "We can't do this here."

"Why not?" I murmur. "And do what?" I add as I glance at her, searching her eyes for any and all signs that she wants this.

"Anything," she says, pulling my hair back slightly. My eyes close in bliss. I love it when she plays with my hair.

"But we've done it here before," I tell her, leaning in to nip at her lower lip, taking it between my teeth. "Why stop now?"

"Not when your grandfather and Maverick are downstairs. You know how thin the walls are."

Good point. And I know how loud she can be when my head is between her legs. And besides, I love her. I want more than just getting each other off. I want to sink deep inside her for the first time.

Somehow, I manage to pull myself away. For the second time today I'm breathless and my skin feels hot, but for completely different reasons. "Let's go for a walk." I turn around and open up my desk drawer, quickly taking a small jewelry box out of there and discreetly putting it in my jeans. I do the same with a couple of condoms.

"A walk? In this weather?"

I shut the desk drawer and turn around, grinning at her. "It's not snowing. It's brisk. We'll go to the barn."

"The barn?" She doesn't look too impressed.

"I have a present for you," I tell her.

"Is it a horse?"

"Just come for a walk with me."

I take her hand and lead her downstairs, throwing on boots and jackets and scarves. Maverick has disappeared somewhere and Grandpa isn't even paying us much attention. Matlock must be on TV.

We step outside into the crisp air. Her present is burning a hole in my pocket. It's not an engagement ring, I know we're too young for that, but it's something along those lines, and once I saw it I knew I had to have it.

The sky is clear, a dark velvet universe that stretches above our heads from snowy peak to snowy peak. Everything glows under the light of the near full moon; we don't even need flashlights.

"It's magical," Rachel says, her breath freezing in the air, becoming a cloud.

We trudge along through the snow, the path to the barn deep with flakes from earlier, hand in hand, breathing in the night that seems like it might stretch on forever. The town across the river twinkles in blurred lights of red, white, gold, and green.

The stable is full of horses right now and as I switch on the lights at the base of the hayloft, a few familiar faces stick their heads out of their stalls, nickering softly at our intrusion.

"Where are we going?" she asks me, and I nod at the ladder.

"Up."

She glances up into the hayloft. "Really?" Rachel isn't a fan of creepy crawlies.

"Don't worry," I assure her. "I was up there earlier. It's fine. No rats, no bugs, just hay."

And also some blankets, which she discovers as soon as she's up there.

"There's a lantern, but I don't know if you can see it," I say as I climb up after her.

She turns the knob and the loft is filled with a warm glow.

That same glow fills my heart.

There's Rachel, settling amidst flannel blankets atop dry, clean hay, her nose red from the cold. She smiles at me, quick and nervous at first as I stand there, my feet on the last rung of the ladder, and then something passes over her eyes. They become serious, grave, not in sadness or something heavy, but there's a depth to them that wasn't there before. A knowing. A wanting.

A yearning.

She starts to remove her parka, then her sweater, her eyes never leaving mine. She's looking so deep into my soul that I feel something inside me stir. It's not just lust. It's not my dick straining against my jeans. It's something much more.

It's a shift.

It's a bookmark sliding in the middle of a novel where the hero's world is blown apart.

Everything that happens before that page is the before.

Everything that happens after is the rest of the hero's life.

This moment is the dividing moment, where a world is halved in two and there's no turning the pages back.

She continues to undress, and our eyes never break apart, not until she's completely naked and lit by the glow of the lantern, her clothes discarded around her like petals.

In my sixteen years, I've seen the most breathtaking sunsets out here on the ranch, the way the sun melts behind the glaciers, casting everything in gold. I've seen sunrises that make you believe in God, all the colors in the world. I've seen the fields come alive again in the spring, so bright and lush you can't believe they'd ever died. I've seen calves being born, eagles that soar higher than the sun, I've seen horses galloping across the plains with sheets of rain chasing their tails.

But I've never seen anything so gorgeous as this.

Rachel is in front of me, naked and bare, all sleek lines

and soft skin and pale places, hidden places, places that only exist for me.

"I'm sorry I've made you wait so long," she says to me, her voice so low it's barely audible above the stir of horses below. "I wasn't ready."

I'm already climbing over her, pressing my finger to her lips. "Please don't apologize. I would have waited forever."

She looks away, breaking our gaze. A flash of shame comes over her eyes.

I kiss her forehead and murmur against it, "We don't have to do this, Raven. There's no rush."

"I know," she whispers, shifting her head back so she's looking at me. Her eyes are brimming with tears. It strikes me so hard, so deep, that I swear it goes right through me like a bullet. "But I want to. I need to. I need to feel your love, Shane. Please. I need to feel how you love me."

I can't argue with that. I get undressed quickly until I'm totally naked, my skin both hot and cold. I take the condom out of my discarded jeans, leaving the gift still inside my pocket.

This is a different gift entirely. Her soul to mine. Mine to hers.

I slip the condom on with shaky hands, hoping I got it right.

I move between her legs as they open for me.

She reaches up, grabbing the back of my neck, my shoulders.

"Tell me if anything is too much," I tell her, my voice already shaking in anticipation. I don't want to hurt her, but I know I just might. "Tell me if you want me to stop and I'll stop."

"I love you," she says as an answer.

Everything inside me blooms and breaks and blooms and breaks. "I love you, too."

I take my time turning her on, making her wet, making her ready. In this hayloft, we have all the time in the world. In this place, this moment, we are the world.

When she's close, her breath short, her thighs tense, I push inside her.

She grips me hard, her nails digging in. There's strain on her brow.

And all I feel is hard tension swirling into bliss.

There's nothing like this.

There never will be.

It's just a spiral of her and me, wrapping around each other, going down, tumbling, turning.

Fucking hell.

I don't even think I can last as long as I need to.

My pace quickens, my hips slamming into hers, and finally her face relaxes, her legs wrap around my waist, her mouth at mine, and I'm fucking *gone*.

I pump once, twice, hoping, wishing on some wild star that this feels as good for her as it does for me.

And then it's over. My mind has melted. My heart is a jackhammer in my chest. My muscles won't stop shaking.

I brush the hair off her forehead, damp with sweat, and gaze into her eyes, searching for a sign that she's okay.

"Are you okay?"

She nods, licks her lips. "I'm fine."

"I'm sorry that was so…"

"It was enough," she says. She smiles. "Believe me, it was enough."

I grin back at her, kiss her forehead, her nose, her lips, her chin.

"But you didn't come."

She gives me a wry smile. "I know. But there's no rush. You've made me come a million times before, and I'm sure you'll do it a million times more. That's not why I did this.

It's not why I wanted to lose my virginity with you. I just wanted to be a part of you forever. I just wanted to feel you inside me. And I did. And I still can. I don't think I'll ever stop feeling you now."

"You promise?"

"I promise."

I kiss her again. Again and again.

Time passes. I hear my dad's truck drive in. But the barn still remains our sacred place, and underneath the flannel blankets, there is no cold. We are warm, we are whole, we are one.

We have sex again. This time I make my fingers go into overdrive and she manages to come at the same time I do. It's like we're spinning out into space together, weightless, dancing in the stars.

But the night starts to get away from us and I know it's time to go. After she gets dressed, shivering as she slips on her clothes, I take the box out of my pocket and hold it out for her.

"Merry Christmas," I tell her.

"What is this?" she asks, awestruck. Her cheeks are still flushed from sex and she's glowing. A woman before me.

"It's a present, obviously. Open it."

She looks at me wide-eyed. "You shouldn't have."

I just nod at it.

She takes off the flimsy ribbon, then the lid. It was just from a store in the mall and I know it's not made of diamonds or anything but...

She gasps and stares.

A tiny rose gold wishbone necklace. The lady at the counter says that all the girls these days love rose gold. I hope that's true.

"Shane," Rachel whispers.

"Do you like it?" I ask, my heart in my throat.

She looks at me and tears spill down her cheeks.

I wasn't expecting that reaction but I won't complain.

"I love it," she says through a sob. "I love it."

I reach over and kiss her through her tears. "Good. I thought you might want a wish for a rainy day."

She wraps her hands around my neck and holds me close to her. "Shane," she whispers and her voice is choked with something more profound than just gratitude. "There's only one thing I wish for."

"What?"

"Run away with me."

I try and understand. This is the first I've heard of it. "Where?"

"Anywhere. Anywhere but here. Shane...I don't want to be in this town anymore. My mother...my father...I need to leave, or else."

My heart rate is picking up again. "Or else what? Raven, talk to me. What is all this?"

She shakes her head, tears spilling in rivers down her face. "I just want to go away. Please."

"Okay," I tell her, grabbing her hand and holding it to my chest. "Your heart is where my home is. I'll go wherever your heart goes."

"Do you mean that?"

I nod. I love it here, but it's not the same without her. If she wants me to run away with her, I'll go. I'll go anywhere if her hand is in mine.

"I promise. Anywhere, anytime."

She seems to calm before my eyes. "I need to leave..."

"I know."

"I can't tell you..."

"Why can't you?"

"Because...it doesn't matter. I just needed to know if you'll leave with me."

"I told you I will. No matter what."

She nods and takes my hand to her lips, kissing my fingers, her bright blue eyes watery and warm and reaching into parts of me I long thought dead and dormant. "Thank you."

A pause.

A whisper.

"Thank you."

CHAPTER 10

SHANE

"Shane," my father says, exasperated.

It takes me a moment to realize he must have been saying my name for the past minute or so.

I pull Polly to a halt and glance over my shoulder at him as he comes forward on Major. Major is a large, dapple-grey half quarter horse, half Percheron and the oldest horse we have. The horse is twenty-six, the same age as me, and in some ways feels like an extra sibling. He doesn't get ridden much but today my father decided to take him out for a stroll, especially as we were only patrolling fences down by the riverbanks and didn't have to go very far.

"What?" I ask him.

I can tell my father is glaring at me under his sunglasses. I don't know why he insists on wearing them on hazy days like today, especially with his cowboy hat. He looks like he's trying to be Jack Nicholson.

"I don't think you've heard a damn word I've been saying," he says to me gruffly as he pulls up alongside me. Polly gives Major the stink-eye and shifts away from him. She's picking up on the tension, and then there's the fact that

Polly doesn't really like the other horses. Which is one reason why I like her so much. She's a challenge.

And that's the reason why I haven't heard a word my father's been saying to me this last while as we've come up from the river.

My mind is fixated on another challenge.

Rachel.

It was only a few days ago that she came to see me by the stable, where I was actually able to have a halfway decent conversation with her. My attempts before were fraught with too many unanswered questions and unsaid words, and I've been too much of a chicken-shit to get real with her.

Time has changed her. In some ways she's the same Rachel that I know, but in others it's like she's slipped on a mask and a new persona, trying to bury the person she once was. If you'd just met her, you'd probably think she's a gorgeous city girl, roughing it in the sticks for a few weeks, a high-powered business person with a full plate. But I'm not really sure that's the person she's become—I think that might just be the person she wants to be.

And above all, the person she wants to be is someone far away from me, from this place.

But, hell, I should probably encourage this. North Ridge doesn't hold anything for her these days, except for her mother who she wants to rebuild a relationship with. There's a better world out there, filled with more opportunities and a faster life. Everything in this town moves at a turtle's pace. There's something I like about it, but it's not for everyone. Most people who leave never end up coming back, not when they've gotten a taste of that big wild world.

And yet, I don't want her to leave. And I don't want things to keep progressing as they are. Sure, I made her laugh but then we separated again. It's like anytime we're brought together for a moment, the both of us make sure to push each other away. One step forward, two steps back.

It's just...it's fucking killing me. It's killing me to know that she's sleeping a few yards away from me. That when I look out my bedroom window, I'm looking at hers. That we're so close and yet light years apart, as if the galaxies above us have drifted down, creating chasms and endless space between us.

Every single moment she's here I'm hit with every single memory, the good and the bad. The sexy and the sweet. She's no longer just a phantasm of my dreams, of the years gone by —she's here. She's here and she's real and I don't know what the hell I'm supposed to do about it. She's got a boyfriend. She's only supposed to be here for a few weeks. And she still fucking hates me. When I look into her eyes, I see pain, and when the pain fades, I see the deep freeze. It's like she's willing her heart to freeze over, to numb herself from the past, from me.

And I can't fucking blame her. That's the worst part of it all.

"Shane," my father says again, and this time his voice is lower, trying out a softer tone. That's the difference between my dad these days and the dad of my past. Though he will always have a hard edge to him, age is making him softer. And ever since Vernalee and Rachel moved into the worker's cottage, I swear he's smiling more than he has in a long time. Believe me, the cattle business is hard these days and there's plenty for us all to be worried about.

I meet his eyes, forcing myself to be in the moment. "Sorry," I tell him. "I'm..."

"I know," he says. "I am too. There's been a lot of change in a short amount of time. It's hard to keep up." He pauses. "What I was saying is next time you go out on the range or into the mountains, you should bring your gun. I saw some bear scat down by the river. Looks like grizzly. You know that normally this isn't something to worry about but with all the fires up north and east, the bears might be out of their usual territory. Plus, this smoke can rile them up."

I nod. "Got it." I don't like to carry my shotgun because it's cumbersome and brings up bad memories. I also don't like to be in the position to shoot anything. I'll bring it to protect myself and the cattle, but I'm rather fond of the bears around here. They're dangerous as hell and terrifying when you see them up close, but they're also a symbol of the wild. I've only once come across them in a perilous situation, and with some luck and a lot of noise, the bear went on its way.

"So how are you holding up?" my father asks me as we start riding again, side by side.

I raise my brow. "Holding up?"

"You know what I mean. With Rachel and Vernalee."

"Well, Vernalee isn't much to worry about," I tell him. "Frankly, I think it makes perfect sense for her to live here for as long as she needs to."

"And after that?" he asks me. "What if she lives here always?"

Is my father asking permission if she can live here permanently?

I shrug. "Sure. I mean, she might have to share the worker's cottage with someone else. When calving season comes, we're going to need someone to help."

"We'll worry about that later," he says. "Worst case scenario, she can take one of you boys' old bedrooms in the house."

I study my father carefully. There's something soft and hopeful in his expression, even though I can't see his eyes. "Honestly, I had no idea you and Vernalee were so close."

His expression hardens but it's forced. He clears his

throat. "We've been friends for a long time, Shane. About as long as you and Rachel have."

"I didn't know that."

He opens his mouth to say something, then stops. Takes a deep breath. "I knew she was in trouble with Errol. Back then, I tried to tell her I was there for her whenever she needed it. But she acted like nothing was wrong. Shit, that still hasn't changed, has it? But when he went to jail, I stepped in. The women in this town, they ostracized her, you know? It was such a damn scandal and it wasn't her fault, but she was caught up in it and she needed a friend. And so we became friends."

I want to bring up the fact that even though they've been friends since then, I've rarely heard him mention her, nor have I seen them together. But I know my dad can be like me sometimes when it comes to opening up and I should be happy I'm getting this much.

When we get back to the ranch, we ride up alongside the worker's cottage. Lo and behold, Rachel is sitting on the porch, immersed in something on her phone.

"Howdy," my father says to her.

She looks up, surprised to see us even though we'd been approaching her for a long time.

"Hi," she says, her tone edgy. She puts her phone down and tries to smile away her frown lines. "Nice ride?"

"Pretty as a peach," he says.

"You're riding bareback," she says to me, nodding at Polly.

I nod. "It's good to mix it up." Not only does it help with your muscles and balance when you ride bareback, but it's much cooler for Polly without the saddle and saddle blanket. "Want to go for a ride?"

She looks at me as if I have two heads, but at least she's smiling. "No way."

My father gives me a quick look. "I'll leave you two." Then he nods at Rachel and steers Major toward the stable.

Rachel looks at him longingly as he goes, and I have to pretend it doesn't hurt that she hates being alone with me that much. But still, I'm feeling persistent today.

I hold out my hand for her. "Come on."

"Shane," she says, "I'm not going bareback riding with you."

"Too busy frowning at your phone? Remember what I said about frowning?"

She cocks her head, studying me with pursed lips. Her dark hair is piled high on her head, a few loose tendrils framing her face which is covered in a thin sheen of sweat and no makeup. She's wearing a white tank top with a red bra strap peeking out, jean shorts, and Converse low-tops. She's still the most gorgeous woman I've ever seen. Time has only amplified this, the fact that over the years no one else has been able to measure up to her, to what we had.

Do you feel it? I want to ask her.

Do you still feel what we had together?

Did you ever think of me on cold nights?

Did you feel that longing in your bones for just one more moment, one more chance?

I don't know if she can read my thoughts, though when we were young it seemed she could. I never did end up making a secret language with her because I never needed to. We just always knew. We knew each other's heart like the back of our hands.

That can't just disappear. That can't just go away. I don't care if she thinks she's changed, that she has an important job, a boyfriend. I refuse to believe I can't reach her.

"You chicken?" I ask, biting down a smile.

She raises her brows. "Chicken?"

That got her attention.

"Yeah, you scared?"

"I'm not scared," she says, raising her chin.

"You forgot how to ride."

"I did not. It's like riding a bicycle."

"Have you been on a horse since you left here?"

"Well, no." She gets to her feet, dusts off her ass.

"So, get on," I tell her, jerking my head for her to climb up. "Stand on the edge of the porch there."

I bring Polly around until she's parallel to the porch and hold out my hand again.

Wheels are turning in her head. She's stubborn. She wants to keep her distance, wants me to leave so she can go back to her phone, back to her life in Toronto.

But then determination sets on her brow and she nods.

She takes my hand.

With ease, I haul her up until she's swinging her leg over and pressed up against me.

"You all right?" I ask, even though I'm the one who feels like I can't breathe. She's barely even touching me and yet the feeling of her so close is lighting my skin on fire.

"I'm fine," she says, a lilt in her voice that tells me she's trying to sound tough.

We'll see about that.

"You going to hold on to me?" I ask.

"I am holding on."

No, you're touching me like I have some sort of fucking disease.

It doesn't matter.

I shift slightly, making a soft cluck to Polly, and she picks up on it in a second.

We jolt forward and start cantering, and with a yelp, Rachel holds on tighter, pressing her fingers into my t-shirt, her arms over my stomach, trying to keep her balance as we negotiate around the cottage.

Polly has a smooth gait, but even so, I take her around

and start heading up the slope, forcing Rachel to hold on even tighter or she'll go sliding right off Polly's back.

I'm being a bit of a dick, I have to admit. I'm only doing this so she'll touch me.

And it's working.

"How are you back there?" I ask over my shoulder, just catching her dark hair flowing behind her out of the corner of my eye. It must have come undone.

We fly over the hill and up into a patch of pine, coming to a walk.

"Where are we going?" she asks. Even though we're going slow now, she's still holding on as hard as she was before.

It feels too fucking good. Not just to be held, but to be held by her. It's like she never left at all, her body molding to mine with ease.

I try and keep my head on straight. "Remember the old settler's barn?"

She grows silent for a moment. I know what she's thinking. What she's remembering.

Our first kiss.

The moment when our friendship twisted and changed into something better. Something beautiful.

"Is that still there?" she asks flatly.

"It is. And nothing has changed."

"Really? We were there, like, when we were thirteen."

"I know. But it's held fast. It's adapted. It's now part of the land. You live here for long enough and you'll see that few things change. The weather swoops in and burns it or floods it or freezes it and winds try and shake what's weak, but most things survive it all. Grandpa says that there are some old structures on the land that have been here for a hundred years. There are trees that have grown for decades upon decades. They're survivors. Just like you."

"Me," she repeats with a soft bitterness.

"Yes, you," I tell her. "You've survived so much and yet here you are."

I hear her swallow behind me. "Maybe I've survived...but is that enough?"

"What do you mean?"

"Nothing." She clears her throat and taps my shoulder, pointing off into the distance. "Hey, there was a pond down that way, wasn't there? We used to catch frogs."

She's changing the subject. I let her. "Except that one time I caught a snapping turtle."

She laughs, squeezing me harder. "I'll never forget your face. That thing nearly took your damn fingers off."

"What was his name again?"

"I don't remember, it was something weird..." She snaps her fingers. "Cleveland!"

Now I'm laughing at the memory. "Who came up with that name?"

"I have no idea."

She lets out one of those soft, happy sighs, the ones she used to make when she was done laughing about something. I lived for those sighs, along with the ones she made as she came. She would cry out my name in a frenzied whisper, her fingers digging into my skin, her skin damp and flushed. She was the most gorgeous creature in the world when I was buried deep inside her and every part of her belonged to every part of me.

Except now, she belongs to someone else. Somewhere else.

The thought rots my insides, like drips of acid, impossible to shake.

I take her down to the old barn, its dark grey and brown wood more weather-beaten than before, the vine now taking over the entire roof. There are more holes punched in it and I'm pretty sure a family of raccoons calls it their home. But despite the hits, it's still standing.

"Want to go inside?" I ask her.

"Are you going to promise not to scare me like you did last time?"

"I don't know. Depends if I feel like kissing you or not."

She hesitates. "Shane," she warns. "That's not funny."

I shrug. "All I was thinking was that if I scared you, you'd jump into my arms and I'd kiss you."

"Instead, I ended up punching you in the face."

"It was a worthy trade. You still let me kiss you in the end."

"I did it out of pity."

"I know. You're going to need to get down first."

She holds on to me and then swings her leg over, lowering herself to the ground. I drop down right after and tie Polly to a post.

"How are your legs?" I ask her. She glances down and brushes the horse hair from her inner thighs. "I mean, they're looking good. Really good. You're so fucking gorgeous, Rachel."

She looks up at me, frowning, a wary look in her eyes. "You've gotten bold. Anyone ever tell you that?"

"I've always been bold," I tell her, taking a step toward her. "I was just quiet about it."

There's only a foot between us. She's doing everything not to look me in the eyes.

I don't even know what I'm doing.

I close the space and reach over, brushing her hair off her shoulders. "I used to have dreams about this hair, you know? It always happened after I saw ravens. They'd come into my dreams and their wings would flow and change into your hair and then you'd appear."

"You dreamed about me?" she asks quietly, her eyes finally meeting mine.

"I always dreamed about you. Every night. Under every moon. For the last six years. The moon would always be changing, but my dreams never did."

I take in a deep breath, catching the sweet scent of her shampoo. My hand rests briefly on her shoulder, and the feel of her skin is warm, so warm, so soft. I let my hand drift down, down, until I'm holding her hand in mine, gently, like I'm holding a bird. "I missed you. Always. You're standing right in front of me and I still miss you."

Her eyes waver with fear, but maybe there's longing underneath, something she's kept hidden away. Maybe that's wishful thinking.

"I have a hard time believing that," she says, shifting her body out of my grasp and walking around Polly toward the building.

I'm right behind her, grabbing her arm and pulling her back to me. "Believe it."

She balks. Her blue eyes are fierce, her mouth set into a near snarl. She's an animal, trapped, ready to fight back. "What are you doing?"

"I'm asking you to believe me."

"And why the fuck should I?"

"Because...I made you think I didn't love you. I made you think you weren't worthy of love when you were always too worthy of it."

"Too worthy?" she says, practically spitting on me. "You know what my father did to me. You know it, and the minute I told you, you know what you did? You broke up with me! You did what my mother did, only it hurt a million times worse because you were all I had. Shane, I loved you so damn much, for so many years, and you just threw it in my face!"

"I made a mistake. Things got out of hand."

The understatement of the century.

She raises her hand. "You know what? No. I don't care. I really don't give a fuck. What's done is done and I don't even care about getting closure anymore. It isn't worth it."

She tries to walk off and I let her go. "Rachel, please. Where are you going?"

"I don't know," she says, going around the structure.

I watch as she disappears around the corner.

I lean my head back and stare up at the sky, trying to see if I have any of that boldness left in me. I know what I have to do. I think I'm just so afraid that it won't change a fucking thing.

I take in a deep breath and set out after her.

I round the corner of the barn, and she's standing right there with her back to me, staring at the ground.

A dead raven at her feet, looking like it's only been dead for a few hours.

She glances at me over her shoulder with tears in her eyes.

"It was just lying here..." she starts. "What happened to it? It's like it fell out of the sky."

I grab her hand and pull her away from it. "It happens."

"We should bury it," she says.

"We should let nature take its course is what we should do."

She shakes her head, takes her hand out of mine. "No. Not here. Not in this place."

I watch as she starts looking around for something to dig with before she brushes past me and goes into the barn.

"Be careful," I tell her, but she's only in there for a few seconds before she comes out with what looks like a rusted hook.

She starts digging a grave.

I search for a suitable rock and then I start digging with her.

We bury the raven quickly, covering it with dirt.

She places a few wild daisies on the mound, then gives me a brave smile. "We should go back now."

I agree. I want her to stay with me, afraid I might not get another chance to talk to her, be with her. But I know the moment is over.

I start out toward Polly, glancing back at the grave as I go.

I'm pretty sure Rachel was just trying to bury everything that we were to each other.

I AWAKE TO A KNOCKING SOUND. FOR THE LONGEST TIME I thought it was in my dream, but now that my eyes are open, adjusting to the darkness of the room, it's not.

I turn my head. The blinds are knocking against the window with each gust of wind that blows through.

Sometimes in the middle of summer we get these mean winds that come down through the mountain passes and don't let up for a few days. Dusty, hot, and dry, these winds put everyone in town on edge. Fights break out at the Bear Trap more easily on those nights, and there are more sirens in the air. The horses are constantly cranky and the chickens don't lay as many eggs.

I get out of bed, glancing at my clock that glows two a.m. as I go and pull up the blinds. Better that than closing the window in this heat.

That's when I notice a figure out in the space between my house and the worker's cottage, dressed in a white nightgown, long grey hair flowing behind her in the wind.

It could be a ghost. It wouldn't be the first time I thought I've seen something unexplainable out here.

But it's not a ghost at all.

It's Vernalee.

I watch her for a few moments as she slowly walks through the knee-high grass, her back to me, and then throws her arms out to the wind, her nightgown billowing around her.

I want to give her space and privacy but at the same time I know she's not well.

I slip on a pair of jeans, a t-shirt and Vans and head out into the night.

The wind is dry and hot, ruffling my hair, making the grass sound like a symphony. I approach Vernalee carefully, realizing she might just be sleepwalking, and if that's the case, I shouldn't disturb her.

"Shane," she says in a low voice.

I freeze as she slowly turns her head and looks at me over her shoulder. "Isn't this beautiful?" she asks.

"What are you doing?" I come over to her.

She closes her eyes and smiles, face to the sky. "I'm finding my wings again. I think if I imagine it hard enough, I might just fly away."

I think about that, looking over the town and the river and the dark peaks against a darker sky. The wind smells like smoke and heat and something from the past, swirling around us, anchoring me in this spot while Vernalee looks as if she's about to take right off.

"Where would you go?" I ask, keeping my voice low, as if I could break the spell.

"I don't know. Nowhere, I guess. I'd stay here. But it's nice to have the option, isn't it?" She opens her eyes and looks at me. "Would you ever go? Leave this place?"

I shake my head. "No reason to. Everything I need is right here."

"Everything?" she asks, and there's a knowing edge to her voice.

"Right now, yes. Everything."

"And when she leaves?" She tilts her head, gives me a soft smile. "I know you're still in love with her, Shane. You have to tell her."

I look away, feeling my throat grow tight.

"And I don't just mean tell her that you still love her," she says. "Although it's a start. You have to tell her everything. I know what you did, Shane, and I know why you did it."

I glance at her sharply, and my knuckles burn with long-forgotten pain. She searches my face, and there's no resentment or anger in her eyes—just a kindness that wells from somewhere deep.

"You've changed," I manage to say.

She lets out a breathy laugh which leads into a cough. "I know. I had to. I couldn't go on like I was. This cancer woke me up. It made me realize that there is an end for all of us and I didn't want to invite it in. It made me realize I have a lot to live for, and for the last six years I haven't been living. I think I died a little when Rachel left town. I know you did too. Have you been living, Shane?"

"No," I say, my voice choking on the word. "I haven't. I've put one foot in front of the other but I don't think that's enough to qualify."

She sighs and grabs my hand, giving it a squeeze with her bony fingers. "All that matters for the both of us is that we get second chances. I've done my girl wrong and that's something I've never been able to forgive myself for. I don't even think I should be forgiven. But I know in order to keep living, to get things right with her, it has to be the start. You, though, you know you have to tell her the truth about what happened."

"How? Why? What difference can it make in her life? It won't get her to stay here. Her life isn't here anymore. She has a home and friends and a boyfriend. She has all she needs."

"I don't believe that. I don't believe she has anything she needs. She needs you, Shane. She needs you to love her, to build a life with her. It's always been you for her and her for you. Time goes on and mistakes happen and lies are told, but when you scratch a bit beneath all that, that's where your truth is. I want Rachel to be happy and I know she's not. And I know she would be with you. But you have to start fresh. Come clean."

I take in a deep breath through my nose, my chest feeling small while the sky above seems to get wider. "I don't even know what to say."

"You tell her what you did. You were trying to protect her. Lord knows I couldn't. But that's my cross to bear, my darkest sin. You were acting out of love and justice and no one can fault you for that."

"The courts would have."

"But they didn't," she said sternly, turning to face me dead on. "Listen to me, Shane. My husband put you in a terrible position, but you did the right thing. It was the hardest thing for everyone, but it was the best thing. Because you finally gave her the courage to leave. You spared her. And the loss of her opened my eyes to what was really going on, all the horrible truths I tried so hard to ignore because facing them would have destroyed me. But it destroyed me in the end. Don't you believe in fate? In luck? In wishes?"

"What does that have to do with anything?"

"She's here. Maybe it's because of me, maybe it's because of you. Maybe it's because of a million wishes made."

I let out a bitter laugh. "She hates me."

"No. No, she doesn't. She hates what you did to her but that's not the same thing. And I'm telling you, I may not know my daughter that well anymore...maybe I never really did. But I do know that just because someone has a broken heart, it doesn't mean the heart doesn't work anymore. It beat for you before, and it will beat for you again. You just have to be patient and honest and true. You have to be brave. You have to."

I nod and close my eyes. The wind feels like ghosts from the past rushing through me.

"I've tried to tell her, but..."

"You have to try harder," she says, adamant. "And I have to try harder too. She's here now and there's a reason she's here. But she won't be here for long, not unless we both give her reasons to stay. Promise me that you'll let her know the truth. Do that and her heart will repair before your very eyes."

It's not that simple. Rachel has moved on. Telling her the truth will only give her closure—it won't open another door. Vernalee has far more stock in our love than I do.

Shit, I didn't even know I was still in love with Rachel until I saw her again.

All those years I spent trying to move on, to find love with someone else, to push her out of my head, dig our relationship a grave and throw dirt on it like she did with the raven. And all of that was for nothing, because deep in my heart, I never stopped loving her. I never stopped thinking about her. The longing became so ingrained in my head, part of my routine, that I never stopped to realize just what—who —I was longing for.

"You better get back to bed," she says to me. "I know you're all early risers out here." She pats me on the arms and walks off toward the house.

"Vernalee," I call out after her. "He loves you, you know."

She stops and glances at me over her shoulder, the hair blowing across her face so that I can't see anything but a slight curve of her lips. A smile.

She doesn't ask who, because she knows.

Then she turns and keeps walking, disappearing into the grass.

CHAPTER 11

RACHEL

PAST – 20 YEARS OLD

I lie back in my bed, summoning courage.

The room is dark. The sky outside my window is even darker.

My heart feels like tar.

Sticky, black, turned over and over a million times.

It lies in wait for the next blow. My soul cowers behind it.

I saw the look in my father's eyes the other night and I know I'm on his agenda again.

It's been years. And it's been months. And I've worked past it and I've tried to thrive. I've stayed behind in this shitty town because I don't want to leave Shane. I know Shane would leave with me in a heartbeat, but I'm not selfish. I know his life is here. And I don't want to make him choose.

So I've stuck it out. And I've tried to put distance between me and my parents.

I've tried. I lived with my friend Jasmine for six months before rent got too high. I've spent more time than ever at the Nelson's. They don't care if I live there, sharing Shane's room.

But it's not enough. Because sometimes I have to come home.

And this is one of those nights. When my mother is drunk, passed out on the couch with a bottle of gin next to her pale, skinny fingers. Those nights where the front door slams shut because my father is home from his shift and each footfall through the house sounds like a jail cell door slamming on my future. On the person I'm trying so hard to be.

But this time I will not play dead.

I will not be invisible.

I will not shrink into the corner and try to take up less space.

I am full of space. I deserve to take up air in this world.

I deserve to be seen.

I won't hide anymore.

No matter how many times I tell myself that, though, the fear runs through me like it's got an iron grip on every single organ. The tightest one is around my soul. Because there's a battle going on in there. There has been since the day my father first touched me, the day he first told me to never tell anyone, the day he made me hate myself.

The day he made me afraid.

You're twenty years old, I tell myself. *You can do this.*

And I think this to myself with silly naiveté, as if the fact that he's the revered chief of police in this town won't matter at all.

Of course it will.

His word against mine.

Still, my limbs go stiff, ready to fight.

The door to my bedroom opens.

A column of cold light shines in.

Footsteps.

The door closes.

The column fades.

"Rachel," my father whispers, and I know it's the devil himself.

He leans over me. Touches my arm gently. He's always so gentle to start, as if he's a nurse, as if he's helping. As if I need soothing.

His hand slides down my arm and I can't take it anymore.

I exist.

I exist.

I exist.

I stiffen all over.

His hand pauses.

"Don't touch me," I manage to say through grinding teeth.

There's a moment where I know he's trying to gather his thoughts.

"What?" he says, shocked.

"I said, don't you fucking touch me."

I don't know what I expected to happen, but I guess I didn't think that far ahead. Maybe if I did, I wouldn't have said anything.

His hand goes to my hair. It grips me there, making a tight fist. He's no longer being gentle, he's no longer being a nurse.

He pulls back in one quick motion, one hardened grunt, and I'm thrown out of bed and onto the floor, screaming as I go.

I hope my neighbors will hear me, but my windows are all closed. I know my mother won't. Even if my cries do wake her up, she'll be too chicken-shit to do anything about it. She'll go on as she has before when I've told her what he's done to me. She'll pretend I'm fucking crazy. Her husband, my father, would *never,* ever do *that.*

I land on the ground with a thud, pain shooting through

me in waves of lightning. All my instincts are on fire, though, and I scramble to my feet, heading for the door.

He's bigger, quicker, stronger. He's a fucking cop.

He grabs me again, this time by the arm, twisting it far behind my back until I have no choice but to pivot around and face him. He rams himself against me, slamming me back until my head bounces off the wall, paintings falling and shattering on the floor.

"You fucking cunt," he sneers at me. "You want to fight back now?"

His hand goes for my waist and I know I don't have much choice in the matter. I will fight back whatever way I can, even if it hurts me.

I bring my head back and slam it forward, headbutting him.

It doesn't work as I planned. It hurts like hell and I'm screaming in pain, my head spinning, but he's pushed back a few feet and it's just enough for me to make for the door and rip it open.

I run out into the hall and to the front door and then I'm out on the street and I'm running and running and running.

It takes a few seconds to feel the cold April air and the fact that I'm in boxer shorts and a tank top, with bare feet. But it doesn't matter. I will keep running until I'm free, I will keep running because that's the only thing I can do.

I don't even bother stopping and knocking at any of our neighbors' doors. They'll only call the police and my father will get the call. What the fuck good will that do.

My feet are bleeding from glass and rocks by the time I make myself stop.

Headlights appear at the start of the street. I'm at least four blocks away, but I'm not taking any chances. I pull back into the shadows and hide in the bushes until the car goes past.

It's a cop car.

My father's.

I watch, holding my breath, as he turns a corner and disappears into town.

Then I turn around and start running back to my house.

I can't even feel anything by the time I get in.

I don't even bother trying to find my phone. I pick up the landline in the hallway and dial Shane's cell.

It's past midnight and I know he's sleeping, doing shifts with Mav and Hank and Dick during the calving season, but he still answers almost right away.

"Hello?"

"Shane?'

"Rachel? What's wrong? Why are you calling...oh it's your home number. What's—?"

"Please come get me. Don't ask questions, don't tell anyone. I'll be on the swing set at the park behind my house. Please hurry."

I hang up and grab my hooded coat from the foyer, slip on a pair of boots, and I'm out the door, running quietly up the street to the park.

I don't let myself fall apart. Not yet. Now is not the time.

I sit on the swings but I don't swing. I don't move. I stay in the shadows and hold my breath and watch.

Minutes crawl by. Somewhere in the distance there's a police siren and I don't know if I should be relieved or not. Maybe my father will be torn away for a while. Or maybe he knows where I am and he's coming for me.

And then, just when I think maybe time isn't on my side, a pair of headlights shine and dim as a truck pulls to the side of the road. I'd recognize the sound of Shane's truck anywhere, the truck he stole from Fox and ended up working his ass off for, for years.

"Rachel?" I hear him call out quietly.

I start running toward him and jump inside the passenger seat.

He looks me over, bewildered, his eyes shining. "What the fuck happened? Are you okay?"

I try and swallow but it's next to impossible. I can only nod frantically.

"Rachel?"

"Please take me home. Shane, your home. Please."

He watches me for a moment.

I finally look at him, pleading. "Please!" I cry out, my voice breaking.

He nods and starts driving.

In minutes we're far from my parents. Then we're far from town. Then we're crossing the bridge over the river and it's only then that I feel I can breathe again.

"Rachel," he whispers again, hand grasping mine as we pull up to his house. "It's okay. You're safe."

Everything passes in a blur. I can't catch my breath, no matter how safe I feel.

Shane leads me up to the tiny guesthouse where he's been living, and I'm grateful at how far removed it is from the main house and the worker's cottage, thankful for the privacy.

He helps me inside, sits me down on the couch, wraps me in a blanket. His dog Fletcher, a gangly puppy, sits on the handmade rug at my feet, while Shane puts on the kettle.

He doesn't say a word to me, which I appreciate. He just seems to know.

He makes me tea with a big splash of rye in it and hands it to me, taking the spot beside me. Close but not too close. He doesn't want to crowd me, doesn't want to pressure me. He just needs me to know that he's there. He brims with patience, with love.

God, I'm not sure I deserve the love of this man.

Finally, after I've had a few gulps of tea, he leans over and tenderly brushes the hair off my forehead that now throbs red with pain.

"He did this to you," he says, his voice tight as he stares at the mark.

I look at him in surprise. "Who?"

His jaw is set so hard I'm afraid it might snap off. His eyes are wild and he's trying so hard to control himself. "Your father."

He knows. He's always known.

I take a moment, trying to breathe. "I did this," I manage to say.

Shane stares at me so fiercely I almost shrink in my seat.

"I headbutted him," I clarify, trying to sound strong and proud but my voice is shaking and I'm shaking, and I'm not sure if I'll ever feel solid again.

I watch his Adam's apple as he swallows. "Rachel," he whispers, licking his lips. "I...how long has this been happening?"

Shame floods me from head to toe, but I can't keep it in anymore. Not anymore.

"Years," I tell him, staring at Fletcher as he breathes at my feet, in a deep sleep. "He...uh...I don't know how to start. Where to start. I don't want to say..."

"Rachel," he says again, his voice cracking as his hand holds mine. "Please. I know this is hard. But you have to tell me. You have to. Everything."

I close my eyes, trying to find the strength. For so long I've kept all of this hidden, locked away in a box inside of me. A place that no one else could find, a place I hoped wouldn't taint my life. But little by little, it leaked. Everything I tried so hard to hide and bury, it leaked like blood from a wound, staining everything I did.

Now Shane sees it all over me. I can no longer pretend

that this isn't destroying me from the inside out, that I'm not living one huge lie.

And so I tell him. I tell him that my father started sexually abusing me when I was twelve, and though it didn't happen all the time, it was enough. And when he wasn't doing that, he was telling me I was nothing more than a mangy dog, ready to be sent to the pound at any moment. He told me that I wasn't fit to be a part of the family, that no one loved me, no one rooted for me, no one believed in me. And no one would believe me. He really drove that part home. That he was someone and I was no one. Just a slut. A whore. Someone that shouldn't have been born.

I saw the abuse spread to my mother in small doses. I saw him hit her and she'd stay home from work to hide the evidence, or he'd start hitting her in places no one could see. I don't know what else he did. I don't know if the attention I got was unique.

But I knew we were both trapped. I knew we had to get out, to break free.

I told my mother one day that I knew what was happening. I told her I was going to report him. I told her I knew he was hurting her and I told her what he was doing to me.

It was the hardest thing I'd ever had to say.

But even harder after that was trying to believe I deserved any love at all. Because when I told my mother, she just shook her head and told me I was lying.

She pushed me away. She told me that it wasn't true, that I was making things up for attention.

She did all this and she wouldn't even look me in the eye.

It didn't matter how much I cried and begged and screamed.

She turned her back on me.

And that's when I knew I didn't have a soul in the world on my side.

"But you have me," Shane says after a few moments of silence. He started gripping my hand so hard that eventually he had to let go. Now he's balling his hands into fists. "You know you have me."

"I know," I whisper. "I was just so afraid to tell you. I thought that you'd be disgusted by me. That you'd look at me differently. I couldn't bear the thought of it."

"Rachel," he whispers hoarsely. He tucks my hair behind my ear, gently cupping my face as he stares into my eyes. "I love you. Body and soul. I will never stop loving you. I will never stop being there for you. You're my whole fucking life, Raven." He pauses. "Did he try to touch you tonight?"

I nod. "And I stopped being silent. I fought back. And he fought back harder. It's been years since he's tried anything with me, maybe he's been afraid now that I'm older, but I could feel it coming. It's like the devil himself is sitting outside your room, biding his time."

He chews on his lip and starts wringing his hands until his knuckles are white. "I'm going to kill him," he says calmly.

"Shane. You can't. I told you this in confidence."

He looks at me, his eyes burning like wildfire. "Your father, the town cop, has been abusing you and your mother for years. I'm going to fucking kill him with my bare fucking hands."

I've never seen that look on Shane's face before. If I were anyone else, I would be frightened to death. "You can't. You can't, okay? No one will believe me. No one. And no one will believe you either. Don't you know by now that he has this fucking town eating out of his hand?"

"Only because people fear him, not because they like or respect him."

"And what's the difference? They'll still take his side no matter what. The police chief being accused of abuse. Do you really think that will fly? And do you think I'll escape unscathed? I've had to live in shame, I've had to will myself to not exist. I've done all I could to prevent this, to pretend it isn't happening. That would put all of it out there for the whole town, the whole province, the whole country to see. And you know it. Do you really want me to go through that?"

"He can't get away with this," he says through grinding teeth. He gets to his feet and I'm sure he's about to put his fist through the wall. "He won't get away with this. I'll make sure of it."

"Shane!" I say sharply enough that Fletcher jumps to his feet, giving us a baleful stare. "Please promise me you won't do anything. You won't say anything. Please."

He leans against the wall, resting his head against it. Every single muscle in his back is tense and ready to go, ready to fight.

"Shane," I say again, getting up and placing my hand on his shoulder. "Please. I told you because I trust you. I trust you to do the right thing and that's to keep it to yourself."

"That's why you wanted to run away," he says softly.

"Yes. It wasn't just this town, it's him. I've been saying it for years, but..."

"But you've been waiting for me."

"I've been waiting for you."

He turns his head and his stark gaze holds me. "I should have listened. I should have run with you. I should have understood what you were saying. I should have dug deeper."

I swallow, thirsty, my throat beyond dry. A fizzy kind of weakness goes through me, making my knees feel like jelly.

"Hey," Shane says, immediately reaching out for me and pulling me against him. "How hard did you hit him? Do I need to take you to the hospital?" He runs his hands gently over my forehead.

I shake my head. "No, I'm fine. I'm fine. I...I've...I've never told a soul. Never told a soul and now I have, and..."

I burst into tears. Tears I've spent so long trying to control. I let them flow, soaking Shane's shirt as he grips me, holding me tight.

"It's over," he says to me. "I've got you. And I'll never let you out of my sight. I'll never let you go. You fly, I fly. I promise."

And I believe his promise, as I believe all of Shane's promises.

Because he loves me.

He loves me.

That's the only true thing I know in this whole world.

I hate to think what would happen if it were ever taken away.

"It's over," he says again.

But despite the conviction in his voice, I know it's not that simple.

It's not over.

It's just beginning.

CHAPTER 12

SHANE

PAST - 20 YEARS OLD

Rachel is asleep on my couch, and I've covered her in a quilt. She's breathing deeply, her chest rising and falling. There's a red mark on her forehead where she had to headbutt her father in self defense, but other than that, there's no sign that anything happened.

And yet I know she's carrying a million scars underneath her skin. They're imprinted on her heart, tarnishing her soul. She hides them deep inside so no one will find them. She believes they make her dirty, but I think they make her strong. She's the strongest woman I know. She's endured years of abuse at the hands of a monster, a man who has been sworn to protect her, to protect his wife, to protect the citizens of this town.

And I'm going to end that all. I'm going to make sure that he protects no one ever again.

Rachel confided in me tonight with something she's kept buried and tonight she let it all out, a hand reaching out from the grave, skeletons rolling out of the closet. She's trusted me with this and I can't break her trust, even when I know I should. Even when I know I have to.

I get it, too. I get that she doesn't want this to come to light, that's she afraid she'll lose, that the town will see her in a different way, maybe as a victim, maybe as a harlot. Who knows. People talk. Rumors spread. I've seen people here turn on each other. It happens all the time. For all the good things that happen in small towns, the very people who wave at you as you drive by, who know you by name, are sometimes the very people willing to throw you under a bus. Small towns don't always breed compassion and solidarity. They breed intimacy, but that's not the same thing, not by a long shot.

There's a chance that Rachel could be dragged through the mud, especially if her mother isn't willing to come to her side. Clearly the woman is also a victim of abuse, but I know she's probably living in extreme denial of what's going on. If she's afraid, she could take his side. And where would that leave Rachel?

No. I know that's the right thing to do, but the right thing usually only pans out in movies. I've got something else I want to do, the justice this man deserves.

"Rachel," I call out softly.

She doesn't move. She continues to breathe deeply. I gave her a lot of whisky and sleepy tea in order to relax her and calm her down. I don't think she's going to stir all night.

Quietly, I slip on my coat and take the shotgun off the gun rack.

I step out into the night, gently closing the door behind me.

The air is crisp and cool, but inside I'm a barely contained fire, just dying to spill out.

I get in my truck and drive across town, all the way to the Waters' house.

I don't really have a plan. My thoughts have slowed to a dull crawl.

I park the truck around the corner.

I leap over the small rounded gate that leads to the stone path up to the house.

I open the door, poking my head inside.

It's dark with only a hall light on. The blue clock of the microwave glows. The house is as still as a tomb and almost as quiet except for snoring coming from the living room.

There lies Rachel's mother, passed out on the couch.

I clear my throat, testing the waters.

"Vernalee," I say.

She doesn't move. Doesn't even stir.

I put my shotgun down against the wall and crouch down, picking her up.

I carry her all the way to the bedroom, placing her in bed. I get a glass of water and some Advil and put it beside her on the table. I know I should hate this woman for not believing her own daughter, for turning her away. But I can't. I only feel deep sorrow and pity that she's stuck in this situation, and until she faces it herself, she'll never escape. No amount of drinking will ever do that.

I leave her in the bed, closing the door behind her, making sure it's latched shut.

Then I switch off the hall light, pick up the shotgun, sit down on the couch in the living room, and wait in the darkness.

I think it's been a couple of hours when I hear a car outside on the street. It runs for a few minutes and then turns off. The engine clicks.

The gate creaks open.

There are footsteps up the front steps.

The door opens with ease. No one locks doors in this town. What's the point when the monsters already live with you?

I know it's a matter of seconds before he spots me waiting in the dark with a shotgun. He might even pull his gun first.

I could just shoot him right now. But that would be too easy and I don't want to get this over with just yet.

He turns into the kitchen and the room glows a cold white as he opens the refrigerator door.

I'm already on my feet. I'm behind him.

The barrel of the gun aimed at the back of his head.

My finger presses against the trigger.

It would be so easy to squeeze.

But I don't.

I pull the gun back, and in the time that Errol Waters whirls around to face me, reaching for the gun in his holster as he does so, I'm swinging the shotgun clear across his face.

Blood sprays on the wall, his cheek collapsing as he's thrown against the kitchen counter, the edge striking him in the ribs.

He cries out as he falls, but I'm already bringing the gun down over his head, striking him right across the crown.

"Help," he cries out, his words garbled with blood and spit, but I'm putting the gun on the table and grabbing him by the collar, hauling him up to meet my face.

"You sick son of a bitch," I sneer at him, spittle flying. The rage I have inside licks me—unrelenting, dangerous flames. "I should fucking kill you right here. Maybe I will."

I slam him back against the fridge, and before he has a chance to duck or move, I strike him in the cheek. My fist cries out in pain but I've learned to ignore it. Errol is taller and bigger than me, but fighting Fox has taught me well over the years.

I start pummeling him, hitting his nose, his jaw, his cheek, his eye. The skin beneath my knuckles is slick with blood and soft, turning to pulp, but I can't stop. The rage is all-encompassing and all I can think about is Rachel.

Revenge for Rachel.

Revenge for the woman I love.

"You sick fuck, you sick fuck," I keep grunting over and over, like I'm in some kind of trance. "I'm going to fucking kill you."

And even though I'm not using my gun, I know if I keep going, I'm going to. I'm going to beat his nose back into his brain and shatter the grey matter with shards of bone. I'm going to end his life like this, lying in a puddle of blood on his kitchen floor, and I know he deserves worse, so much worse. I could go on like this for hours.

I just might.

Then I hear someone behind me, and even though I don't hear a gun being cocked I know one is pointed at my head. That's something you can feel deep in the seat of you.

"Stop," a man's voice says. "Put your hands up. Now."

The man isn't calm. His voice is weak, shaking, and I know it's the voice of Constable James Zimmer. He's not about to fire his gun on me, but if he's as panicked as he sounds, he might.

I raise my hands in the air and Errol slumps to the floor, spitting out blood and teeth.

"Turn around," Zimmer says.

I slowly turn around, my chin raised along with my hands.

The look of shock that comes over his face is almost humorous. "Shane Nelson?" he asks.

I don't say a word.

And Errol, he's not done. He's not knocked out, though he should be after what I did to him. He shouldn't even be able to breathe even though he's slowly getting to his feet beside me.

"Errol, are you okay?" Zimmer asks him.

But Errol is not okay. He's able to stand if he's holding on to the kitchen counter, but he's not okay.

"Shane, what the hell are you doing? What happened?" Zimmer asks me.

But I don't know what to say. I'm supposed to keep this to myself.

I can't anymore. I've gone too far. I pray Rachel can forgive me.

"Justice," I tell him. "Why don't you ask him what he's been doing to his wife and daughter for years? I'm sure if they had the strength, they would have done the same."

Zimmer is beyond puzzled, the shadows on his face deepening in the darkness. "What the hell are you talking about? Errol?"

Errol raises his head to look at me.

I meet his eyes and it's like looking into the face of hell itself.

His eyes blaze with a shining blackness, like this whole thing has excited him instead of breaking his spirit. "This man," Errol says hoarsely, slurring, barely able to move his jaw, "broke into my house with the intention to murder me. He had a shotgun aimed at my head before I fought back, and then he attempted to beat me...to death."

Everything inside me seizes. I look to Zimmer. "I came here because Rachel, his daughter, said he's been—"

"This man came here with the intent to fucking kill me," Errol cries out. "Arrest him."

Zimmer moves toward me, one shaking hand holding the gun, the other going for his handcuffs. Maybe I can fight off both of them, but I'm not about to hurt Zimmer. I knew his son from high school. He's a good man.

But he's in the position beneath Errol. And he'll do whatever Errol says.

"I'll throw your fucking ass in jail and you'll never come out," Errol seethes, blood pouring from his cuts. My knuckles throb, scraped raw from his face. "You hear me? You'll fucking rot in there, pretty boy."

The cuffs shake in Zimmer's hands.

I'm fucked.

Completely fucked.

"Unless," Errol adds slowly, "you can do me a favor."

I try to swallow but can't. I look to Zimmer but he's paused, waiting, looking just as confused as I feel.

I don't want to do this man any fucking favors.

"I'm not doing shit for you," I tell him. "I know what you did. I'll make sure the whole damn world knows it."

"No one in this whole damn world would believe you," Errol says. "Not Zimmer over there. Not any other cop, or cheap lawyer in this town. Not even my own wife. No one."

He can't be right. That's not supposed to be how this turns out. He doesn't just win because he's a cop. He doesn't get to get away with it. With all the sick and terrible things he's done...

"Now, I won't repeat myself again," he says, and he fucking sounds like a man who's holding all the cards. "But I need you to do me a favor. And I won't press charges. And Zimmer here will pretend like he never saw a goddamn thing. Ain't that right, Zimmer?"

"Uh, yes sir."

"Good." His eyes peer at mine, hate coming from a place I would never dare explore. "If you break up with my daughter and I never see your face around here again, I'll let all of this slide."

I balk. "Why the fuck would I do that?"

"Because I'll put you away for good. Take a good look at me, boy. Hey, Zimmer, you take a good look, too. You came here to murder me and I'm pretty sure that if Zimmer hadn't stepped in, you would have finished the job." He spits a lump of blood onto the floor and then smiles at me with missing teeth. "I think Zimmer deserves a promotion for saving my life."

I look over my shoulder at Zimmer. He's standing up straighter, and like most simple cops in this town, he would love nothing more. But he's still confused as to what's going on.

I'm not, though. What Errol is asking me to do is not the better alternative than jail.

And that's why he's asking it.

Because it would destroy me even more.

He's seen me around his daughter, day in and day out since we were both nine years old. We have eleven years of history together, eleven years of love. He knows that giving that up will destroy me, destroy her.

"You don't have much time to think," Errol says, sounding weaker. "Don't be a martyr. If you go to jail, you'll be sent up to prison in Kamloops. Your daddy and grandfather will lose a hand on the ranch. Your family's reputation will be ruined, I'll see to that. And you'll leave your precious Rachel all alone. You hear me? She'll be all alone...and small towns can be cruel."

My heart thuds slowly in my chest as I try and grasp what he's saying. If I go to jail, she has no one. Her only alternative is to move, but would she? Not unless I push her away. If I break up with her, if I push her away, she'll leave this town for good. I know she will. It's all she's been talking about for years. She's only staying here for me.

I'm not worth it. I never have been.

And her father isn't a stupid man. He knows if I go to jail, there will be talk over what I did and why. People love to find the motive, especially when it comes from someone like me. I might be a wild card, but attempted murder is not something that people would see coming. They'll want to know. And people will talk. Maybe even Rachel and Vernalee will come forward.

Or I can break it off with Rachel and tell her to leave. To go. The only thing is, that poor girl loves me. She won't go easily. If I slip for even a second about what's going on, she'll stay.

"Time is ticking," Errol says, slouching into the kitchen chair. "What will it be?"

CHAPTER 13

RACHEL

PAST - 20 YEARS OLD

The Bear Trap is alive tonight.

Saturday night and everyone's here, including Shane's brothers who are home for the weekend. Fox sits at the bar with a beer, his dark eyes scanning the room like he's looking for trouble. Maverick is playing pool with some guys from town, his loud laugh carrying over the music and conversation.

I'm tucked into our usual corner booth, nursing a beer and watching Shane at the bar. He's been acting strange all day. Distant. Like he's wrestling with something heavy, something that's eating him alive from the inside out.

I know what it is.

Ever since I told him about my father two nights ago, ever since he held me and promised me that everything would be okay, there's been this darkness following him around. I know he's angry—I could see it in his eyes when I told him what my father had done to me. The way his hands shook, the way his jaw clenched so hard I thought it might snap.

But this feels different. This feels like something else entirely.

"You okay, Raven?" Delilah asks, sliding into the booth across from me. She's been working tonight but it's finally slowed down enough for her to take a break.

I touch the wishbone necklace at my throat, the one Shane gave me for Christmas. It's become a habit when I'm nervous. "Yeah, I'm fine. Just tired."

She follows my gaze to where Shane is standing at the bar, his broad shoulders tense beneath his flannel shirt. "He's been weird tonight."

"You noticed too?"

"Hard not to. He looks like he's about to punch some-one." She pauses, studying him. "Or like someone already punched him."

My stomach clenches. I hadn't noticed it before, but now that she mentions it, there's something different about the way he's holding himself.

Like he's in...pain.

Shane turns then, as if he can feel me watching him, and our eyes meet across the crowded bar. For a moment, his face softens and I see my Shane—the boy who's held my heart since I was nine years old. The man who promised to run away with me, to protect me, to love me forever.

But then something shutters closed behind his eyes, and he looks away.

Cold settles in my chest like winter fog.

"I'm going to go talk to him," I tell Del, sliding out of the booth.

I weave through the crowd of locals and the few tourists who've wandered in. The closer I get, the more I can see that Del was right. There's something wrong. His knuckles are scraped raw, barely healed. A ranch injury? Or something else? His jaw is set in that stubborn line that usually means he's made up his mind about something.

"Hey," I say softly, touching his arm.

He flinches away from me.

Actually flinches.

Shane has never, not once in all the years I've known him, pulled away from my touch.

"Shane?" My voice comes out small in the din of the bar. "What's wrong?"

He drains his beer and sets the bottle down hard on the bar. Too hard. "Nothing's wrong."

But everything about him screams that something is very, very wrong.

"Don't lie to me," I say, stepping closer. "You've been acting strange all day. Ever since—"

"Ever since what?" His voice is sharp, cutting. I've never heard him use that tone with me before.

"Ever since I told you about my father."

Something flickers across his face—pain, maybe, or guilt—but it's gone so fast I might have imagined it.

"Yeah, well, it's a lot to handle," he says, his voice strained.

The words hit me like a slap. I actually take a step back, my hand going to my chest where it feels like something vital has just been ripped out.

"What? A lot for *you* to handle?"

Shane looks at me then, really looks at me, and there's something in his golden eyes that makes my blood turn to ice. Something desperate and pained, like he's drowning.

But now I'm drowning too.

"I'm at a crossroads, Rachel," he says quietly, almost to himself.

The bar suddenly feels too loud, too bright. I'm aware that people are starting to look our way, that Maverick has stopped playing pool, that Fox has turned on his stool to watch us. We aren't making much noise and yet everyone can tell that something is wrong.

Because something is so terribly wrong.

"I don't understand," I whisper.

Shane lets out a harsh laugh that doesn't sound like him at all, as if it's put on for show. "Of course you don't. Look, Rachel..." He runs a hand through his hair, a battle raging inside him that shines through his amber eyes. "This isn't working anymore."

Each word is like a knife sliding between my ribs. "Shane, what are you talking about? What's happening?"

"What's happening is that I can't do this," he says, his voice carrying over the suddenly quiet bar. "I can't...we can't keep doing this."

The world tilts sideways. I reach out to steady myself against the bar, but Shane doesn't move to help me.

"You don't mean that," I manage to say, though my voice is shaking now. "Shane, you don't mean that. You love me. You said—"

He closes his eyes like I've just caused him physical pain. Him! When he opens them again, they're hollow. "I can't love you the way you need to be loved."

One sentence.

One fucking sentence.

That's all it takes to shatter my entire universe.

"What does that mean?" I breathe. "Shane, what does that mean?"

But when he opens his eyes, Shane's face has gone carefully blank. Like he's forcing himself not to feel anything. "It means I'm not good for you, Rachel. It means you need to get out of this town and find someone who can give you what you deserve."

He meets my eyes briefly before he looks away. Cold and controlled like he's fighting some internal war. Nothing like the man who made love to me just three nights ago. Nothing like the boy who held me while I cried, who promised to protect me.

I don't know who this stranger is at all.

"I'm leaving North Ridge," he says quietly. "After graduation. I'm getting out of here and you...you should too. Far away. You always wanted to leave anyway."

I'm dimly aware that the entire bar has gone silent. That everyone is watching this play out like it's some kind of twisted entertainment, a soap opera. I can see Del at the edge of my vision, her face pale with shock. Maverick has put down his pool cue. Even Old Joe has stopped drinking to stare.

"But you said—" My voice cracks. "You said you'd run away with me. You said your heart was where my home was."

Shane flinches like I've slapped him. For a moment, his mask slips and I see raw agony in his eyes. But then he straightens his shoulders like he's bracing for impact.

"I was wrong," he says quietly and his voice sounds like it's being dragged over broken glass. "We're too young, Rachel. This is too much. Your father, what he did to you...I can't fix that. I can't be what you need me to be."

The wishbone necklace feels like it's burning against my skin. I reach up and touch it with trembling fingers, and Shane's eyes follow the movement.

When he sees the necklace, something breaks in his expression. Something that looks like pure devastation.

"Rachel," he whispers, and for a second he sounds like himself again. Like my sweet Shane.

But then he straightens, and the walls go back up.

"You should keep that," he says roughly. "Make a wish on it. Wish for something better than this place. Better than..." He stops himself, jaw clenching. "Just wish for something better."

My hands are shaking so badly I can barely form words. "Shane, please. Please don't do this. Whatever's wrong, we can fix it. We can work through this together. We always have."

"No!" The word explodes out of him, desperate and raw. "We can't fix this, Rachel. Don't you understand? Some things can't be fixed." His voice drops to barely above a whisper. "I can't be the man you need me to be. I thought I could, but I can't. I don't...I don't love you anymore. I can't."

Each word is cold water down my back. I'm gasping now, struggling to breathe as everything I thought I knew about my life crumbles around me.

"You're scared," I whisper, grasping for anything that makes sense. "You're scared because of what I told you about my father. But Shane, that doesn't change us. That doesn't change how we feel about each other."

His face contorts with something that looks like pain. "It changes everything," he says hoarsely. "Can't you see that? You deserve so much more than what this place can give you. More than what I can give you."

The air feels thick, suffocating. "Don't tell me what I deserve. I get to decide that. And I choose you. I choose us."

"Well...I don't." The words come out flat, final. "I don't choose this anymore, Rachel. I can't."

I'm crying now, ugly sobs that shake my whole body. The necklace feels heavy against my chest, this tiny symbol of everything I thought we had. Everything I thought we were.

My fingers find the clasp and I struggle with it, my hands shaking with grief and rage.

"Twelve years," I whisper, looking up at him through my tears. "Twelve years, Shane. Since we were eight years old. Was any of it real?"

Shane's composure finally cracks completely. His face crumples and for a moment he looks like he's about to reach for me. Like he wants to take it all back.

"It was all real," he whispers, so quietly I almost miss it. "Every second of it was real."

But then he steps back, shaking his head. "But it's over now. It has to be over."

Something inside me breaks. Not cracks—breaks. Completely and utterly shatters into pieces so small I know I'll never be able to put them back together.

I look around the bar, at all the faces staring at us. At Fox, who looks like he wants to say something but doesn't know what. At Maverick, whose cocky grin has disappeared entirely. At Del, who has tears in her own eyes.

At all these people who just watched the person I love most in the world walk away from me.

The necklace finally comes free in my hands. I stare down at the tiny wishbone, this symbol of everything we were to each other.

"You know what?" I say, my voice surprisingly steady now that there's nothing left to break. "You're a coward, Shane Nelson. You're too scared to fight for us, too scared of big problems, real problems, so you're running away." I look directly at him, memorizing his face for what I know will be one last time. "But I'm not going to beg you to stay."

With as much force as I can muster, I throw the necklace at his feet. It lands with a tiny clink that somehow carries over the silence, the wishbone breaking in half on the peanut shell-covered floor.

Just like us.

Shane stares down at it for a long moment, and I see his hands shake as he bends to pick up the pieces.

When he looks back up at me, his eyes are full of tears.

"I'm sorry," he whispers. "Rachel, I'm so fucking sorry."

But sorry doesn't fix this.

"Goodbye, Shane," I say quietly.

And then I turn and walk toward the door on unsteady

legs, expecting—hoping—that he'll call my name. That he'll come after me, tell me he was drunk, scared, panicked. That this is all some terrible nightmare and I'll wake up in his arms and everything will be okay.

But he doesn't call out.

He doesn't follow.

He let's me leave him.

And when I push through the door into the cold October night, I know with absolute certainty that I'll never come back to this place. Never see him again.

Because Shane Nelson just taught me that the person you love most in the world is capable of hurting you in ways you never thought possible.

And I'll carry that lesson with me forever.

CHAPTER 14

RACHEL

Some things never change.

One of those things is the Bear Trap pub.

The moment I turned nineteen and could legally drink, this damn pub became like a third home to me (I say third because Shane's was my second). I was here almost every night, not drinking to get wasted, though that sometimes happened when I had too many Jaeger bombs, but just having a beer or two and enjoying the company of my friends.

Tonight, it looks the same as it ever did. Back then, Del worked here too, only she wasn't the owner and manager of the bar like she is now. But there were still peanuts in the little yellow bowls, the shells casually discarded on the floor, and the lighting was still dim (combined with beer goggles this place was quite the hook-up spot), and the walls dark and covered with faded mountain memorabilia. There's even Old Joe, still in his regular booth.

It's Old Joe who actually bought me the beer I'm drinking right now, though Fox promised to get me the next round. He's sitting beside me at the bar, such a giant hulk of a man.

"Cheers," Fox says to me, raising his beer and clinking it against mine.

"Cheers," I say, taking a sip.

"You didn't look me in the eye," he teases. "You know what that means. Seven years of bad sex."

Del snorts from across the bar. "Hogwash."

"Hogwash?" Fox repeats, his dark brows raised. "Since when did you start saying hogwash, Del?"

"Since I started dealing with people who say hogwash on a daily basis. You two are the youngest people I've had in here in a while. I know the Bear Trap is supposed to be for the locals, but how come the locals have to be so damn old?"

Fox laughs. Fox doesn't laugh much. In that respect he's a lot like Hank and Shane, though he's a lot more brooding. But tonight he's been laughing and smiling at pretty much everything Del says.

"Is it me?" Del says, looking down at her tiny faded ringer tee with the bar's logo on it, which her boobs are stretching to the point of being illegible. "Maybe I should dress fancier."

"Are you kidding me?" Fox says, sitting up straighter, bouncing his foot on the rung of the stool. "Don't you ever change, unless your clientele starts having heart attacks. Those breasts *are* pretty dangerous."

She scrunches up her wet rag and throws it at his face, but he catches it one-handed. "Nice try, baby," he says.

"You're a pig," she volleys back, but she's smiling.

I can't help but smile, watching the two of them like I'm watching a TV show. I have a hard time believing that these two haven't slept with each other yet. It has to have happened at some point. Then again, there's too much sexual tension between them.

"Uh oh," Del says under her breath, her eyes trained on the door.

I look over my shoulder to see Shane walk in. He's

wearing dirty jeans and a white thermal that's too hot for this weather but nonetheless makes his taut muscles look fucking fantastic. He stops in his tracks when he sees me and Fox.

"Sorry, Rach," Del says under her breath.

I just wave her off. "It's fine. We're fine."

"Fucking hell you're fine," Fox mutters under his breath.

"Hey," Shane says, hovering at the bar. He nods at me and Fox. I haven't seen him since we buried the raven and rode back to the ranch in complete silence. That was yesterday, and I've been grappling with what happened since then. The feel of his abs through his sweaty shirt, my legs pushed against his, the smell of his skin, the look in his eyes when he told me he dreamed about me every night. The sound of his voice when he told me he misses me.

I felt it. I shouldn't have, but I did. It worked its way past the lock on my heart and buried itself inside until I realized just how badly I've missed him too.

And the awful part is that it's too late. We had our moment in the sun, we had our young love. Whether he regrets it or not, he pushed me away and we broke apart, and you can't go back and change that. You can't change the past any easier than you can change your feelings.

Now I'm a fucking mess, knowing that I have to stay mad at him, then getting mad at myself as if that's the only big reason we should be apart. The reason why he shouldn't touch my skin like he did, setting off fireworks in my chest. There's Samuel, my boyfriend. We may not be head over heels in love with each other but that has to come with time —it has to, and I can't tarnish that potential just because being around Shane stirs up all those old feelings, just because he has such a pretty way with words.

But they were honest words. You know it. They were the most real words you've heard in years.

I suck back on my beer and try to pretend it's okay that

Shane's here, but it's not. It's why I'm at the damn bar to begin with.

Fox gives me the side-eye and gets up. "I'm going to go put some money in the jukebox."

"What can I get you?" Del asks Shane after she watches Fox walk off.

Shane gives her a half smile. "Why do you even ask?"

She rolls her eyes and grabs a bottle of beer from the fridge, passing it to him.

Then Shane turns to me. "Mind if I sit down?"

I shake my head, unable to find the words, and Shane takes the seat on the other side of me.

"I didn't expect to see you here," he says to me before he takes a swig of his beer. "You're looking beautiful."

And I didn't expect for him to say something like that right out of the gate. Things were left so awkward between us and yet he's moving on without skipping a beat.

"Thanks," I tell him. I guess I did go out of my way to try and look good tonight instead of that sweaty dirty farmgirl mess I've been lately. I put on a strappy, tiered cornflower blue maxi dress that matches my eyes, my hair loose around my shoulders, even though I keep brushing it back in a loose braid to keep the heat off my neck, and just the tiniest bit of mascara.

He leans in closer and I try not to freeze. "I just wanted to say I'm sorry about the other day."

I give him a funny look, moving my head back an inch. "You have nothing to apologize for."

He stares at me, deep into my eyes, with so much intensity that it renders the next thoughts in my head to dust. "I just want us to be friends."

Oh. I wasn't expecting him to say that.

I glance up at Del who immediately turns around and

busies herself at the bar, pretending like she's not listening. I call hogwash on that.

Friends. Well, I guess I can do that. It's how we started anyway.

"Okay," I tell him. "Friends it is."

But do friends know what it's like to kiss each other, to fuck each other, to give each other over and over again in the name of love?

"Friends, it is," I say again, as if I'm convincing myself that I can do this. Fuck, even ignoring each other has become incredibly hard lately. There's rarely a minute that goes by when he doesn't occupy my head. Everything here reminds me of him because everything is him.

"You need another drink," he says to me, nudging my elbow. He looks at Del. "Two whiskies."

"Cherries in mine," I tell her.

He gives me a smile that I feel in my core, a sweet flash of heat. "You still love your whisky and cherries."

I shrug, conscious of how he's leaning into me, as if we're trading secrets, conspiring to be the people we used to be. "It makes it sweeter."

He nods, palming his beer. "I remember you used to love that Jaegermeister shit."

"I was, like, eighteen," I tell him. "Every underage drinker loves that. Except for you. You were an old soul even then. Drinking your whisky or rye straight, sipping from the glass, just like your dad and grandpa."

He seems to think that over, staring at the bar for a moment, at the condensation gathering at the bottom of his bottle. "I know," he says gravely. He exhales heavily. "I wanted to be like them. I knew I'd be working on the ranch. I knew that's what I was born to do. Fox, Mav, they got to run free, scale cliffs, jump out of airplanes. And I stayed."

Something prickles at the back of my throat and I try to swallow it down. "Did you ever want a different life?"

He turns his head toward mine, eyes just inches away, more amber in color than his red ale. To anyone else it would look like we're having an extremely intimate moment. Maybe because we are.

"I told you I'd run away with you," he murmurs, his voice so low it sends faint shock waves through me. "I meant it. I would have gone anywhere with you. I would have tried any other kind of life, so long as it was with you."

This stuns me. Completely. I always thought he was paying lip service with empty promises.

"But you love being a rancher," I say softly.

"I do now," he says. "I really do. But I knew growing up that I was expected to be the one to take it over, to help out, to become one of them. When I say I was born to do this, I'm being literal. Fox and Mav did their own thing, and it was up to me to pull the ranch together, to keep the ranch going. And maybe...maybe I felt I owed it, you know. Because of my mother. Because I had to do something to make up for...that."

Fucking hell. I don't want my heart to break for Shane all over again, but it does. It is. All through the years I saw him grapple with those demons and I had no idea how serious and life-changing they turned out to be. He stuck with the ranch because he felt he owed it to his own family, just for being born.

"But," he goes on quietly, chewing on his lip for a moment. "After a while, it stuck. I started to like it, I started to love it. I drank the whisky like my dad and granddad because I wanted so badly to be like them, to prove I had what it takes to do what they did. The drink stuck, every-thing else stuck. And now it's my life."

I watch him, taking him all in. The cut of his jaw, his lips, the pull of his eyebrows as he frowns at his drink. He's changed so much and yet he's still the same boy I fell in love with. The boy who was my protector, my savior, my world.

Friends. I'm supposed to be *friends* with him?

The man might still have most of my heart.

"But are you happy?" I whisper.

He stares at me for a moment, his gaze resting on my lips in such way that I know what he's thinking.

And I want him to think it.

"Almost," he finally answers. "What about you?"

I should give him the stock answer I give everyone. The answer I give myself.

But I can't lie to Shane anymore.

I give a simple shake of my head. "No. I'm not."

"Sorry to interrupt," Fox says, suddenly appearing behind us. He rests his hand on my shoulder and gives it a meaty squeeze that brings me back to reality. "Rachel, I'm going out for a bit to see a few friends. I'll be back later if you need a ride home."

"Not drinking tonight?" Shane asks him.

"Nah, I might be sent out tomorrow, so I need to be in good shape. See you in a bit."

Then he leaves. I watch him go because it gives me time to get myself in order, to put some distance between what was just happening with Shane and me. I don't even know what that was, but it was getting dangerously close to something I'm not sure I could pull back from.

So I drink instead.

I finish my whisky and cherries.

Shane finishes his.

We have two more.

Then two more.

And then Waylon Jennings "You Ask Me To" comes on the jukebox and Shane springs to his feet, nearly knocking over his stool. He grabs my arm and pulls me to the dance-floor which is already crowded with people.

He slips his arms around me and starts singing into my neck. "Let the world call me a fool but if things are right with me and you…"

I sing the rest of the chorus back to him, laughing as I go. It reminds me of our high school grad party, drinking moonshine my father confiscated, sitting on bales of hay outside the dance and having our own private party via a tiny speaker. This song came on and Shane started singing it to me, every single word done in a dead-on impression of Jennings.

I fell in love with him even more that night.

Just like the nights before it.

Just like the nights after.

And it never, ever stopped.

"Come with me outside," Shane whispers into my ear, the warmth of his breath shooting right through me to my toes, bathing me in a helpless warmth.

I nod, letting him steal me away. I can feel Del's eyes on me and I don't care.

I don't care about much right now except the man holding onto me.

His hand meant to meld with mine.

Shane leads me into the parking lot until we're standing beside his truck.

"You're too drunk to drive," I tell him.

But that's all I get to say.

In a flash, my face is cupped by his large, warm hands and his mouth is enveloping mine and every single bad part of me flees my soul. It's replaced by his lips, soft and hungry against mine, his tongue, the way his hands grip me, holding me in place, possessive and strong.

I struggle to have thoughts. I can't find that hard place

inside me from which to push back from. I succumb to him because it's so fucking easy to give myself to Shane Nelson.

My hand goes to his waist, tentative at first, then aggressive as our kiss amplifies, turns frenzied. All these years, all these years.

He moans into my mouth.

I grab the back of his head, feeling the heat on his neck.

He pushes me back against the truck door, the handle digging into my hip, but I don't care.

His lips go for my neck, sucking and kissing and licking as if he'll never get his fill and I'm digging my fingernails into his shirt because I'm afraid to let go, afraid to see what lies beyond this moment the minute we stop.

I don't want to stop.

I'm wet already, everything is throbbing, aching for him. He's always had that ability with me and now it's on ten-fold, rendering me completely powerless in his throes.

I want him so fucking bad.

I need him.

I've needed him all this time.

He whimpers, this primal, desperate sound as his mouth finds mine again and his tongue slips in, sliding against mine until I'm driven wild. Wild for him, always so wild.

"Rachel," he whispers, breathless, hungry. He licks up a path to my ear, takes my earlobe between his teeth and pulls, hot breath enveloping me.

And I'm melting.

Melting.

Right here in this parking lot.

The same parking lot that he broke my heart in.

And just like a needle scratching across a record, everything comes to a wretched stop.

The anger I thought was shoved aside has shot right back

up and I pull back, pressing my fingers into the hard mass of his chest, pushing him back. "No," I manage to say.

His eyes are glazed with lust in the lights above the parking lot but they quickly snap out of it while he reads my face. "What?" he says, voice thick.

"No," I say again and manage to squeeze out between us, stepping away. "No, just no. No, Shane you don't get to do that."

He studies me, trying to regain his breath. Adjusts his erection in his jeans.

I ignore the hot stab of want that rolls through me at the sight.

"I'm sorry."

"Stop apologizing!" I yell, pulling at my hair. "Fucking hell, Shane."

He almost says it again, I can tell. So Canadian of him.

Then he says, "It's because of your boyfriend."

"No. Yes. It's everything...Shane...for crying out loud, don't you see where we are? Don't you know, remember, realize the last thing that happened here?"

He closes his eyes, leans back against the truck, kneads his forehead with his knuckles. Doesn't say anything.

"Shane. You broke me. You changed me. You did that, here, and it's something I'll never be able to get over because I'll never understand why you did it. Why you told me, in front of all our friends, your brothers, everyone, that you didn't love me anymore, that you never loved me and you wished I was gone for good. That's what you said Shane. And I still can't...I can't believe it because that's not who you are. And yet I can believe it because...who has ever fucking loved me, and meant it?"

He looks up, his eyes sharper than a mountain peak. "That's not it, Rachel. Don't say that. Don't you fucking say that."

Tears rush to my eyes and I throw my hands out in frustration. "Then why? Why did you do it?"

"Because I had no choice," he says, voice like steel.

"What?"

"I had no choice, Rachel. No, wait, that's not true. I had two choices. And I picked the one that I thought was best for the both of us."

I blink at him, tears rolling down my face, my heart lurching around in my chest, trying to find a place to land. "What are you talking about?"

He takes in a deep breath and looks away, a quiet kind of madness flashing in his eyes. "Do you remember the night before? Your father...attacked you. You called me. I took you home. You told me everything. You fell asleep..." His eyes swing to mine. He swallows. "Do you remember how when you woke up, I wasn't there. I was down at the barn. I had bandages wrapped around my knuckles because I had one of the horses spook on me when I had the reins wrapped around my hands."

I remember. I remember everything because that morning was the last morning we had together. You always remember your last day with someone you love, like it's your last day on earth. Every look, every smell, every touch. I remember that day he acted like he was wrestling one of his demons. I assumed it had something to do with what I told him the night before, that he didn't know how to deal with it. I couldn't blame him.

"Do you then remember that your father was severely beaten by a couple of junkies who tried to rob a house?"

I just stare at him and in my heart I feel the puzzle pieces come together before my brain can even catch up.

"There were no junkies. That was me. You told me what he did to you and all I wanted to do was kill him. And so I almost did. I fucked up, Rachel. And in the end...I didn't have a choice."

I can only shake my head, my hand at my chest, my heart throwing itself at my ribs. "You broke up with me..." I say faintly.

"I broke up with you because your father told me to. It was either that. Or it was jail."

"He...he told you to break up with me? Why?"

He gives me a sour smile. "Because he knew that would kill me more than throwing me in jail would. He knew how much I loved you. He knew how to get to me. What would really make me suffer. And so I had to do it. I had to be as cruel and ruthless to you as possible. I wanted you to rip off your necklace and throw it at me, and you did. I wanted that kind of hate from you, because only then would you not question me. And only then would you finally leave this place. Only then would you be safe." He licks his lips. "It worked. You left. And he couldn't hurt you anymore."

I can't believe this. The parking lot is starting to spin around me, the lights swirling like galaxies.

How can this be? How can everything that happened be based on a lie? And while my heart is trying to sing for what Shane did, how it wasn't about the loss of love but the protection of life, it's beating to a different beat. Trying to catch up, trying to understand.

The last six years have been rewritten.

Everything I've based my new life on has been ripped out from underneath me.

I'm both elated and confused, angry...lost.

"I shouldn't apologize again because I know you don't like it," Shane says. "But I've been dealing with this truth every single day since you left. It killed me to know that I had to hurt you like that and the only trade off was that you were somewhere safe and free. But, fuck, Rachel. I'm so sorry it came to that. I was young, I wasn't thinking. I could only think of hurting him for hurting you and because of that, I fucked both our lives up. And I know it's going to take some time to come to terms with it."

I nod, glancing at him briefly. I can't be here anymore. I can't deal with him.

"I'm going to go," I tell him absently, trying to find words. "See if Fox is back and can drive me home."

"Are you sure?"

"Yeah, I... I need time to think." I suck in a breath, my chest tight. "Jesus, Shane. This changes everything."

"For good or bad?"

I look at him and frown, sick to my stomach. "I have no idea."

And then I walk off, unsteady at first, then quicker, until I'm back inside the bar.

Everything already looks different.

CHAPTER 15

SHANE

I have dreams of blood and guns. Of toothless grins and devil eyes. Of prison bars over beating hearts. Of Rachel's lips. Those beautiful lips, the taste of whisky on them, maraschino cherries. Hope. So much hope.

Did that really happen?

The world seems different under the veil of truth.

A thud shakes the whole room, sending knives into my brain.

"Holy hell, Shane," Maverick's voice booms. "Did you tie one on last night or what?"

I groan and open one eye. The room spins. I'm no longer dreaming even though fragments of last night settle around me like dust.

"What time is it?" I mumble into the pillow.

"It's nine a.m., sharpshooter," he says, kicking the edge of the bed, blunt objects splintering through my head. "I thought you cowboys were up with the fucking roosters."

"Most cowboys don't drink their weight in whisky," I manage to say. My mouth tastes like sour dirt.

"What the fuck are you talking about?" Mav says. "Of

course they do. The only difference is they know how to handle it and you obviously don't. I'm starting to think you ain't a Nelson at all."

"Why are you here, standing in my room, yelling at me?" I slowly ease myself up, ignoring the spins.

"Because dad said you needed my help today. He's off on a ride, says you need to do the irrigation pipes. I know you need help for that."

I nod. Irrigating is an all-day job and time-consuming. Usually we hire someone to do this but it's a tough role to fill and we've already gone through three different guys this year so far. The pipes have to be moved every day to ensure the fields (which we use for hay or silage) get water and some of our lines are hand lines, so we have to manually move each forty-foot pipe over sixty feet to ensure the entire field gets water. It's hard, tedious work.

So I'm surprised that Maverick volunteered for the job. Surprised but not at all complaining, especially when I feel like ass.

"Well I'm glad you're here," I tell him, moving slowly as I put on my jeans so as not to disrupt all the loose sharp stuff in my brain. "You do remember how to ride, right?"

He grins at me as I throw on my tee shirt and hat. "Fuck riding, brother. We're taking my new truck."

"That's not technically yours," I remind him. "And this field is all the way to the east, down by the lake."

"Then we'll see just how this baby will handle."

As it turns out, it handles really well. Maverick loves his vehicles and he's driving this truck with a big, shit-eating grin on his face, laughing maniacally as we careen over potholes and bumps.

Finally, we reach the field and get started, carefully moving the long, rusted pipe along the tall, green grass in sections. It's a lot of lifting and shuffling and the sun beats down on us harder with each hour that passes.

We take a break at the truck, leaning against it as we drink sun-warmed water straight out of plastic jugs.

"So are you going to talk about what happened last night?" Maverick asks, dipping over to sprinkle some water on the back of his neck.

"What do you mean?"

"I was there for a minute, you know," he says, giving me a steady look. "Saw you and Rachel dancing like it was old times."

"We were just dancing," I tell him, looking off toward the crop of alder and birch where our land meets the lake. Waylon Jennings plays in my head.

"Uh huh. That's not what it looked like to me. You know, man, you and Fox are exactly the same."

That brings a sharp look out of me. "What do you mean?"

Mav looks at me like I'm dumb. "You and Rachel, Fox and Delilah. Two sets of couples that should just shut the fuck up and admit that they love each other already."

"Fox is in love with Del?"

"Don't change the subject. I knew you never got over Rachel. I didn't see how you could, to be honest. And I never believed for a second that you willingly broke up with her. The Shane I know would never do that to her. Especially in front of everyone like that. You were fucking vicious, man, and that's not you."

I stiffen, hating that I've had to keep reliving that moment so much lately.

"What happened?" he asks, his voice lower. "Look, I get it. Water under the bridge, maybe. But it's something no one has ever understood, especially Rachel."

"She understands now," I tell him, looking him square in the eye. "Last night I told her."

"Told her *what*?"

It's not my place to say but since the truth has been coming out...

"Errol Waters use to abuse her. Sexually. Emotionally. Physically. He was abusive to Vernalee too."

Mav's jaw sets in a hard line. He's almost as protective over Rachel as I am. "Why am I not fucking surprised," he seethes quietly.

"Because he's a fucking piece of shit, disgusting scum on this good green earth. And Rachel dealt with it for years before she finally told me. That night...I wasn't thinking straight. I couldn't. I just wanted to murder him and that's all that I could see, all I could do. If I had just stepped back and took a moment and tried to control myself but...she's Rachel, you know? I couldn't let it slide. I had to take matters into my own hands. I was blind with rage. Just fucking blind."

"What did you do, Shane?"

I take a deep breath and I let it all out. I don't hold back on anything, just lay the truth bare.

"Holy fuck," Mav whispers when I'm done. "Why didn't he just throw you in jail?"

"Because he knew he was at fault. He wanted to keep what he did hidden. He knew that if he pressed charges against me, the town would talk. They'd wonder why I did what I did. Why did good ol' boy Shane Nelson nearly beat this man to death? The truth would leak out that way, which wouldn't be a bad thing. But it would be for him. If I told the truth, there might be a trial. A trial might bring out a testimony from Rachel, even Vernalee. There's a witness too, Zimmer. Sure he kept his mouth shut but under oath? In court? Would he still keep quiet about what he heard? Errol knew that he couldn't risk it. He wanted everything to be shoved under the rug so things would go on as they always did. He wanted to keep his position of power."

My heart is still galloping in my chest, making me feel lightheaded under this sun. "And most of all, he knew that breaking Rachel's heart would be far, far worse. He hated me. Hated her. He wanted the both of us to suffer. And he got what he wanted. His crimes never came to light and I broke up with her and I knew that if I wasn't ruthless and vicious and cruel to her that she wouldn't believe it. I couldn't let her know why I was doing it. So I broke up with her in front of everyone. I humiliated her and I broke my own heart and ruined everything because I had no fucking choice."

My fists ball, then uncurl. "There hasn't been a day where I haven't wished I finished the job, you know. That he got away with it all, then went on to kill that kid and who knows who the hell else in the so-called name of the law. In the end, he fucked himself over but he shouldn't have even had the choice."

A solid silence hangs over us, both of us digesting this poison from the past.

"Fuck me. That is some heavy, heavy shit, Shane." Mav runs his hand down over his face, tugging at his features. "What did she say after you told her this last night?"

I exhale loudly, feeling the frustration roll through me. "She didn't know what to say. How to handle it. She said she needed time to think. And then she went back into the bar. I got a cab, came back here and finished a bottle of Grandpa's whisky."

"Just like old times."

"Pretty much."

"I can't believe you've kept that inside all this time. Why didn't you tell me? Why didn't you ever tell her?"

"I don't know. I couldn't reach Rachel and I guess I thought it didn't matter. Why bring up the past? What good would it do? And to be honest, even though parts of me wish I killed him, I'm not proud of what I did. I should have gone about it another way, that way I would have never had to break up with Rachel. I just wasn't thinking. I was young and brash and stupid."

"With balls of fucking steel." He slaps me hard on the shoulder. "If I'm ever screwed over by someone, I'm calling you for your own brand of vigilante justice."

I smirk at him. Maverick is pretty much all muscle. He hangs off the side of cliffs every winter like Stallone in *Cliffhanger*, risking his life to rescue people. He has no problems dealing with anybody. That said, he often puts himself in situations where extra support may be needed. Confidence is a virtue, being a cocky fucker is another thing entirely.

"Is that Pa?" he suddenly says, squinting in the sun and I look over to see our father cantering over the ridge toward us.

"Shane!" he yells to me, riding over on Basil, his prized paint quarter horse.

"Something wrong?" I ask as I put on my hat, striding toward him. He doesn't sound overly panicked but there's still something wrong considering he's rode all the way over to us. Normally there's a radio in my truck that we use to communicate since cell phone service over here doesn't reach but we took Mav's truck instead.

"I need you to head west over Pastor's Peak," he says to me, coming to a stop along the edge of the field. "Neighbor's plane spotted some of our cows too far onto Crown Land. It'll be a bitch to get them back later if they don't get turned around right now." He gets off of Basil and hands me his reins. "Here, take him back and go. I'll help Mav with the irrigation."

I nod and swing up on Basil, adjusting myself on Basil's broad back. "Do you know how far around the peak?"

"I think closer to Arrow Lake," he says.

"I should bring an overnight bag then."

"Shouldn't take you that long but just in case. It's only a handful so just take Fletcher with you."

I tell him I will, thank Mav and then turn around galloping toward the ranch.

I'm there in no time, though Basil is frothy with sweat, and I quickly take the time to rinse him off with the hose before I tack up Polly.

It's when I'm about to lead Basil over to the pasture that I hear a strange whimpering sound coming from the hayloft.

I leave Basil and head over to the ladder. "Hello?" I call up it.

A sniffle.

"Rachel?"

I haul myself up the rungs and peer out over the edge.

Rachel is sitting amongst the hay, her knees drawn up to her chest, her phone beside her. Her head is turned away from me and I can see she's trying to wipe away tears.

"What happened?" I ask her, climbing up and coming over, hunching down from the roof. I crouch right in front of her and think about putting my hand on her leg, wondering if she'll flinch.

I do it anyway, my palm pressed against her warm skin.

She doesn't flinch.

A small victory.

"Did something happen to your mom?" I ask softly.

She shakes her head. "No. Yes. Not like that..."

I reach out and hold her chin, bringing her face around so I'm staring right into her eyes, red-rimmed and shining with tears. "What happened?"

She sighs and shakes her head, eyes closed, tears spilling down her cheeks until they run onto my fingers. "It doesn't matter."

"Rachel. Everything you do matters to me. You know this

now. Is it...something to do with me? With what happened last night?"

She takes in a deep breath and I tuck her hair behind her ear. "Yeah."

My heart feels heavy. I sit down right next to her, copying her pose, my arms resting on my knees. "Lay it on me."

"I, uh...I broke up with Samuel."

I shouldn't be feeling joy right now, especially when she's upset, but that's what's burning in my chest. "I'm sorry," I tell her. "That was probably my fault."

She gives me a weak smile. "Yeah. It was. But...it was also mine. I called him, you know, because I wanted to check in. Reception here sucks, so I took mom's car and drove into town until I could get a better signal. I felt guilty about last night, I can't help it. And just off the bat, I could tell he didn't really care when I was coming home. So I knew it was pretty much over. I mean, it's been over for a while but I... well, anyway, then I told him the truth. That you kissed me and I kissed you back and he didn't even sound upset." She lets out a sour laugh. "I mean, what does that say?"

"Says he didn't know what he had when he had it. How long were you together?"

"Half a year or so," she says, picking up some hay and playing with it. "Never said I love you. Never felt it. But I figured that eventually I would, you know. I was used to not falling in love...I couldn't fall in love after you, Shane." She rubs her lips together, glances at me. "You were it for me. I gave my heart to you and I never got it back. I don't even think I wanted it back. I just prayed that I could love as big as I did the first time I loved you."

I'm holding my breath as she talks, my own heart swelling and stretching with each word that falls from her lips.

"And I didn't," she goes on. "My heart just couldn't do it. I didn't have it in me because it's only you that could get me to love like that again. Your heart is the only one that mine responds to."

Are you talking in past or present tense? I think. Please, please God, let this be about the here and now.

"Funny thing is, Samuel says he wasn't surprised at all. He knew this would happen. I never talked about you to him, I did my best to pretend you didn't exist, but he still knew that my heart belonged elsewhere. Said that when we were, well, together, I was never in the moment. Never present. He said it was as if I was always somewhere else but it was never with him. And he was totally right."

I clear my throat, wanting so badly to just push her back on the hay and kiss her, have her, take her. Revel in her sweet, sweet words.

I manage to hold it in. "Sounds like it needed to happen, though you know I'm biased."

"It did," she says and then rolls her eyes. "And then I contacted work because I was all paranoid that my boss was going to break up with me too."

"And?"

She gives a half-hearted shrug. "He said that he's thinking of bringing Pete up to my level so when I go back, I shouldn't be surprised if I'm officially sharing my clients now. Actually, I think by the time I get back…I won't have any clients at all."

"I'm sorry."

"Yeah. Well. I knew that was the risk in coming here but I wouldn't change anything. Still, I was upset and angry and frustrated at everything, just every fucking thing. And I came back to the house and my mom and I got in a fight and I think everything I kept bottled up just came pouring out. It was last night, what you told me. It reminded me that she was never ever there for me and yet here I am for her, sacrificing everything. I know I'm her daughter and I'm doing what good daughters do but fuck!" She slaps her knee. "She was never there. She turned her back on me. You were the only one who went to bat for me, Shane. I'm just so fucking confused."

I grab her hand, holding it, trying to give her comfort. "I know it's hard."

"I told her some really horrible things," she cries out softly, looking at me with pained eyes. "I was so mean."

"It happens. This is what families do. You don't think I haven't fought with every single member of my family?"

"Not your grandpa."

"Yes my grandpa. Rachel, you knew me when I was young. I could be a little shit sometimes. I'm not anymore but that's the point of getting older. Maybe I still want to duke it out with Fox every now and then and maybe we should but even so, it's just life. You said some mean things and your mother probably deserved it. She hurt you. She was your mother and she failed for a while because she was hurt too and she hurt you and that's valid. But in time, you'll both get over it. I promise. No one's heart repairs overnight, it takes time to put the pieces back together."

If they even want to try, that is.

"Why are you so good to me?" she whispers.

Because I never stopped loving you.

"Because you deserve all the good this world can bring," I tell her, sliding my hand behind her neck as I lean in, my lips finding hers.

"Shane," she whispers against my mouth but her words drop away. The world drops away as I sink into the sweetness of her tongue, as we fall back into the hay, my hands roaming over her body in quiet worship. Each section of skin my palm skirts over is a section of my heart I'm shocking alive again, willing it to beat. Her body makes me feel like I'm just being born, over and over again.

I want to give her everything.

I kiss her, deeper, sweeter, with a longing I can't hide as I start to pull down her shorts, slipping my fingers under the front of her panties.

She tenses. I know it's moving fast and backwards all at once but I keep going because I know what she likes, I know how she likes it. I need to know that I still know her as intimately as I once did.

"Shane," she says again but her words drip with sex and then I'm pulling her shorts and underwear down, yanking them aside and parting her soft thighs, diving right in.

I need to taste her, messy, hot, and wild. I want her body, her touch, her soul, everything I once had and lost. I need to put my cock deep inside her, make sure she really feels me, knows me, knows I'm hers. Always *hers*.

But this isn't about that right now. Right now, I just want to take her mind off of everything. I want to make her come in my mouth, thighs squeezing my face, whispering my name.

"I'm on the pill," she manages to say as my tongue, flat, wide and wet, licks up her thighs, her taste is sweet and salty and sinfully good. "I mean, an IUD. And I'm clean...I..."

"Shhhh," I tell her, murmuring into her skin. "Don't worry about that right now. This is just about you."

At that, she squirms underneath me in anticipation and my mouth fucking waters at the sight. I push my lips into her, groaning as my tongue swirls around her clit, building and building, just the way she used to like it.

I think she still does. She's growing wetter by the second, her hands are first in the hay, making fists and then they're reaching down, in my hair, holding tight, and her legs are splayed wider, wanting more. I pull back, wanting to be a tease and gently blow on her until she's whimpering.

"Do want it soft or wild?" I whisper, air skirting over her clit. I'll give her anything she asks for.

"Wild," she says and I love how bold she is. There was no hesitation at all.

I smile to myself, the sight of her spread before me, then I attack her with my tongue, pulsing it in and out of her, flicking and licking up a frenzy until it's wet and messy and my mouth is cramping. It's not long before she's coming, her thighs wrapped on either side of my head, her skin throbbing beneath my lips.

I smile against her and look up over her chest rising and falling, frantic. She's gripping the hay for dear life, her back arched and her mouth is gaping open as she cries out my name.

I've missed this. It's like witnessing a miracle. Hard to find in an ordinary world.

I pull back and watch her as she comes down from the high, her cheeks rosy, her skin glistening with sweat.

Eventually she sits up, pulls her underwear and shorts back on.

She's avoiding my eyes at all costs.

That ain't fucking good.

My heart seems to drop out of me.

"Was that okay?" I ask her. She sure acted like it was okay in the moment but now that the moment has passed, she looks like she's struggling with something.

"It was..." she starts. She looks at me. "I'm not sure if that was a good idea."

I swallow uneasily. "Okay. Why?"

"It's too much...too fast." She rubs at her forehead. "I don't know how I feel about anything right now. An orgasm isn't going to fix anything, it's just going to complicate things and we're already complicated enough as it is."

An orgasm? I want to say. That wasn't just an orgasm. That was everything.

But I don't say it because she's fucking right and this just proves it. Things are complicated as hell.

Still, "I hate to break it to you, Rachel, but we're going to be complicated for a while yet."

"And when does it stop?"

When you love me again. When you stay.

If you stay.

Our eyes lock with each other and I know that she knows what I'm thinking. She has to feel it off of me. Rachel feels everything.

And because of that, I know I have to tread carefully. I don't want to push her away, I don't want to scare her off. She has to work things out on her own, even though I would give anything to help her. I gave her closure, I reset her past, but that doesn't mean that I'm her future.

I get to my feet, breaking our gaze, and start heading down the ladder.

"I better get a move on then."

"Where are you going?" she asks, staring over the edge as I jump down on the barn floor.

I look up at her. With the way the sun is streaming in, the dust motes floating around her head look like a halo. "I'd just finished hosing down Basil. Now I gotta get Polly, tack up, head out on the range. Some cows have wandered too far."

"How long are you going to be gone for?"

"I don't know," I tell her as she starts climbing down the ladder. "Maybe overnight. Maybe not."

"Can I come?" she steps onto the ground and turns to face me.

I'm beyond puzzled. "Why would you want to come?"

"I don't want to stay here. I don't want to talk to my mother after that, I just need to get away for a bit. I don't want to be alone."

I raise my brows. For someone who doesn't want complications, she's certainly complicating things.

But like hell I'm complaining.

"Of course you can come," I tell her. "I'll saddle up Sybil for you. Go put on some jeans, boots, grab a sweater, maybe a toothbrush and I'll get us some saddle bags just in case."

She nods, looking nervous at the thought of having to go back into the worker's cottage and the scene of the crime. Then she turns and runs to go get her stuff.

I watch her ass as she goes, the taste of her still on my lips.

I'm welcoming this complication with open fucking arms.

CHAPTER 16

SHANE

A lot of time may have passed since Rachel was young and on this ranch but one thing remains the same. She's cute as fucking hell on horseback.

And a natural, too.

Even though we'd gone bareback riding the other day, now seeing her sit proudly on the back of Sybil, a slow and rather ornery mare (just like the *Fawlty Towers* character she was named after), as we ride up into the mountains, she looks just as she did back in the day.

"What?" she asks me, adjusting the brim of the black cowboy hat I'd given her.

"Nothing." I smile.

"You keep staring at me. Am I doing it wrong?"

"You're doing it great. You belong on the back of a horse."

She snorts. "Yeah, well after we went bareback, I couldn't walk very well the next day."

"Kind of like the day after we've had sex."

She narrows her eyes at me and lets out a puff of air in disgust. "You and your ego."

I shrug. "Not ego, just the truth."

I know it's making her uncomfortable for me to talk about sex but I just had my head between her legs so I don't think it matters all that much what we talk about. She can pretend that what happened was a mistake but I know that meant something to her, even if she won't admit it.

"Don't act like your other partners ever measured up to me," I add. I bite my lip, watching for her reaction.

Her eyes roll far back in her head and she clucks at Sybil to pick up the pace, trying to get past me.

"You trying to escape?" I call after her.

She glances at me over her shoulder and then yells at Sybil, "Come on girl!" and starts kicking like crazy.

Sybil perks up and starts off at a canter, turning to a gallop as soon as the two of them find their rhythm together. I take a moment to watch Rachel fly across the grass like she's sailing on top of a ghost. I can hear the freedom in her voice as she whoops and hollers over the hoofbeats, the big sky and mountain peaks stretched out in front of them.

I look over at Fletcher trotting beside me, his ears perked up and focused on Rachel as she gets a bigger and bigger lead.

"You ready cow dog?" I ask him.

He wags his tail.

And I join in the chase.

In a hot second, Polly is up to a gallop under my saddle and we're flying down the slope after her. The reins are slack as I lean forward, one hand holding down my hat, Polly's ears pinned back as she's given 'er.

I can't wipe the smile from my face, the pure joy that filters through me like sunshine as I chase down my love. It's all open spaces and heat and horses and heart. That girl has my fucking heart.

"You can't get rid of me that easily," I yell at her as I start to catch up. She may have had the headstart but Polly is as fast as a thoroughbred and streamlined like a whip. Soon we're overtaking them and I'm laughing into the sky as I pull Polly around in a circle, going around them.

"Fuck you," Rachel says but she's smiling uncontrollably. "You're literally riding circles around me."

"Trying to ensure you won't ride off again."

"Don't give me any reasons," she retorts as we both slow to a trot, then a walk.

"Don't spook so easily."

"Spook?" she says. "Please."

"What? You've been all jumpy ever since I tongue-fucked you."

She balks at that, looking at me with an open mouth. "Shane."

"What?"

"That's no way to speak to a lady."

I grin at her. "You ain't no lady."

"Fucker."

"I stand corrected. Besides, I remember you used to like the dirty talk."

Her cheeks flush and she pulls down at the brim of her hat to cover her face.

"You did say I'd gotten bold," I add. "I reckon you might just like it."

"Stop," she says, sounding exasperated. "Let's just put all that past us."

"Why should we do that? You have something against orgasms? You used to never get your fill. Greedy little thing you were."

Another sharp look. "Because. I told you. It's complicating things."

"Funny," I say, gesturing between the two of us riding side-by-side, Fletcher loping on the outskirts and the wild land beyond, "this seems like the easiest thing on earth. Just you and me. Out here. It's where we both belong."

"It's where you belong," she says softly.

"And you belong with me."

"Shane..."

I sigh. "Look, I know I'm coming on strong and I know you think things are getting complicated but...you need to give me a chance."

"A chance?"

I gnaw on my lip, wondering how to proceed. How to lay everything bare. It seemed so easy last night but that was everything from the past. It's the present that matters most.

"A second chance," I tell her. "There's nothing stopping you anymore."

"Are you serious? Shane. I can't just...uproot my whole life. Maybe Samuel and I broke up, okay fine. And maybe I'm not happy in Toronto or with my job and maybe I won't even have a fucking job when I get back home but...I have to go back home."

I shake my head, my heart feeling tight. "No. You don't have to."

"Shane."

"Damnit, Rachel," I tell her, bouncing a fist off the saddle horn as the frustration rolls through me. I shouldn't be getting mad but I can't help it. "This isn't over. You know it isn't. You can't just come here and tell me that I'm not worth another chance. You can't pretend that you don't want me, need me. Fucking hell, I've been needing and wanting you every single day since you left and I refuse to believe that you haven't felt the same way. Yeah, I fucked up but it's over. You know the truth now and it's over."

"You think I can just turn it off?" she snaps. "While you've been so-called pining for me, I've been fucking *hating* you."

Her words cut like paper, quick with a deep sting. "Ouch."

"Well I'm sorry," she says. "But you ruined me and I know

we've been over this but I can't just forget that it ever happened!"

"But you have to. You have to if you ever want to move on. You have to let it all go."

"You try being in my shoes. I get it that you broke your own heart when you broke mine and I feel for you but you weren't in my shoes. What you're asking me to do isn't easy."

"I know it isn't, I know. But aren't I still worth trying for?"

She presses her lips together and looks off and my heart, it fucking sinks.

Maybe I'm not worth it in the end.

"You know what," I tell her. "It's fine. I get it. I'll back off."

She exhales, her shoulders slumping. "This was a mistake."

Whether she means coming along on the ride or coming to North Ridge in general, I don't know. All the options hurt.

We ride for the next few hours in silence, the air heavy and thick with tension that neither of us seem to shake. Even the horses are on edge, their ears flicking back and forth, giving nervous snorts.

As we approach September, the days are getting shorter. It's seven o'clock and the sun will be going down in an hour or so. I've seen signs of the herd but haven't actually seen them and it looks like we'll be spending the night.

One long, awkward night, I'm betting. I only have one sleeping bag. Seemed like a good idea a few hours ago.

"We'll ride for a bit more," I tell Rachel as we skirt alongside a green lake, a forest of pine on the other side. The elevation here is higher and there's a bit of bite to the air. "Then set up camp."

I can tell she's nervous about the whole thing and I don't think it has to do with being alone with me. I'm not sure if she's ever been out in the wilderness overnight. For me, it's pretty much second nature.

"I need to go pee," she says, pulling up Sybil to a halt and looking around. In front of us a patch of alder and shrubs lead into the hill of pine.

"I promise I won't look," I tell her, ready to shield my eyes.

But she dismounts and fishes some toilet paper out of the saddle bag I'd given her and heads out into the trees, not even looking my way. I don't know how she's still mad at me or even what for but time doesn't seem to be helping.

I watch her disappear and look around. This isn't a bad spot to camp but I don't like the proximity to the forest. I'd rather keep riding and find another spot, maybe beside a creek so the horses have access to water, some place open so I can see from all angles. It's not going to rain, so we just need a place to tie up the horses and some flat ground to spread the sleeping bag on and that's about it.

I actually love camping under the stars. Sometimes I go on overnights just by myself. Usually there's a purpose to them, like traveling to other ranch lands to meet with ranchers or just driving cows or checking fences and making repairs, but I'm always the one going. There's something about lying beneath a blanket of stars, far from the comforts of home, that makes you feel immensely connected to the land. It's that connection that keeps the love of the job going.

Polly shifts nervously underneath me, her ears flicking back and forth. Sybil does the same. Fletcher is looking alert in the direction of where Rachel disappeared.

A coldness builds in my chest and I straighten up, instinctively reaching for my shotgun at the back of my saddle. "Rachel?" I say loudly. "You doing okay?"

I wait, listen.

I hear nothing.

Then rustling.

Unease trickles through me.

"Rachel!" I yell. My hand grasps the gun and I carefully bring it forward.

No answer.

I look at Fletcher. "Go find Rachel," I tell him urgently.

He springs into action, trotting off into the forest until I can't see him either.

Something isn't right.

No, not right at all.

Sybil's head suddenly lifts and she starts backing up, as does Polly, spooked as fucked.

Fletcher starts barking and barking like crazy from somewhere in the trees.

A heavy rustling follows.

"Rachel!" I yell, ready to jump off.

Then, a growl.

No, a *roar*.

It makes all my hair stand on end, freezing me on the spot.

There's a rapid onslaught of sounds.

Fletcher barks, growls, snaps.

And something large and menacing growls back, a low, guttural cry that nearly shakes the ground.

Sybil rears.

I keep Polly in place.

Fletcher keeps barking, twigs and branches snap.

So do jaws.

Snarls.

Another roar and then Fletcher's high-pitched howl, a cry of absolute pain.

Fucking hell, not Fletcher. Not my dog.

"Rachel!" I yell. "Fletcher!"

There are no more barks.

The trees start moving.

The ground is shaking.

Yards ahead, a mammoth-sized grizzly bear comes thundering out of the trees, a big, scary fucker that comes to a stop a yard away, dirt flying around his massive body.

Sybil pulls her reins out of my grasp and gallops away and Polly wants to do the same, even though a grizzly bear can run as fast as racehorse for short distances and there's no doubt he would charge and bring us both down. I do what I can to keep Polly in place because I'm not fucking leaving Rachel or my dog behind.

I aim the shotgun at the bear, trying to keep calm, keep steady.

The bear opens his mouth in a deafening roar, showing off a pink mouth, rows of sharp teeth, then rises up on his hind legs so he's a beast of eight feet tall.

Jesus.

It's the most horrifying and majestic sight I've ever seen. A true testament to power, to nature, to the wild.

And it can so easily kill me.

I keep the shotgun trained on his head, ready to pull the trigger.

I don't want to. And I know that even with a shotgun blast to the head, grizzlies don't always die on the spot and the chances of me taking him out before he can get to me are slim.

But so help me God, if he did anything to Rachel, I will blast his fucking brains out.

My finger touches the trigger but doesn't pull it, Polly dancing back and forth beneath me as I try to keep the grizzly in my sights. The panic inside me wants to well up and scream but I can't pay it attention, can't feed it, I push it down and act instinctively. Having the gun in my hands like this brings me right back into the Waters' kitchen, pointing it at Errol.

I stare at the bear. Deep brown eyes.

The bear stares back at me.

I might see my whole life in that look. Gone in a horrible flash.

The moment stretches forever and all that loss knocks at my door.

But this wasn't like facing off with Errol.

This is something else entirely.

I take a deep breath.

Prepared. Determined. And ultimately torn.

Yet I will do what I have to do.

But, it changes. The bear lowers himself to the ground, huffing and slapping the earth with its paws, its long black claws raking the dirt before it gives another low growl.

And then, with a shake of its head, it lumbers off in the opposite direction along the lake, disappearing around the bend of the hill.

Gone.

I exhale and eventually lower the gun. Then as the reality comes back, I'm shaking, the adrenaline and fear ravaging through me.

"Rachel!" I scream and jump off Polly, running into the forest with the gun.

I look around, yelling her name over and over again but she's nowhere to be found.

Then there's a bark.

I whip around to see Fletcher limping toward me, tongue hanging out.

"Fletcher!" I cry out, dropping to my knees to examine him. I was so certain he was dead. Miraculously, he isn't that hurt. He's limping and the fur at the back of his neck is wet with saliva and blood and there's a small wound but that's about it. My guess is he attacked the bear and the bear got him by the back of the neck and threw him off. It could have been so much worse.

I stand back up, cupping my hands over my mouth, trying to ignore that panic but fuck it's going to kill me. "Rachel!" I yell. "Can you hear me! Please?"

I look down at Fletcher. "Where is she? Where is Rachel?"

Fletcher whines and I'm not sure he understands but when I ask again, keeping my voice as steady as possible, he gets my intentions.

He lopes a bit further into the brush and I follow until he stops at the base of a tree.

And looks up.

CHAPTER 17

RACHEL

*H*elp, help, help.

The words repeat over and over, screaming inside my head.

Help, help, help.

I don't want to die.

Not now, not now. Not when I haven't really lived.

I haven't really lived.

I haven't really lived.

Help, help, help.

My arms are numb, my legs too, everything. I'm not sure how much longer I can stay up here, holding onto the tree trunk. Or maybe I'm forever molded to it, like moss. Maybe I'll never come back down.

My mind shifts back in time.

Me lying on my back amongst the hay.

Shane devouring me.

Against my better judgement, I opened my legs and let him in.

I let myself be vulnerable again, only for him.

And it was at that moment I realized I was alive.

He was trying to bring me back to life.

And it scared the shit out of me.

To open that door and stick my neck out and hope for the fucking best.

But I was alive.

And now I'm in a fucking pine tree, my limbs scraped and bleeding from the hasty climb and I'm wondering why I was so afraid to be alive when the alternative is so much worse.

"Rachel!" Shane's voice cuts through my head.

It's real, I have to tell myself. *He's real. The bear has to be gone by now.*

When I went into the forest to do my business, a bear was the last thing I expected to see. To be honest, I just wanted time away from Shane. To prepare for the night ahead, to grapple with the things I'd said earlier. The mean way they left my lips. I hurt him. It hurt me.

But there it was.

The grizzly.

It hadn't seen me yet.

I didn't know what to do. I thought that unlike black bears, grizzlies can't climb trees and I knew that if I ran for Shane or called for Shane, I would be fucking dead.

So I went for the nearest tree and climbed and didn't look back.

Except when I did, the fucking bear was trying to climb too.

So much for that myth.

And then Fletcher came bounding toward the bear and I closed my eyes, not wanting to watch. The poor dog bought me time and I climbed up a few more branches until I saw him grab Fletcher by the neck and throw him where I couldn't see. The sound of the dog's yelp burrowing into my brain. Then the bear ran off.

I couldn't breathe, couldn't speak, couldn't cry.

I could do nothing but do what I'm doing right now.

Hold on tight and pray.

Help, help, help.

"Rachel," I hear Shane's voice again and I know I have to move, to say something, but I'm so fucking scared.

I manage to move my head and look down through the branches, the bottom ones broken off by the grizzly. It's left deep grooves in the bark from its claws.

Shane and Fletcher stare up at me.

"Rachel," he says again, his voice lower. "Are you okay?"

I can't speak.

"Please, come down. It's not safe to stay up there. We need to keep moving." His voice is pleading yet so calm, like he's got control of the entire situation. "Please. Nothing is going to happen to you. I've got you."

And that's all it takes. His words sink in. He means them. He always has been my protector. I've never not been safe in his arms.

"Okay," I whisper and after a long moment I slowly start making my way down the tree, my muscles cramping as I go.

I have to jump the last bit and he catches me, arms strong and warm, immovable.

"Shane," I cry out, holding onto him, so fucking terrified. "Oh god."

"It's okay," he says, his hand cupping the back of my head as my legs wrap around his waist. "I've got you. I'm not letting you go. Not again."

I don't know how I manage to keep it together. I just want to cry and scream at everything, the fear of death still lingering. I want to unravel, completely, and I know if I do, he's going to have a hell of a time putting me back together.

So I hold on and then I let go.

I'm lowered to the ground and he takes my hand and with

his shotgun in the other, that shotgun that changed everything, he leads me out of the forest and back to the horses.

Of course, Sybil is long gone but somehow Polly is still around, standing nearby, ears flicking back and forth. She snorts softly when she sees Shane, relaxing visibly when she realizes she's safe. He has the same power over her as he does over me.

We're too close to the bear's territory, so he puts me up in the saddle and then leads us away, Fletcher limping at his side but otherwise alert.

We walk into the setting sun and it might be the most brilliant sunset I've ever seen. Each wash of gold, purple, pink, orange looks like strokes of watercolor paint, constantly changing, thickening, fading. Everything looks more alive.

You're alive, you're alive, you're alive, I tell myself. And then I don't have to tell myself because I feel it.

When dusk settles in, purple-grey, we stop. A small creek runs past and Polly and Fletcher have a long drink. I stay up on Polly's back, watching in silence as Shane takes off the saddle bag and starts to set up camp beside a stand of four ponderosa pines. Beyond it, the mountains rise up higher and higher. I have no idea where I am but I don't think it matters.

Shane works quickly and with ease. Every movement is natural to him. He's part of this earth, breathing in the same heartbeat. There's something almost magical about him, otherworldly. I think about what he did for me, even though it broke me, he did it for me. He wanted nothing more than to protect me because he loved me so much.

And I was so lucky to have his love. No one else did. It was mine to hold, to nurture, to take care of. He trusted me with his heart and I trusted him with mine.

In the end, he never broke that trust. Not really. Just on the surface. But underneath, where the truth lies, that trust never wavered.

His love never wavered.

"Shane," I whisper to him.

He looks up at me. Even in the hazy twilight, I can see him perfectly. The way his sweat makes his olive shirt cling to his muscles, the tawny gold of his skin, the longing in his eyes as they fix on me.

And yet he knows what I want.

What I need.

He's all I need.

He puts down the sleeping bag and walks over to me. Grabs me by the waist and lifts me off the horse until my feet are firmly on the ground. Doesn't say a word. Doesn't need to.

He bends down and kisses me. One hand at the back of my neck, sweetly possessive, telling me I'm his. That I need to be his.

His lips move against mine, soft and tender, building slowly until my mouth matches his. I feel the kiss all the way in my toes, the way he holds me, the way his tongue slides against mine, stoking a fire. My nerves fizzle and snap and with each second we become more in-sync with each other. It feels right. So right.

"Shane," I whisper against his mouth and he takes my lower lip in his teeth, tugs, then runs his tongue inside the rim. Shivers explode along my spine like a row of roman candles.

"Shhhh," he says to me, his hands, large, wonderful hands, hands that love, hands that protect, they glide down over my body like he's sculpting me, relishing the curves, the way I flow. One hand goes under my top, sliding up against my skin and I'm melting all over again. It's like last night but I'm not going to stop it this time, not going to pull away. His touch, his kiss, he's bringing me back from the past and becoming my future.

I let out a small moan as his rough palm goes over my

breast, pulling down the edge of my lacy bra until he brushes against my nipple. More fireworks radiate outward, a small but powerful heat that I know is taking over me, second by second.

He tugs at the edge of my shirt and pulls it up over my head, throwing it on the ground beside us. His eyes meet mine and I only see a fevered, burning want in them, like he's lost to his own desire. He gazes down at my breasts, taking a moment to hold them with his eyes, then swiftly undoes my bra until it drops at my feet. My nipples harden in the air.

"You're so fucking gorgeous," he says, sounding awestruck, as if he's witnessing something transcendent. It makes me feel like a fucking queen on a throne, a ruler with only one subject. He runs his hands up and down over my sides, trying to memorize me, skin remembering skin.

And I remember him. His touch that could always set me free. It hasn't changed. We both have in small ways but the way our bodies respond to each other hasn't.

Then he dips his head, gripping my breasts, eyes on me as he licks and sucks, tongue flat and teasing. I keep his carnal gaze until my eyes pinch shut with pleasure and I cry out, my fingers threading through his silky hair. "Don't stop," I manage to say, my words floating on the air.

But he does stop.

He pulls back and stares at me, raw determination on his brow, his eyes stealing my breath away.

Look at how he looks at me. The way he sees me. No one else ever saw me like this.

"Rachel," he says, voice low, rich, deep, a whisky-voice that intoxicates my blood. "If you don't want me to stop...I won't stop. I promise you I won't stop until I've given all I have to you." I watch his Adam's apple as he swallows, my eyes drinking in the thickness of his neck, his broad shoulders, the veins and muscles on his biceps, forearms, hands that give and give.

He is so beautiful.

And he's mine.

It's time to let go of the past. It's time to move forward. Just for these minutes. If not just for tonight.

I'm Rachel and he's Shane and we go together, fit together, because we always have. We worked then and we work in the here and now.

This needs to happen.

It needs to happen like we both need the air we breathe.

It's been building, twisting, turning to this moment for far too fucking long.

I stare at him and without breaking our gaze, I take off my boots, socks, jeans, underwear, until I'm standing naked in front of him. It doesn't matter that my bare feet are in dirt, that there's a horse behind us, that we're in the middle of fucking nowhere.

Nothing matters but us.

I have been so damn starved for him.

Six fucking years.

"Don't ever stop," I tell him.

I'm ready.

His nostrils flare and then he's at me, capturing my mouth in a brutal, commanding kiss.

I gasp, overtaken by his strength, the elegant violence of his lips as his tongue fucks my mouth.

This is wild, so wild. I'm shaking as he works me, our kiss is messy and hard and full of anger and loss and hate and love and so much history and so much time. So, so much time.

I'm making whimpering sounds against his mouth and then I'm breathless as he grabs me by the waist and spins me around until I'm up against the tree. My back is pressed against the rough bark and his shirt is coming over his head, the rest of his clothes – jeans, briefs, boots – are cast aside.

He stares at my body for just a moment, but in that moment, he sets me on fire and everything is urgent now, so urgent, and I'm burning for him.

He drops to his knees and lifts one of my legs over his shoulder, shoving his face between my thighs for the second time today. Unlike earlier where he was tentative and unsure, now he's a feral creature devouring his prey, rough and raw. His mouth presses into me, moaning, grunting against my skin. Just his breath, his heat, the slide of his tongue against my clit pushes me already so close to the edge, every muscle in my body winding and winding and winding up.

He groans again, the vibrations rolling through me.

"Shane," I whisper, breathless, going fucking crazy as his tongue lashes at me relentlessly until I'm so spread, so swollen, I start writhing with pleasure, my body famished. I hold his head in place, not even minding the way the bark scrapes at my spine. Even the pain feels amazing.

"I'm going..." I start to say but my words trail off and I can't focus on anything anymore, too many sensations are coming at me from all directions. The slick fuck of his tongue, the suck, suck, suck of his lips, his fingers pressing so hard into my thighs I know they'll leave bruises, the raw skin of my spine.

A sweat breaks out at my temples.

My fingers yank at his hair, trying to hold on before I'm gone but...

I'm gone.

So gone.

I cry out, loud, shrill, his name is offered up over and over again and I'm not even myself, not even here. I'm in his mouth and everywhere. I've melted and been put back together.

And I don't even have room to think.

"I've been craving the taste of you for years," he says, voice breaking as he gets to his feet. "Now that I've had you again, I don't think this will ever be enough."

He takes my hands together until it looks like I'm praying and then turns me around, placing them on the tree. "Hold on, raven girl. There's only one ride and it's wild."

I weave a bit on my feet and grip the tree as he spreads my legs with his hands, one hand coming forward underneath me and gripping me, fingers splayed so I can feel how large his hands are. He holds me tight, possessive – mine, this says, all mine – applying pressure until I'm less sensitive, then let's go and positions himself behind me.

"I've waited for you," he murmurs to me, running his wet fingers down my spine and I shiver, my body beyond my control. "God, I've waited for you, wished for you, Rachel. Just like this, just for me. Just us." His voice is rough with emotion. "I've missed you so much."

My heart trips at his words.

But before I can say anything to that, he grips my hips and pushes in, a sharp hiss escaping his lips as he goes.

I cry out, my nails digging into the bark, holding on tight as he slowly eases in, spreading me wider and wider from the inside out. It takes forever to feel the full length of him slide into me and then he's in so deep, in so right, I swear I feel him pulsing, his heat coming through.

I've never felt so full of him before, I'm both starving for him and satisfied, filled and indescribably desperate.

"You like that?" he asks in a quiet rasp as he leans over to kiss my neck, my shoulders. The skin of his chest brushing over my sensitive back. "Did you miss that?"

"Yes," I hiss, closing my eyes, my back arching as he eases out and deliberately pushes in again, inch by inch.

"Tell me you want this."

"I... I want this," I whisper, my words catching as my breath does. I can't seem to convey what I'm feeling, just how he's rendering me, shaking and a little wild. "Fuck, I want this Shane. I want you. Give me all of you."

"Rachel," he murmurs and then slams into me until I'm pressed against the tree.

I cry out, not from pain but from everything. It's everything, I'm feeling everything and he's relentless. He starts to rut into me, his hips slapping against my ass in a slowly building rhythm. Inside I'm glowing, everything getting hotter, tighter, my noises louder and louder.

Shane's inside me.

So deep inside me.

He fits with me like no one else ever could.

My brain wants to focus on the future, on tomorrow, my plans and the what-ifs but I pull it back. I force it to be here with him. I force it to feel the things it doesn't want to feel, the scary things, the things that mean the world.

The fact that I love him so much.

Too much.

Can you love someone, want someone too much? Can you go crazy from it?

I'm afraid if I let go, I just might.

"Stay with me," Shane says, breathless as he thrusts into me. "Be here with me, now."

He starts pumping hard and fast, fucking me so roughly that it's digging splinters into my hands, his sweat is dripping onto my back. Each thrust renders me thoughtless, until I'm just a body and a soul and I'm needing, needing, needing more.

More.

God.

"Shane," I cry out.

I am so impossibly full which makes me realize how

hollow I was before. Empty, carved out, not sure what I was always yearning for when the truth is I always knew his name.

His hand reaches around, sliding over my clit, still slick, and I whimper because it's too much and he's too much and this is too much.

Don't ever stop. Don't ever stop.

Please, you have to stop.

Keep it coming.

I'm almost there.

I don't want it to be over.

Don't let this be over.

Fuck me forever.

My beautiful cowboy.

"Can you come?" he whispers to me.

I try to nod but I'm gasping, feeling the cool sweat run down my breasts, my neck. I'm on a tightrope ready to snap. My pulse skips when he groans, tells me he wants to hear me come.

"Rachel," he rasps, voice straining.

His fingers slide.

I go off like a buckshot and I'm soaring, speeding through time and space and then expanding until I'm confetti, slowly drifting down to earth on shaking legs, barely standing up and holding on.

Shane's hands become steel around me as he starts pumping harder, the sweat flying, grunts and groans rolling out of him as he comes.

He calls out my name and I don't think I've ever heard it sound so revered, his voice almost pained.

Then his hips slow against me.

He loses a bit of control, shaking now, and leans over me, reaching for the tree to take the pressure off of me, his hot, slick chest pressed against my back.

"Fuck," he says. "Fuck. Rachel, that was..."

There are no words.

My mind takes its time coming back into the present, to the now, to the fact that I was just thoroughly fucked from behind by Shane Nelson. Not for the first time, not by a long-shot, but fucking hell.

What could ever top this?

Who can ever top him?

And it hurts and pinches and stings that I know the answer to that one very well.

Shane pulls out and his cum drips down my legs and he's trying to catch his breath.

Suddenly I can't breathe either.

Before it was just want and need and a desire that never wavered.

Now there's just my pulse pounding in my head, my legs throbbing, my hands cramped and raw, and that pure, sharp twist of fear deep inside.

"Rachel," he says to me as I straighten up, trying to find my balance as I push off from the tree. I turn around and he's stepping into me, his hand at my jaw, the other holding my arm. "Please tell me that...that..." He swallows, the sweat glistening above his lip as he gazes at me. "Please tell me that meant to you what it meant to me."

There's a strange fluttering in my chest.

Fear. Hope. Love. Loss.

"What did it mean to you?" I whisper.

"The world," he says before he kisses me, quick and light and laced with tenderness. "It meant the whole entire world."

Everything inside me brightens, warm and delirious. Because that meant the world to me too.

But when someone hands you the world, don't tell me it doesn't scare you.

"Hold on," he whispers to me and walks over to the saddle bags he strung up on the neighboring tree. Even though the light is dim, painting him in lavender and grey, I can't help but stare at his gorgeously bare ass. No wonder he was able to fuck me so hard, that ass is made out of steel.

He comes back with a handful of tissues and slowly glides it up my leg, cleaning me off. He then kisses me on the forehead, discarding the tissues and getting back in his boxer briefs.

"I know it's early but…I'm fucking spent," he says with a wry grin, spreading out the sleeping bag on top of the mat he rolled out earlier. Then he tosses me my underwear and t-shirt, and lifts the edge of the bag. "After you."

I put my underwear and shirt back on, quickly go pee behind the trees, not dawdling this time because, you know, bears, and then get inside the sleeping bag.

When he gets in beside me, his body spooning mine, holding me flush to him, it's only then that I realize Polly and Fletcher had seen us having sex. Thankfully they don't seem all that fazed, though poor Fletcher won't meet my eyes.

"Is he going to be okay?" I nod at the dog who is curled up at the foot of the sleeping bag. "Not because he saw us fucking, I mean, from what the bear did."

Shane pulls back and I look over my shoulder at him as he gives me a funny look. "You were worried about the dog watching us have sex?"

"No. I mean, for a second. The horse too. But I mean, will he be okay?"

Shane nods and kisses the back of my head. "He'll be fine. Bright and early we'll head back to the ranch. My dad and I can go back out later to get the cows. Right now, we just need to get everyone home and Fletcher to the vet. It's all going to fine."

I exhale, feeling more relieved. "What about Sybil?"

"Well I briefly saw her just as we came into this site. She

was trailing behind us. My guess is we'll see her tomorrow. Don't you worry about a thing, you're safe tonight."

I close my eyes, sinking into the feeling of his arms around me, a feeling as strong and old as time.

Safe.

I'd spent years in therapy learning how to function after what my father did.

I'd worked through it all until I could learn to love myself, learn to feel safe.

I don't live in that fear anymore, except for the fear of losing myself to Shane all over again.

But being in his arms makes me realize how safe I really am. With him, without him.

I am safe.

CHAPTER 18

SHANE

I awake just after dawn to birdsong.

My face is buried in Rachel's soft neck, her silky hair around me like wings.

I smile. Breathe in the smell of her. The morning air. Fresh and cool with only a hint of the heat to come.

She stirs, letting out a little moan.

"Good morning," I murmur, kissing the back of her head. "How did you sleep?"

She sighs dreamily. "Best sleep I had in years."

"You didn't dream about bears."

She pauses, as if remembering. "No. No, I dreamed about you."

"A good dream, I hope."

"You're only in good dreams," she says and then shifts so she's gazing at me. "This isn't a dream, is it?"

"No. This is all real." I look up and my eyes scan the horizon, the sun barely lifting above the peaks. Polly is grazing nearby, Fletcher is sleeping. The world looks new, is new. Everything is different now with Rachel in my arms. Better, brighter.

I smile at her. If she's feeling different after last night, I can't tell. But what I can tell is that I'm not rushing out of this sleeping bag. Last night was amazing but that's not the end of us, it can't be. Not when I'm dying to be back inside of her, to watch her come this time while I'm deep within.

I kiss her softly, running my hand down over the swell of her breasts, to her belly, testing the waters. She kisses me back, making sweet little noises at my touch. I'm so darn hard and ready to put this morning wood to good use.

The only problem is a sleeping bag doesn't leave much room, especially with two people.

"Hold on," I tell her, reaching over and unzipping it until it's lying flat on the mat and we're exposed to the new world. In seconds, I'm naked.

"Lie back," I tell her as I crawl over her, my hard, bare cock bobbing between us. I put my hands on her shoulders and nudge her back while I settle over top of her. I run my thumb over her lips, pushing gently until her lips wrap around it. With an achingly beautiful smile, she sucks softly and I feel the jolt right through me, all the way to my toes.

"I don't think you realize what you do to me, what you've always done to me," I murmur to her, one hand moving her underwear down her legs as she shimmies out of it. I remove my thumb and pull her top over her head as she arches back to let me.

I stare down at her tits, so perfect, spilling to the sides. They seem to glow in the light of sunrise, pure and flawless, her dark pink nipples hardening before my eyes. I bite my lip, trying to control my hunger, and gently blow air across her breasts. She arches her back again – so fucking gorgeous – and I watch her skin prickle as I trace the goosebumps across her chest with my flat tongue.

She makes this breathless gasp—we're both so drowsy still with sleep—and I press my body down on top of her so she can feel how hard, long, and ready I am, the weight of me. Her eyes widen but they aren't afraid. Not of this. She knows that she can handle it and handle it well, take me for all that I give her.

I kiss her neck and spread her legs apart with my knee. I breathe her in, the smell of our sex from last night hitting me like a fucking bomb, causing my dick to grow hot, my skin to get tighter.

I pause, even though my body is like a gun with a quick trigger, and take it all in. Rachel Waters. My raven girl. Here on my sleeping bag, surrounded by my land. She's under me, naked and vulnerable and willing. She stares up at me with trust, with want, need, and submission. She's giving herself to me as I give myself to her.

It means a lot more to me than she could possibly know.

I take a shaking breath at how real this all is, and while keeping all my weight on one arm, my free hand snakes between her legs. My eyes close at the feel of her warmth—she's hotter than the summer sun and I could drown in her arms.

I bury my head into the crook of her neck making small, quick bites along her delicate skin until I find the soft, delicate lobe of her ear. She likes this. She always has. I lightly tug on it between my teeth until she moans, her fingers digging into my shoulders.

Trying to steady my breath, I slide my hand up to her clit and a low, guttural groan rises up from my chest. She feels like heaven—just as soft and silky as last night, and absolutely wet.

"You're so perfect," I tell her as I push two fingers inside her.

A gasp catches in her throat.

Tight. She's so fucking tight.

The way she squeezes around my fingers, holding me,

makes my eyes momentarily roll back in my head. My cock swells to the breaking point and I'm not sure how much longer I can hold back. I'm practically panting, working her like this, and she squirms, her head rolling from side to side, that mouth of hers wet and open. Wanting more.

I can watch this for days.

Look at what I do to her.

Her breath catches, and her round tits heave upwards, the skin even more pale against her summer tan. I run my tongue over her nipples, hard pebbles that respond to my every touch, every smooth lick, and she groans again, louder this time. I want to take her to the limit, I want her inhibitions stripped bare.

Out here, in the wild, I want her wild.

I want to watch it all under this rising sun, watch her glow and radiate until she's blinding me. I want her light to banish all the dark years.

I push my fingers in further and the groan deepens. Her hips jerk upward, again and again, nearly desperate. Watching her writhe and moan underneath me, from just my fingers, feels better than any shot of whisky.

I can't take much more. I make a fist around my rigid shaft and position it at her entrance. Her eyes flutter open as I slowly rub my swollen head up and down her silky cleft, taking my time to tease her, to tease myself.

I don't need the teasing.

I suck in my breath, trying to hold back.

It's the hardest thing. Every nerve in my body is ready to slam deep inside and fuck her until we're off the sleeping bag and rolling in the dirt. It takes all my strength to slowly ease my way inside her. She's so hot and wet as I slowly push in that I begin to shake, my muscles contorting, trying to regain control. I pause and take in a deep, wavering breath before I continue.

Her face twists as I sink deeper.

"You feel me?" I whisper hoarsely to her. "You feel all of me?"

She tries to nod but she's moaning, caught up in delirium. She's so fucking tight, like a vise. Both of us are breathing hard, sweat building on my brow, our skin damp. When I'm in deep, I slowly pull out again, watching my cock as it withdraws, glistening with her wetness.

There are no words. No thoughts. Just this. Just us, making love under an early sky.

She grabs the edge of the sleeping bag, curling her fingers around it.

I reach down, gliding over her stomach, and place my finger on her clit and rub in small, lazy circles, making her wetter. I work at her until I feel her widen, her legs spreading more, and then I push in again, deeper. Her hips buck up against me and now she's even tauter. I can plunge deeper and I know I'm hitting all her sweet spots. She gasps and I grab her hip, holding on tight, my fingertips sinking into her soft skin.

She's so wet and lush, I could lose my body, my heart in her forever.

But I don't have forever.

The sun is rising higher.

The birdsong fades away, buried by our labored breaths.

I'm close now. So close.

My pace becomes quicker as my balls rise, tighten, threatening to let loose inside of her. They smack against her skin, the slapping noise filling the air as I pound her in and out, in and out, quick and relentless, bringing me to the edge. Droplets of sweat trickle off my forehead, splashing onto her below me.

I groan loudly, unable to keep quiet. Out here, we can scream all we want. The need in me to come is too sharp, too hard, too much. I slide out slowly and watch my thick shaft, shiny with everything she has, then I plunge back in. My whole body shudders.

"Come for me," I murmur roughly. "Come with me."

Her eyes meet mine and I'm in love, I'm so in love with her, still in love with her.

Oh fuck me.

I work my fingers into a frenzy, her face contorting, her mouth opening like a flower while I slam into her harder and harder.

"Oh my god!" she cries out. "Oh god, Shane!"

She's shaking.

I'm shaking.

I swear the ground is shaking too.

Then I'm coming.

Hard.

I take in a deep breath and let out a low, guttural cry as my strained muscles let loose and the orgasm rips down my spine, shooting out through every vein. I see the fucking stars. The moon. The sun. The world.

Then there's nothing of me left.

I'm empty. Sated.

Spent.

I lean against her, trying to feel my limbs, my grip on her hips slick with sweat. I brush the damp hair off her forehead, grinning at her beautiful face and kiss the small beauty mark on her jaw. She used to hate that mark and Maverick, such a dick, would tease her for it when we were younger. She'd try and cover it with makeup but I always wanted her just like this, clean-faced, flushed and letting me see the real, beautiful Rachel.

"Good morning," I whisper to her.

She grins at me lazily. "You already said that."

"But now it's a *real* good morning."

"You can say that again." She reaches up, running her fingers down my face. "I never thought this would happen."

I close my eyes at her touch. "What do you mean?"

"I mean when I decided to come back here. You, me...it was never a possibility. I planned on hating you until the day I died."

I swallow hard. That's not the best thing to hear after sex, or anytime, really.

She exhales sharply, looks away. "I'm sorry. I didn't mean to sound so harsh."

"I get it," I tell her. "I really do."

"Just because I didn't think it was a possibility, doesn't mean I didn't want it to happen." I frown. She looks at me with big eyes, glacier blue, and I see her truth in them. "I used to wonder about all the what ifs. What if you hadn't broken up with me, what if I stayed in North Ridge, what if you had run away with me. I would wonder if I'd ever truly love someone the way that I loved you. And I tried. I tried to love. Turns out the hardest person to love was myself."

"Ain't that the truth," I say under my breath, knowing that struggle all too well.

"And I thought, what if I came here and the past was erased and I could just use my heart again to its full extent. But I pushed it away because it wasn't real. It wasn't possible. The best I could hope for was closure."

"And did you get it? Closure, I mean?"

"I thought I did. But then, Shane...what are we doing?"

"What do you mean?"

"This," she says, pressing her hand against my chest. "Us. This isn't closure Shane. Is it for you? Is this putting something to rest so we can both walk away, unchained? Or is this slipping the chains back on? This is just opening another door, maybe one that should stay closed."

I shake my head, not liking this fear in her voice, how she

doesn't see what's really burning between us. "Love isn't a chain, Rachel. It's not a shackle. Love is what sets you free, love doesn't confine. What I feel for you...it's wild and it's raw and it's as fucking real as that sun above us."

"And what do you feel for me?" she asks so quietly I lean in to hear her better.

Her question stuns me.

"It's not obvious?" I ask, running my thumb over her lips before placing my hand at her heart, her soft bare skin warming my palm. "Rachel, I love you. I loved you then, I love you now, and I loved you in all the light and darkness in-between. I love you with a wildness I can't tame." I pause, my chest tightening as I feel everything hang in the balance, resting on my words. "Please tell me you feel that from me, that you feel it too. Tell me you'll at least run with it for a while."

She stares up at me, her eyes searching mine, looking for all the answers I've already given her. "Shane..." she says softly. "This isn't my home anymore."

"Yes it is. *I'm* your home. I've always been your home even when you've been somewhere else, even when you were hating me, trying to forget me, my heart has been your home."

God, can't she see that? See that she always has and always will belong with me?

She closes her eyes and gives a quick shake of her head. "I have to go home soon. I have to."

"You don't."

"Shane, please," she says, staring at me, pleading with her eyes. "Put yourself in my shoes. I have a life over there. I have a condo, a job, a —"

"Yes, I've heard it all before," I snap at her. I inhale deep and sharp, trying to keep my cool. "Look, I know that this isn't easy and that you've worked really hard to build that life there. All I'm asking is that you try and build that life *here.*"

Her brows knit together delicately. "You say that like you have an idea what it's like to start over. And how could you? You never left this damn place."

"Rachel..."

"It's true."

"You'd have me every step of the way. You'd have your mother. You'd have Mav and Fox and my dad and grandpa and Del, even Jeanine."

"But it doesn't fix everything."

I stare at her. "What do you need to fix?"

"You think that by coming back here my life will get back on track? Let's say I find a job here that I do like. Let's say a bunch of wonderful things align. Do you think that's going to fix what's wrong with me, fix this hole inside, fix all the damage that's been done? Your love is a start Shane, but it's not enough."

Whoa.

I jerk my head back, shaking inside.

My love is not enough.

Not enough.

I'm not enough.

"Okay," I tell her, pushing off of her and getting to my feet. I quickly slip on my briefs and start getting ready. No sense in just lying on a sleeping bag all morning and throwing barbs at each other when there's important shit to be done.

"Shane," she says, getting dressed. "I didn't mean it like that."

"Yes, you did," I tell her, glancing at her as I pull on my jeans. "You have a sharp fucking tongue sometimes, you know that?"

"I know. I'm sorry. Look, I—"

"It doesn't matter," I tell her quickly, practically ripping the sleeping bag away from under her feet. "We need to get moving. Take Fletcher to the vet, deal with the damn cows some other time." I glance over at Fletcher who has been snoozing in the grass by Polly all morning. He actually seems a lot better but he's going to the vet anyway just to make sure. "Fuck, I wouldn't mind finding that bear right now and giving him a real piece of my mind."

"Shane. Please. I hate it when you're mad at me."

I give her a look. "Then quit saying shit you know I'll get mad at."

"You have to understand how fucking broken I am!" She throws her arms out, features strained and red with frustration.

"I do understand!" I yell at her. "I've understood from the day I first saw you. The day I decided I was going to protect you no matter what. That I was going to be there for you no matter what. And I know that maybe my love isn't enough to fix all the horrible shit that was done to you and I know I tried in my own way and I just made things worse and I get that being here is hard and it's not just about me. Okay, I know. But why can't I be there for you in the here and now? Why can't we work through this together? You don't have to repair yourself on your own."

"Maybe I do," she says, rubbing her lips together. "It's what I've been doing so far. Six years is a long time."

"But it's not as long as the rest of your life." I study her, my chest feeling like I've got a jackhammer inside, all my nerves on fire. I'm high as the fucking sun one minute and the next I'm slipping in a raven's grave. "Rachel. Everything you feel you need to do, you don't need to do it alone anymore. I'm here for you whether you like it or not."

She watches me for a moment and I can't tell if she's just weighing her options or letting anything sink in. Then she just nods at me. "I'm going to go pee." She goes behind the pines just a few feet away and I turn, giving her privacy, feeling like my heart has been trodden on by a million hooves.

When she returns, I've got mostly everything packed up.

Since Sybil didn't make an appearance during the night, she gets on Polly, I stay on foot and lead the way, Fletcher on the other side of me until I've decided he's had enough and put him up on the horse with Rachel. He's a pro at this, a dog that can ride.

We do this for hours, until my feet are screaming with pain inside my boots from walking for so long, but I want to give Rachel her distance. She needs it, even if it's just her up on a horse and me in front of her.

We're a kilometer from the ranch when I spot the ghostly form of Sybil grazing on the dry grass to the right of us.

"And there she is," I say, mainly to myself.

Sybil raises her head, eyeing us and I pretend to ignore her, hoping it will spur on her interest. If I go after her and push her, she'll just back up and run. Usually this tactic doesn't work as well with horses as it does with humans but after a few moments she slowly starts walking behind us, not wanting to be left behind.

It's then that Rachel finally says something. Guess it works on her too.

"Shane."

"Yeah?" I look over my shoulder at her.

She stares at me, her expression open, almost...hopeful. "No matter what happens, I don't want to leave it like this. We owe each other more than that. After all this time. Can we keep being with each other like this?" She licks her lips, nervous. "Do you think we can just try and make every second count?"

I know what she's asking. Let's be together until she

leaves. But if my heart is barely holding on now, what's going to happen to it when she's gone?

How the fuck can I go through that all over again?

But I'm a fool.

And I'm in love.

So I say yes.

We'll make every damn second count.

CHAPTER 19

RACHEL

The next few days crawl past.

The worker's cottage is thick with dust and heat and all the angry words I'd exchanged with my mother before I left on the ride with Shane.

It's laden with guilt and hurt and the two of us are too stubborn to break it down, to deal with it, to face it head on.

I faced a bear and lived to tell about it and yet facing truths with my own mother seems scarier than anything else.

We avoid each other. My mother spends a lot of time in the main house with Hank and Dick. I spend my days with Shane, including going to the vet with Fletcher. The lucky dog only needed a dose of antibiotics for the small wound and some time off his sprained leg. The rest of the time, it's like the old days, me helping Shane around the ranch with whatever he needs.

And then there's the sex.

Oh yes.

I knew that when we had come back to the ranch after being out on the range that things would be different between the two of us. I knew that as good as the sex was, as *needed* as it was, it was something we should probably avoid doing again. It made us intimate and through intimacy we fought.

And made up.

Again and again.

Making every second count.

Even though I know being with him is just going to make things harder in the end, I can't stay away from Shane any more than he can stay away from me. My hands yearn to touch him, my lips burn to kiss him. As swift and help-less as a raft on the river, I am drawn to him repeatedly, ignoring where the current is leading us. It's in his arms where I feel myself becoming more alive, where I transform.

I grew up feeling like a weed in the garden, unwanted, cowering, left to die. Bit by bit, year by year, I worked through it and tried to grow, to blossom, and it came, slowly, but surely. I learned to let myself bloom. But when I'm with Shane, it's more than letting myself take up space and shine. He makes me want to grow wild, to run rampant, to unapolo-getically *thrive*.

I just wish it didn't scare me so damn much.

Because even if this is for a short time, how on earth is my heart going to survive when I leave? He told me he still loved me, something I'd slowly come to realize out here at Ravenswood Ranch. He told me he never stopped and I felt it in the marrow of my bones, a truth that I can't shake, that I can't escape from. He loves me fiercely, with abandon, the kind of love that sets fire to things until we're standing in the ashes.

And in those seconds we have together, I'm trying so fucking hard to keep myself together, to not let his love consume me.

Because, god, how easy that would be.

Then, good news comes in. My mother has a surgery scheduled.

I decide to drive her. I know it's not ideal but like hell I wouldn't be there for her. That's the thing about family, about loved ones, is even when you're at odds with each other, even when there are more negative emotions rolling out of you than good, you won't abandon them. You'll be there for them.

At least that's what I'm learning.

I've been learning a lot these days.

The drive to Vancouver is long and awkward. Painfully so. We barely talk. She's lost in her own thoughts and I'm lost in mine.

To be honest, I'm not just scared because of what's going on between Shane and I, I'm scared for my mother. I know that the surgery is routine, that she should be fine. That this is about nipping something in the bud, taking out the cancer before it has a chance to ravage her. But sometimes she just seems so weak and unhealthy that I'm not sure how strong she really is. She's been thriving too while being at the Nelson's, but even so, she's not quite optimal. I think, for the both of us, the road to recovery is a long one.

We go straight to the hospital where we're introduced to Doctor Fielding and the nurses. He explains to us, as Doctor Cooper did back in North Ridge, exactly what the surgery entails. It's a pre-emptive strike, especially for patients who haven't yet experienced the mass effects of cancer yet. He explains how it will leave my mother in a much weaker position than before we started, but the alternative is, of course, cancer. We don't have a choice.

She'll be in ICU for a few days after surgery, assisted by a breathing tube and, if anxious, heavily medicated, then will be recovering. After a week or so, she'll be discharged and we're free to go. In the meantime, I'll be renting a room in a hotel around the corner and spending most of my days in the hospital.

It doesn't sound so bad but what makes it worse is that my mother is barely looking at me, even when the doctor is laying out all the potential complications, and for a woman of her age and health, there are a lot.

It isn't until the next day, the day of her surgery, when both of us are waiting around in a small, sterile room, that she taps me on the back of the hand and brings something out of her purse.

It's a bunch of tissue and I watch, enraptured, as she carefully starts unfolding each piece until I'm surprised at the sight.

A dried wishbone sits in the middle of the tissues.

"What is this?" I ask her.

"It's for you," she says, picking it up with shaking hands. "When we first came to Ravenswood Ranch a few weeks ago and Hank had made us that chicken, I took the wishbone aside and saved it."

Tears are already starting to well up in my eyes.

"I remember that necklace," she goes on. "The one Shane gave to you for Christmas that one year. You loved it so much, never took it off until you did. I knew it meant something to you." She pauses, looking down at the wishbone with fondness. "I saw this and I knew you should have it. You should have something to wish on again."

I press my lips together, trying to keep my sobs in check. No dice.

"I'm so sorry mom," I cry out, wrapping my arms around her. "I'm so sorry for the things I've said to you. I don't mean any of them. I love you. I don't want to lose you, I don't." I whisper, "I'm so scared."

"Oh, sweetie," she says to me, holding me back. Even though she's fragile, she has some strength to her, strength and warmth I can feel seep into my bones. Even after every-thing, there's something about a mother's hug that sets the world back on its axis, makes it spin, brings back the days and the nights, a balance. "You don't have to be sorry. I know you're angry and you have every single right to be. You can be angry with me for the rest of your life and I know I deserve it and more."

I pull back, wiping at my face. "But I don't want to be angry anymore. I understand. It took me a long time but I understand. I know you loved me, you were just afraid."

"I was afraid and I was a coward," she says, her voice warbling though she's trying to sound strong. "No mother should ever choose her husband before her daughter, should never choose herself. Darling, I was in such denial over what was happening to me, to hear what was happening to you...I couldn't bare it. I couldn't deal. It just – *poof* – my brain spit it right back out. But I knew, I knew deep down you were telling the truth, I just didn't have the courage to face it. I will never, ever forgive myself for it. I've betrayed you in the most horrific way possible and I'll spend my whole life making it right even though I know it won't be."

"It's okay."

"It's not okay," she says and now she's crying, big tears that spill down her pale face and onto the linoleum floor. "It's not okay and it will never be okay. And that's something I have to live with. I can never go back and change the past and what I did, or didn't do, will stick with me. But going forward, I can only love you and pray you'll give me a second chance."

"Of course I will," I sob to her, leaning against her shoul-der. "You don't need to ask. It's just there. I don't want to lose you, not now, not after this when we go back to North Ridge. I want to get to know you, the real you, I want a real relationship and all the time in the world to make up for all the time that we lost."

"And so you'll stay?" she looks at me hopefully.

I grasp her hand. "If that's what you want, if that's what you need, I will stay. For you."

She frowns, looking saddened, and shakes her head. "My baby girl. You'll stay for your mother, your mother who turned her back on you and didn't protect you when you needed her most, you'll stay for her but not the man who has always been there. How come you'll stay for me but you won't stay for Shane?"

I blink at her, my blood whooshing in my head as I try and grapple with it.

She's asked a damn good question.

"Because you're my mother," I say softly, struggling for words.

"And he's your man. A man that loves you. A man who never stopped loving you."

"It's not the same."

"When it comes to the heart, when it comes down to love, it all weighs the same amount. Rachel, Shane is in love with you and I know you're in love with him. Don't throw that away because you think you belong somewhere else."

"But I have a life there," I tell her and even now my excuses, valid or not, are starting to sound stale. "I have everything I've worked hard for."

"And you'll work hard again and you'll get those things you want, if you even want them anymore, if they really matter. But love like yours, that's not something you can just show up for, or even earn. Love like that, you have to hold onto it when you see it. It's a once in a lifetime love, my baby girl. And we both know how short those lifetimes can sometimes be."

I grow quiet. I could argue forever. I could bring up the

millions of excuses. But against my mother, I'm not sure how far I'd get.

"Let me ask you something," she says, taking my hand into hers. "What feeds your soul?"

"What feeds my soul?"

"You heard me. What feeds it? What gets you up in the mornings? What makes you want to be a better version of yourself, to keep on growing? What makes you feel alive? More than that, what makes you want to be alive forever, finding the lust and the joy for it day by day?" She pauses. "Now change that around. Not what, but who? *Who* feeds your soul?"

I try and swallow. I'm thirsty and exhausted and scared, still so scared. I want to give her different answers and yet I won't lie. I won't bother. There's only one answer.

Who feeds my soul?

Shane.

Shane feeds my soul.

She squeezes my hand. "You know. I can see that you know. You don't have to make a decision about it now, but eventually you will. And when you do, just remember what I asked. Just remember what you feel. Your soul is part of your heart and your heart is a part of the world. Who feeds your soul, feeds all of you and in turn you feed them back. And this funny little world rolls on and on and on."

I manage to give her a smile. "You know, I wasn't expecting all the self-examination."

"You thought I would be the one to re-examine my life choices?" She rolls her eyes. "Please, I'm getting surgery, I'm not on my damn death bed."

Then her features harden and she stares at me, serious. "But there is one thing I'd like to talk to you about before they wheel me away and start with the pain meds."

"What?"

She takes in a deep breath. "I know one of the reasons that you're struggling, why you've always struggled, is because you don't have closure. And I'm not talking about your boy Shane. I'm talking…I'm talking about your father. He went to jail but he didn't go to jail for what he should have. Granted, I'm sure he didn't go for a lot of things he should have but the fact is…he tried to destroy us. And for a while he did. And I know that time has passed but I don't want him to get away with it anymore."

My heart starts to beat faster against my ribs. "I don't want to see him."

"You don't have to see him. He'll rot in prison for what he did to that boy but he should also be in there for what he did to you. And me. Now, I can't and won't make you do anything that you don't want to do but, and it depends on how long you plan on staying, I want to press charges. When we get home, I'm going to file a police report against him. I won't mention your name unless you want me to, I won't do that without your permission baby girl, but I'm going to give a statement about what he did to me and I'm going to make sure it gets to him."

Funny. Even just hearing her say that, as horrifying to even think about the past, the situations, what he did, the fact that she can still do something, that justice can still be served after all these years, that he won't get away with it…the heaviest weight has been lifted off my shoulders. I'm immediately lighter. Scared, but lighter all the same.

"I'll do it," I tell her, frightened and determined and bolstered all at once. "I'll come forward and I'll file. He's gotten away with it for this long and I'm no longer ashamed of it. I want him to know he's caught, that he didn't destroy us like the way he tried. I want to do this. I'll do it with you. Together."

"Are you sure?" she asks, studying me.

"I'm sure." I nod, again and again, each time with more conviction. "I'm more than sure. This needs to happen, for both of us. *This* is closure."

"You're damn right," she whispers, kissing the back of my hand just as the door opens, Doctor Fielding peering at us.

"Are you ready, Vernalee?" he asks

She looks at me and smiles knowingly. "More than ever."

She hands me the wishbone and I hold onto it as hard as I can without crushing it.

He wheels her away to surgery.

And I wait.

CHAPTER 20

SHANE

"Can't sleep?" I ask as I approach the porch.

It's past midnight and there's a big ol' full moon casting a silver sheen over the ranch. My father is sitting on the porch swing, a glass of whisky in his hands, staring out at the stars. For the first time in a long time, there's a hint of coolness in the air, a promise that fall is around the corner. That, or more storms.

It always gets worse before it gets better.

He looks to me, shadowed in the magic light. "Nope. How about you?"

I shake my head, lean against the post. "I've texted Rachel but you know how our service is here. I'm not sure if they're getting through. I know that if anything bad happened, she'd call."

Because that's what we're both thinking, my dad more so than me. He's worried sick about Vernalee, I can tell. He hasn't said as much, but lately as I've become more aware of my love for Rachel, I've started seeing his feelings for her mother.

As for me, I'm worried about Vernalee but I'm missing

"

Rachel fiercely. It burns inside my chest, not a longing anymore, but this desperate need to see her, to have her in my arms again. When she gets back I have to do what I can to convince her not to go and I'm not sure it will be enough.

"Why don't you tell her how you feel?" I ask boldly.

My words hang in the air for a moment and I'm not sure if my father will just brush it away like he usually does.

Then he says. "Maybe I will." His voice is softer than I've ever heard it. He clears his throat and sighs, looking back at the moon. They seem to have a staring contest with each other. "I should have told her before she left. I had the chance. I didn't have the courage. I'm not brave like you."

That catches me completely off-guard. "Brave?" I've never heard my father call me that before.

"Yeah, son. You're brave. You know it too. We all know it. You can look any problem dead in the eye and do what needs to be done. And do so without ego. Without armor. I've seen you with Rachel, the way you're nothing but open with her and that takes guts, son. Love takes guts. And you've got that in spades."

I sigh and sit down on the porch steps, resting my head in my hands. "What good is love and guts if your love runs away in the end."

"I don't need to answer that," he says. "You know it's worth it. Worth it to have loved and lost than—"

"To have never loved before," I fill in.

"No, you dolt," he says gruffly. "Than to have loved and kept that shit to yourself until you died from it."

I smile in the darkness. "I'm not sure that's the saying, dad."

"It's *a* saying." He takes a sip of his drink. "Anyway. You know what I mean. No one said loving someone is easy and Rachel has a boatload of issues that are only going to make things more difficult for you. That's why when she pushes you away, you can't walk away. You can't give up. You have to keep at her. In reality, what you should have done is followed her to Toronto the moment she left and told her the truth. But you didn't. I don't know, maybe that was for the best. Maybe she needed to be on her own, far away from everyone else, a place she could reinvent herself and discover that she was more than what her father did to her."

"When did you find out?"

"Vernalee told me. She told me everything one night. Cried her eyes out until she fell asleep on my shoulder. I'm not saying that Rachel doesn't have the right to be angry and hurt by her momma, but Vernalee was a victim too. Both of them are, still. And it takes a special person to work with that. Luckily, I know you're that kind of person."

"So are you," I point out. "Apparently."

He smiles over his glass. "I'm trying. I got to say, and I know it's hard to hear but maybe you understand better than Fox and Mav because you never got to know her as well but... Vernalee is the first woman since your mother that I've felt any part of me come alive. Shit. It's been twenty-six years and now, only now, am I finally ready, finally moving on."

"It's worth it, though."

"I think it is. It's never too late to learn to use your heart, son. That's what I keep telling myself."

"What on earth are you two knuckleheads yammering about, eh?"

We both look behind us to see my grandfather standing in the doorway, his white hair all wild from sleep, pulling his robe closed just in time. Thank god.

"Just watching the stars, grandpa."

"Well can you both watch the stars with your mouths shut? Walls are thin, you know."

And with that he turns around and walks back into the house.

Dad and I exchange a grin. I laugh.
We both start looking for shooting stars.

THE NEXT MORNING RACHEL FINALLY CALLS.

The surgery was successful and Vernalee is doing fine.

I decide to be brave. I tell her I miss her.

She tells me the same thing right back and it sounds as real as that sun in the sky but I can't be sure, not yet. Words mean some, actions mean more.

A week later, after Vernalee's stint in the hospital, the two of them arrive home.

Home.

Because how can my heart not be her home?

"They're here," Delilah says, staring out the front windows.

Everyone is over, including Fox who is back in town for a few days before he's sent out

again.

Hank heads out and I follow as Rachel brings the Ford Tempo to a stop in front of the house.

She gets out and grins at me so big, it steals my heart and breath, then she quickly goes to the other door to help her mother out.

We join in. Hank reaches in and helps her to her feet and she leans on both Rachel and my father for support.

She looks weak, frail, but she's smiling.

"I know I didn't have cancer long enough to know, but damn this sucks," she says. "Barely survived that car ride with all that terrible music Rachel listens to."

Rachel manages a smile. "The driver gets to choose. Next

time, when you're driving, you can listen to Céline Dion and Michael Bublé all you want."

Vernalee wrinkles her nose in disgust and I laugh. She's an old country lover, through and through.

We help her into the house, set her down in grandpa's chair and everyone starts running all over the place, fetching her stuff. Del brings her lemonade, Maverick offers up magazines like Redbook and Good Housekeeping, and I can only imagine how embarrassed he would have been buying them at the grocery store, especially when he's always hitting on the checkout girls. Fox brings her a blanket, making sure she's comfortable. It's a sweltering, stuffy day, the kind that hinges on a thunderstorm, but even so, Vernalee seems cold.

When everyone is settled and Vernalee starts singing the praises of the nurses at the hospital to Grandpa, I take Rachel by the arm and pull her out onto the porch.

I'm pretty sure everyone here knows we're back together but even so, I like to keep it quiet and just between us. We just aren't a sure thing.

Yet.

Maybe never.

Maybe...

"Hey," I say to her, wanting so badly to hold her in my arms, to feel every soft inch of her. I've been craving her so badly, an addict in front of his fix. "How are you holding up?"

"Good," she says and smiles. She looks good, more at peace now than when she left.

"How was she? Any complications?"

"Well, she might be saying wonderful things about those nurses and doctors now but I tell you a few days ago she was pretty close to issuing them death threats."

I laugh and then wipe the smile from my face. "That bad, eh?"

"You better believe it. A bit of cabin fever. She was drugged for the first few days too. Every time she saw the breathing tube she started freaking out. Thankfully it wasn't in there for long."

"And how are you both? I mean, are you okay now, did you talk?"

She nods. "Yeah," she says quietly. "We had a good talk." She pauses, licks her lips. "Before I leave..." And my heart fucking sinks at those words. "My mother and I are going to file a police report."

I frown. "What happened?"

"Against my father. You know, that closure I needed? It wasn't just from you. It was because he got away with it. And now, finally, we're not going to let him."

"Rachel," I say with a sigh, relief coursing through me. "That's amazing. Seriously. This is going to be so good for you."

"We won't mention what happened with you, what you did."

"Even if you did, I'll handle it. The point is, you need this. More than anything."

"I do. I really do. And then, then I can move on. My mother can move on."

I grab her hand and hold it tight. "Want to hear something funny? Maybe it's no longer a family secret but...it turns out my father is in love with your mother."

She lets out a sweet laugh, her eyes dancing. "I know. And I know she feels the same way. They just need to fess up to it. They don't have all the time in the world."

"No one does."

"Yeah." She looks away, smiling shyly.

"Let's hope they don't get married though. Or we'd be brother and sister."

"Shut up," she says, pulling away playfully. "Hey, is your house empty?"

"That's a strange transition," I say, letting her lead me off the steps and into the grassy path toward my house. "But yes it is."

We head inside and I open the windows, trying to move the hot stuffy air. It's another scorcher, stifling and thick.

She stands in the doorway to my bedroom and wags her finger at me.

"Come here," she says, backing up until she's at my bed.

I raise my brows. I don't know what I was expecting but I don't think it was this.

"Your wish is my command," I tell her, discarding my hat on the dresser and following her in.

She grabs me by the back of my neck and pulls me down to her mouth.

My legs feel weak. I kick off my shoes, my mouth still pressed to hers, kissing her hungrily.

"I've missed you so much," I whisper to her. "This last week has been unbearable without you." My hands slide down her sides, feeling the fabric of her sundress, wanting it off so I can see and touch and lick her warm, bare skin.

I want more. I want her every day, all the time, until she leaves.

God, please don't leave.

"I've missed you too," she says and her throaty tone makes my cock stiffen, hot and thick and pushing against my jeans. She stands on her toes and kisses my jaw, then my cheek, then my mouth. Her lips open against mine, and I slide my tongue in, tasting her.

"Oh, my raven girl," I murmur, running my thumb over her breast as she arches back, her body begging for more. "I might lose my mind if I can't get inside you right now."

She smiles coyly. "I had a very long drive to plan exactly what I was going to do with you."

I cock my brow at that. "I'd hate to borrow a line from Uncle Jesse, but...*have mercy*."

I know that she's putting up a front, that she's taking on the sex kitten role because she doesn't want things to get real, because there are so many variables and she holds so many answers I may not want to hear. But god, I want her. I want her so bad, I'll let her do anything, be anyone.

"Mercy for the merciless," she whispers against me.

I shiver, though so much heat is pumping through me. "Fucking hell. Get on the bed. Take off your damn clothes before I take them off for you."

"Oh no," she says, putting her hand on my chest and pushing me back. "You get on the bed. Take your cock out."

I grin at her. "What?"

"You heard me," she says, pushing me flat on my back. "Take that gorgeous cock out or I'll take it out for you."

"Is this a trick question?" I ask but I sit down and start undoing my belt buckle.

She stands in front of me and watches as I remove the belt with one quick snap. Then unzip my jeans, slowly taking my cock out of my briefs. She runs her nails over the hard planes of my stomach, my abs tensing from the abrasion, before she drops to her knees.

My cock juts straight up and I lean back on my elbow, not wanting to miss this view while my other hand sinks into her dark hair, wrapping the silky strands around my fingers.

She takes my length in her hand, and my blood pulses against her palm. The feeling is nearly too much to bear. Her mouth opens, those sweet lips sliding over the tip, pushing me into a flurry of lust that sends my eyes back into my skull. Fuck she's good, better than I remembered, imagined, dreamed, sliding her tongue over the veins, over every hardened ridge, like she can't get enough of me.

"Fuck," I mutter, eyes pinched shut, pulling on her hair. "Don't fucking stop, Rachel, don't stop."

She pulls her mouth off, a wet sucking sound, and I think for a terrible moment that she *is* stopping, and every part of me tenses in frustration. Then her hand comes down over my cock, sliding like silk, pulling back to the base until I think my head might explode. I jerk my hips up, craving release.

But she has more planned. She tugs down at my jeans and I lift up my hips so she can pull down my briefs. She lowers her head and slowly, gently takes my balls into her mouth, while stroking me off with her hand.

Good lord.

Even though we lost our virginity to each other, even though we experimented a lot when we were young, our sex drives have changed dramatically. Rachel used to approach sex with understandable apprehension, always shy and self-conscious. We made it about trust, we made it about love and it should always be about those things but damn. Now, she's approaching sex with pure lust and desire. She knows what makes her come, knows what she wants and, more than that, knows what I want.

She's a fucking *genius* at giving head.

I don't want to come in her mouth though, not right now. I lift my head, trying to speak. My throat is so dry, my thoughts scrambled. Everything is being redirected to primal instinct, the drive to come and come as hard as I can, and it doesn't help that I have this shadowy view of her head between my legs, tongue and lips sucking my thin skin until I don't know where I am.

"I want to be inside you," I manage to say, my tongue feeling heavy.

She shakes her head, the vibrations driving me mad. I grip her hair tighter. I want her to stop and I don't at the same time, but she's the one in control.

"Please, I need it," I say, before I moan as another wave of pleasure robs me of speech.

She just pumps her fist harder, and I know I'm a goner if I don't do something.

"Rachel," I tell her gruffly, tugging on her hair until my cock falls away from her open mouth and she stares at me with hooded eyes. "Get fucking naked right now or else."

Quickly, before I lose it, my body hair-trigger sensitive, I pull her down toward me, ripping off her dress while she undoes her bra, slips out of her panties.

She grabs my shoulders and climbs on me, straddling my waist. With one firm grip at my cock and the other at her hip, I slowly lower her on top of me, pushing my cock up and inside.

"Fuck," I mutter, forcing myself to open my eyes and watch her expression when all I want to do is close my eyes and drown in this feeling.

So.

Fucking.

Good.

I tell her this.

I tell her how wet she is, how tight.

I tell her how much I've needed her, how hard I need to fuck her.

I won't be able to get her out of my system but I don't fucking care.

She starts riding me, her tits bouncing and god, I want to take them in my mouth.

And just like before, my own release is sneaking up on me.

Before I can get as carried away like I did when we were teenagers, I pull back and kiss and suck my way down her body. From her shoulder, across to the soft hollow of her throat, down between her breasts, my hand cupping them perfectly, one at a time. I love teasing around her nipples, love how she always arches her back, pushing her breasts up, so ravenous for my lips, for my touch. I like to prolong it as long as possible, doing long, circular laps with my tongue and then blowing lightly. I watch her skin erupt in shivers, her nipple becoming harder, darker, and it's torture not to put it between my teeth and give it a sharp tug.

"Oh god," she cries out, her hands running through my hair and pulling on the ends as she slides up and down my shaft.

"Tell me what you want."

She grabs my head and places my lips on her nipple. "There. Make it hurt."

I smile at her command and do as she says, nipping the hardened end and giving it a long, hard suck into my mouth. She yelps, then settles into a low, throaty groan, her vibrations rattling me to my very bones. The rigid ache of my cock is almost unbearable now, it's all I can think about.

With borderline desperation, I quickly lift her off my cock and throw her back on the bed, then prowl over her like a beast, parting her legs. My fingers slide against her cleft, so hot and slick. I grab the base of my dick and straighten up, gripping her hips, pulling her toward me. Sitting back on my knees, I thrust into her, her legs spread wide.

She cries out, her eyes widening, but I can't help it. She started it and there's no time to do this gently. There is a fire raging inside me and she's the only one who can put it out.

I take a firm grip of her thighs, my hands sinking into her soft, smooth flesh, and hold her legs back while I pull out then push myself in again. She's watching my cock slide in and out of her, and I'm watching too, crazed by the raw, primal sight of our bodies giving each other pleasure and how we fit so perfectly. We've always fit, since the very start.

Fuck, I hope we always will.

It's that desperation, that longing, that need, not just for her body but her big red heart that's driving all of this.

"Please don't stop," she says. Her voice is raspy, quiet, and so disarmingly beautiful when I'm turning her on. I remember the first time we had sex, the way she looked as she came, and I knew I wanted this until my dying day, just this endless give and take, this exquisite pleasure I get from seeing her features soften, her body respond to me on a pure, primal, instinctual level. It's a vessel continuously being filled, though never empty, not so long as I'm with her.

"Hold on," I whisper to her, briefly pulling out and putting my hand beneath her left cheek, rolling her until she's on her side. I grab her leg and with my grip on her thigh, I slowly push myself in and out of her, sliding in even deeper than before.

Fuck.

Fuck.

Fuck.

I'm hitting a sweet spot, and her mouth is falling open while her eyes pinch closed. She's soft and as my thrusts become harder, I'm reveling in the look of her beneath me, her dark hair spilling around her. She's mine, for now, she's mine.

I slip my hand down to her clit, so swollen, pink, and wet, and begging for my touch. Her body tenses and she lets out a shaking breath as I rub my finger around in taunting, teasing circles, light as air.

She begins to jerk into me, wanting more pressure, wanting so badly to come.

I can tell she's close to coming. Her body is shaking with strain, her breaths short and quick, her muscles taut. Her hands grasp the sheets so hard I think they might freeze like that.

I work my fingers into a frenzy and her muffled moans get

louder and louder while I slam into her harder and harder. Her back is arched, nipples pink peaks, and I know she's close.

"Fuck!" she cries out. "Oh, Shane."

Because I'm starting to pound into her so hard, shaking the bed, shaking her breasts, I can't tell if she's coming or not, but then I feel her clench around me, pulsing, and I know she's there, lost in the spiral.

I take in a deep breath and let out a low, guttural cry as my coiled muscles let loose and the orgasm rips down my spine, shooting out through every nerve ending. I'm fucking her so hard I think I'm going to push the bed right through the wall, right into the field and then I'm white-hot, wild, undone.

It sneaks up on me, like someone tackling from behind. I'm thrown into space, going off like a detonation, light bursting behind my eyes, and the groans out of my throat are loud, hoarse, and deafening.

It takes a few moments for me to catch my breath, for my heart rate to stop galloping, and slowly I collapse on the bed. My thoughts won't gather; I can only lie here while Rachel lies down next to me, fingers running over my sweat-soaked skin

"Hey you," she says, staring up at me through her thick lashes.

I clear my throat a few times, my throat feeling like sandpaper. "Howdy."

"I like to think that went as planned," she says. "But you sure as fuck know how to surprise me, Shane."

I lick my parched lips and tilt my head to stare at her. Her eyes are so wet and blue, and I know I have a bad habit of staring into them for too long, but I can't help it. I never could.

I reach over and take a strand of her damp hair between my fingers and gently brush it off her face.

I'm so fucking wild about you.

Please stay, please stay, please stay.

I don't even have to say it out loud. She knows.

She opens her mouth to say something, eyes grappling with things I probably don't understand. Then she says, "I think I'll sleep well tonight. Can I stay here?"

"You can stay here," I tell her, kissing her gently on the nose. "You can stay here forever."

Please stay here forever.

CHAPTER 21

RACHEL

I wake up with a start.

My heart is thudding in my chest, making me wonder if I was in the middle of a bad dream.

The room is hot, dark. Shane is beside me, sleeping on his stomach, one arm draped across my chest. I'm surprised he can't feel how fast my heart is going, that it's not waking him up.

I take in a deep breath and will myself to calm down.

After my mother and I came home, I stole away to Shane's place, seduced him like I was some sort of goddess. I can't explain it. I just wanted him so badly, wanted to give myself to him in the event that it was our last time.

Was that our last time? I think, staring at him, how beautiful he looks when he's sleeping, the soft curve of his full lips, the plane of his nose, his strong jaw. He has such a classic face, the ones you see in the old paintings, then later on Hollywood actors who could say a thousand words with just a glance, the last of a dying breed.

Shane feels like one of the last true men. Someone honest and true, shooting straight like an arrow every time. He's alpha when he needs to be and vulnerable when doesn't. There's no pretention when it comes to him, no front or façade. He's like a motherfucking cowboy legend, drinking whisky, fighting off bears and telling the woman he loves that he'll move mountains for her. He'll move them all for me.

If I stay here with Shane, I'll be beyond lucky.

I know this.

And maybe that's why I keep thinking about leaving.

Because I have to.

This whole entire time I've been holding back, guarding my heart like a stray dog guards his food. I know I could let go but I also know I have to leave.

I haven't lost my job yet. I worked so hard for it and, yeah, maybe the longer I'm here the more I realize that it doesn't feed my soul. Neither does the condo, or the nightly dinners with friends who only talk about fashion and celebrity gossip and getting the most likes on their Instagram posts, nothing from their hearts. Neither did Samuel or any of the boys I dated. None of it fed me. It kept me alive but it didn't give me a lust for life.

A lust for love.

Shane does that.

He was part of my past.

Now he can be part of my future.

If I take that leap and leave everything I worked for behind.

Shane and I were young and in love.

I thought we were unstoppable, as those who are young and in love do, believing it's enough to weather any storm.

Now we're older and...

I sigh, feeling like I can't get enough air. I slowly pick up his arm and lift it off my chest, then get to my feet.

Flash.

The room turns a shade of white.

Lightning.

I go to the window and look out.

The wind is picking up, blowing in the curtains, the air dancing with the smell of electricity and change.

Thunder follows with a long, loud bellow, like God is shouting across the land.

There's a reckoning afoot.

I slip on my underwear and one of Shane's t-shirts and I run out of the house, like I'm being drawn outside, a magnet to the storm.

It's fucking unreal.

I throw my arms out and laugh as the sky dances with more lighting, flash after flash, fork lightning over the town, over the river. Thunder rumbles and shakes and I feel like I might just fly away from here, spread my wings and become the storm itself. Swirling, tumbling, twisting – all that power.

I run a bit further, the tinder dry grass hot under my bare feet until I can see everything perfectly. The dark clouds roll in, obscuring the mountain range on the other side of the river, though they bring no rain.

The wind blows my hair behind me and I can't stop smiling.

I pretended to be a goddess earlier but I feel like a goddess now.

This is real.

And my heart is shocked alive when I realize Shane's love for me is as real as it comes.

As real as this storm and the lightning and this land.

As real as it's ever been.

Changing, churning, becoming and yet always staying true.

It's never too late, the words flit across my head, *never too late to start again.*

I'm ready, I'm ready, I'm ready.

To fight my demons, to fight for love.

I'm going to stay.

Lightning fills the sky, my skin and hair buzzing as it strikes the ponderosa pine by the road.

I jump, let out a yelp.

"Holy shit!"

The tree goes up in flames immediately and I stand here, staring, trying to realize that this is also real, my nostrils filling with the smell of charred wood and smoke.

The lightning strikes again and my world goes white.

I'm vibrating, every cell in my body jumping like I'm being hit with resuscitation paddles.

With hair standing straight up and out, I whip around in trance to see where the lightning hit.

Behind me.

The worker's cottage.

Where my mom is sleeping in her bed, drugged on pain medication after her surgery.

Oh fuck no.

I scream and start running up hill to the cottage as it starts to burn.

"No!" I yell. "Mom! Mom! Wake up! Fire! Oh my god, oh my god, fire!"

I keep running toward the building, my heart trying to leap out of my throat, my arms waving in the air even though there's no one to see me. The lightning struck at the back of the cottage, where the kitchen is, and the orange flames already start licking the roof, spreading down the sides.

"Help!" I scream and my words barely travel over the lightning and the thunder and the flames and I don't know what I'm doing but I'm not about to stand and watch.

I run right inside the house, heading for her bedroom.

I stop and scream.

The kitchen is completely on fire and even standing in the

middle of the house for a second I can see the flames travel along the ceiling, eating way at the dried-out wood and spreading like greedy red fingers, consuming everything in sight.

"Mom!" I cry out, the smoke already filling the rooms. Jesus, help me, this house is going to be completely gone in a few minutes.

I run to her bedroom, just as flames reach out to grab me.

I scream, my skin so hot I might ignite and start looking for something to cover me.

"Rachel," my mom croaks through the smoke. Alive!

"I'm getting you out of there, can you get up?" I yell back.

My mother starts coughing loudly and I can't even see her in her bedroom, the smoke is so thick.

"Rachel!"

I turn around to see Shane standing at the door in his briefs, staring at me wide-eyed. "Get back!" he yells, running in and grabbing my arm, pulling me away just as flames leap across the doorway.

"Shane, please," I plead, tears streaming down my face while smoke fills my lungs. I try and tell him I need to see my mother but the words are buried by a coughing fit.

"Vernalee!" he yells into the bedroom. "Stay where you are, I'm coming."

He starts to pull me out of the house and I'm fighting him, needing to help.

"Rachel please," he says, pushing me out onto the grass. In the distance, the fire from the ponderosa pine is spreading along the grass toward the barn. Sirens ring through the air, coming from town. But none of it matters, none of it sinks in.

I have to get to my mother. I have to, I have to.

We've come so far, it can't end now.

"Listen to me, Rachel." Shane is in my face, shaking me back to him. "Go into the house, wake up dad and grandpa, get the hose, buckets of water, get as many thick and big blankets as you can get."

I shake my head, swallowed by panic. "I'm not leaving you. I'm not leaving my mom."

"I'm getting your mother out, okay? But it's not going to be easy. It's going to hurt. Do you understand?"

"Shane, please," I cry out.

"I'm getting her out. I promise you that. Now go, now!"

He yells at me and then turns, running back into the inferno.

I can't even move. I'm just staring at him as he goes, disappearing into the burning building without even any clothing to protect him.

"Rachel!" Hank's voice rings out from behind me, barely audible above the flames. "Jesus, the barn! Dad, call 911, get the hose."

I can't even turn around. I can't breathe. My lungs feel closed up with soot and the heat from the cottage is growing deeper and deeper until it feels like my hair is burning.

I stumble backward, right into Hank's arms.

"Rachel, is Vernalee in there?"

"Yes. And Shane's in there," I gasp. "He went to get her."

"Oh dear god. Oh god," he cries out. He looks at me. "We need a first aid kit, blankets. Under the sink."

I blink at him, my eyes are burning.

"Rachel!" he yells in my face. "Do it!"

I snap out of it. A jolt to my heart.

Everything I love is at stake.

Everyone I love.

I start running toward the house just as Dick is running out of it, moving fast for his age.

"I called 911, they were already on their way," he says, heading for the hose by the barn.

There's too much to do at once. I know that no horses are

inside the stable right now but even so, Dick has to protect it and get that other fire under control. Meanwhile Hank and Shane are trying to get my mother out.

I grab the heavy-duty first aid kit from under the kitchen sink, then pick up a stack of thick quilts that Jeanine made ages ago, stacked along the backs of the couches, and start running back.

The sight nearly ruins me.

The whole cottage is up in flames and rafters and pieces of the room are starting to fall down, sending sparks up into the dark sky. Against it is Hank's silhouette and only Hank's.

He stares at the building and I know what he's thinking, what he fears.

In the distance, the sirens get closer.

I manage to walk forward until the heat blasts me like opening an oven. I drop the blankets at my feet and go to Hank, grabbing onto his sleeve, holding on for dear life.

"What do we do?" I croak. "What do we do?"

"We pray, sweetie," he says to me, his voice choked. He puts his hand over mine and presses down. "We pray that they'll make it out."

How can this be happening?

How can everything I love possibly be gone in a second?

I hold onto Hank and watch and wait as the flames jump into the sky, as the seconds tick down, as it looks like they might never come out.

They might never come out.

CHAPTER 22

SHANE

Hell.

I'm in Hell.

There's no other way to describe it.

This is a place that most men would run away from, a place where all living things flee. Even now I can see a spider on the ceiling, moving rapidly, trying to escape the flames that threaten it.

But I don't have that luxury.

Vernalee is inside here and I have to get her out.

When I woke up, it was to Rachel yelling, screaming and I was so sure that it was a horrible nightmare that I almost went back to sleep. Then I remembered that she had fallen asleep in my bed and when I opened my eyes and looked for her, she was gone.

In fact, the whole room was bathed in a horrible, flickering light, my ears finally tuning into the sound of thunder and crackling flames and that's when I knew something terrible had happened.

I got out of bed and saw the burning house, saw Rachel's figure inside, her silhouette so stark against those red, hot flames. For a sickening moment, I thought maybe it was too late, maybe she was burning alive right in front of me.

She wasn't.

I ran in and got her out and went back in to get her mother.

Only now, as I stand here and the world is collapsing around me, my body boiling to a million degrees, my eyes feeling like they're being sucked out of my skull, I know that I might not make it back out there.

Vernalee might not either, but that won't stop me from trying.

"Vernalee!" I yell but my voice is caught and I cough, the smoke filling my lungs. I squint, hovering down close to the ground, trying to find the cooler air. "Vernalee!"

There's no answer. Or if there is, I can't hear it over the roar of the flames. The sound of the wood being consumed is a deafening, alien-like crackle that floods the ears.

Both sides of her door are covered in flames and they are spreading inside the room like a violent disease, intent on getting her. I know I have to go in there if I want to get her out and already I feel the hair on my bare arms and legs getting singed, my eyelashes too.

The couch is starting to smoke but there's a doily resting on the arm, so I grab that and hold it over my nose and mouth, trying to filter out the smoke.

Here it goes.

I take in a deep breath and close my eyes, running through the flames into her room. They lick at me, burning my skin but then I'm through, her room already filled with thick smoke, like something forgotten in an oven for too long.

I cough violently, making my way over to the bed where she's lying in her nightgown.

Motionless.

"Vernalee," I try and croak before my lungs seize. I erupt into a coughing fit that nearly takes me out and I stagger forward, my fingers going for her neck. She's breathing, she still has a pulse, but she won't for long.

I pick her up in my arms, carrying her around the bed. The door is completely engulfed now and there's no way we can get out alive that way.

I move to her window, already open from earlier in an attempt to beat the heat, and see my father and Rachel on the other side.

He pushes Rachel back and comes running forward, even as flames start spreading from the roof, coming down by the window, lashing out at him, attempting to block the only way out.

But we have no choice.

I can't speak but I hold onto Vernalee and push the window pane the rest of the way up, then as carefully and quickly as possibly I lift up Vernalee higher and pass her through.

She collapses into Hank's arms and if I could breathe a sigh of relief I would. She's out of the fire. But from the way my father is staring down at her, feeling for her pulse, I'm not sure if she's going to okay after all.

"Vernalee," he cries out, taking her away from the house as Rachel runs over sobbing. She looks up at me and says, "Shane, get out of there!"

I nod, almost frozen, my lungs don't even seem to work anymore, there' s no air, just thick black smoke that fills me up and up until there's nowhere for it to go.

I waver on my feet for a second, holding Rachel's eyes.

My father is performing CPR on Vernalee.

My world is just fire and flames and that horrible roar of consumption.

Then I manage to snap out of it, slowly, like a sick man getting out of bed, and I try to climb through the window.

Flames reach down from above, a blast of hellish heat that sends me backward onto the floor.

Then there's a CRASH as the rafters behind me fall down, smashing onto the bed, sending up more sparks and smoke my way.

Then there's another CRASH.

A slice of burning pain on my shoulder as part of the ceiling falls on me.

I try to scream but everything is singed and raw inside me. The impact knocks me to the floor, the cool floor, and I rest my cheek against it, closing my eyes, relishing this feeling. I know it will be the last good feeling I'll ever have, this beautifully cool floor.

No.

No, my last good feeling is of Rachel.

Rachel who is so close but far away.

Safe.

I love you, I think to myself.

My heart slows, my lungs start to slog.

I don't have much more in me.

Then I hear a yell, far off, a new voice. Low, commanding, in control.

Fox.

It's Fox.

I hear the smash of wood and glass and then arms around me hauling me up, pulling me out of the fire.

But I'm still so hot, so hot, every part of me is cooked.

"Shane." A slap at my face. "Shane, can you hear me?"

Somehow, I manage to open my eyes and at first all I see is white and maybe this is heaven and then Fox's face comes into view and I know he wouldn't be there, so I'm wrong.

He removes his mask, peers down at me. "Hey little

brother," he says to me. "Stay with me, okay? You're safe, you're going to be okay."

His voice is completely steadfast and strong, confident. It gives me confidence.

I open my mouth to speak but I can't.

"Don't try," Fox says as a pair of hands give him an oxygen tank and he puts the mask over my mouth. "Focus on me," he says. "Watch what I do. Breathe in," he breathes in, "breathe out. Do it Shane. In and out."

I try and end up coughing, my lungs as tight as a fist.

"Take your time, okay?" he says, taking in a deep breath again to show me. "In and out. Slowly."

I try again. Air, pure clean air starts to fill my lungs until soon I'm gulping it like water.

"That's it," Fox says, resting his hand on my good shoulder and giving it a squeeze. "You're doing good. Keep it going."

And I do, lying on my back, staring up at my older brother and the dark clouds above him. I blink. I swear a bit of water just fell in my eye.

Fox looks up at the sky and then back to me, smiles. "You felt that huh? Rain. That'll make our job easier."

Then Rachel's face comes over my vision, tears pouring down her face.

I reach up for her and she takes my hand.

I want to tell her I'm okay but I don't think that's why she's crying.

She's crying from pure panic.

I roll my head over to see a couple of firefighters giving Vernalee CPR.

My father holds her hand as they do so.

He's crying.

Sobbing.

"Please don't leave me," he cries out to her. "Please don't

leave me Vernalee. I love you. I love you, I love you. This isn't the end. This is only the beginning. God, please, this is supposed to be the beginning."

My breath hitches in my throat, not from the smoke, but from the noose around my heart.

My poor father. My poor Rachel.

"Vernalee," he cries out, kissing her palm as his tears spill down. "You can't go. You can't go. This was supposed to be our second chance."

I look back up at Rachel. She's covering her face in her hands, my grandpa now beside her, putting his arm around her. I meet Fox's eyes and his are watering too.

He gives me a tense smile. "Keep breathing, Shane. You're going to be okay."

But even as he says that, I see him frown at me.

Then my eyes start to roll back in my head as pain, exquisite pain, starts to tear through my body.

I cough and gulp for air, my heart beat slowing and slowing until I think it's covered in quicksand, and then Fox is yelling for someone, sounding panicked now.

I take in a breath but I don't think it does any good.

Everything goes black.

My world goes quiet.

And cold.

CHAPTER 23

RACHEL

I remember when I was nine years old and my parents first told me that we were moving from our suburb outside of Edmonton down to a tiny town in the mountains of British Columbia.

They told me over dinner and like usual, I didn't react. The most I would do was nod my head and silently agree, no matter what it was. At that time, my father wasn't sexually abusing me. That started when I was about twelve. But I was still frightened to death of him, probably egged on by the fact that my mother was too.

He would often pull me aside when my mother wasn't looking or listening and tell me wonderful things only to knock me down at the end. He would do this repeatedly and I would believe it because I didn't know any better. He was my father. He was my protector and provider, my ruler, my world. What he said was gold. It was the last word and the only word.

The day he told me we were moving, that he'd gotten a new important position at the RCMP station in North Ridge, was the day I first felt hope.

I thought, maybe, maybe if we went to North Ridge, that life would get better. I thought maybe he would love his job and be happy and if he was happy, he would be nicer to me. I thought maybe my mother would smile more. I thought a lot of things.

The drive down to North Ridge took two days and a lot of driving and I knew better than to ask for any restroom breaks or to take pictures of the elk on the side of the road and we kept going and all I could think about was pulling into town (at the moment I think I had a picture of a Swiss alpine village in my head) and having my life really begin again. New friends, new school, new parents, a new life.

North Ridge was my second chance.

And I remember it still felt like that, even as we moved into our new house. It even had a white picket fence, just like the movies, and the house itself was painted a brilliant blue with red trim.

That day I truly believed that everything was going to be better.

My parents were all smiles.

They even looked in love.

That night I went to bed and my father came in.

He normally didn't tuck me in at night and I guess I should have thought it was odd but I thought maybe this was the new dad, the one that cares.

"Rachel," he said to me, sitting on the edge of the bed.

I nodded because I still wasn't brave enough to speak.

"I hope you like your new town. I think we might fit in here just fine. You'll have new friends and new teachers and it will be like starting fresh, don't you think?" I kept on nodding, smiling even a little. He cleared his throat and his piercing eyes swung to me. "Just remember one thing. It's a fresh start but it's our only fresh start. I'm in charge of this town now and people will respect me. They will. You'll see.

I'll have all the power and the privilege a little place like this will give me. So don't you dare screw anything up for me."

I blinked at him, scared at the tone of his voice.

"If you're going to be my daughter, you have to do as you're told. You have to work hard and keep your head down. You don't need friends, you don't need distractions, you don't need anyone but your mother and your father. You need to stay out of my way. You need to not exist, you understand what I'm saying?"

My father didn't want me as a distraction.

But I became a distraction anyway.

I tried so hard to not exist.

And I failed.

Until I met Shane.

When I sat next to him in class, my world changed.

Slowly, very slowly, day by day, Shane pulled me out of my shell. He was the only person in the world I could truly be myself with, even when I didn't know who I was. He helped me discover everything I could be.

He taught me how to exist.

I owe him the world.

I owe him my life.

And now I'm sitting in the North Ridge hospital waiting room and waiting for the news about him and about my mother.

The fire burned the worker's cottage to the ground.

Even a whole team of firefighters and a spattering of rain did nothing to stop it from happening. The only thing they were able to save was the stable, though the ponderosa pines are just charred skeletons.

I knew that when Shane ran back into the house, that I might not ever see him again.

I can't describe the terror that gripped me, a dark, malevolent fist gripping me from the inside out. The fact that I might lose both of them.

They were both rushed to the hospital. At first it seemed like Shane was doing okay. While Hank was crying over my mother, pleading for her not to leave him, Shane was looking up at me. Fox had revived him.

But then his eyes rolled back in his head and he was gone.

Just like that.

One team was trying to revive my mother, the other was trying to revive him.

And if Dick wasn't holding onto me, I'm sure I would have had to be revived as well.

Now, I'm waiting.

Waiting for good news, any news.

My mind wants to run away on me, it wants to focus on the dark, and I have to fight it tooth and nail to keep it out of the shadows. I can't think about those horrors, so I do my best to stay calm, to keep everything at the surface.

I'm not alone. Everyone else is here: Hank, Dick, Fox, Maverick, Delilah, even her mother Jeanine. We're all waiting in this damn room, our breath held in our throats, trying so hard to not fall apart.

Finally, a doctor appears with a nurse beside him. He looks grim.

It's at that moment I realize that everything is lost.

One of them is gone.

Maybe both.

We all get to our feet, though I'm hanging onto Hank as I do so and he's hanging onto me.

The doctor clears his throat and looks at the two of us. "Hank Nelson. Rachel Waters."

I make a breathless sound, like all life is draining out of me.

"I have good news."

I stare at him. Still, I can't breathe.

"What?" Hank whispers.

"Good news?" Dick says loudly. "If you have good news then why on God's green earth do you look so grim?"

The doctor looks at Dick and I didn't think it was possible for his frown to get any deeper but it does. "Come again?"

Obviously this is just his face. You'd think they'd get a doctor with a better one.

"What's the good news?" Fox asks impatiently.

"They're both on the mend," he says and everyone exhales one collected breath. "It was touch and go with Vernalee for a while. Her surgery and reduced lung capacity made the smoke inhalation that much worse. But they were able to revive her on the way over here."

"And Shane?" I ask. "How is he?"

"He's going to be okay. He's got a lot of second degree and some third degree burns, mainly on his shoulders and legs. He's going to be in a lot of pain for some time but he'll have medicine to manage it."

"Can we see them?" Hank asks.

"You can see Shane in a few hours. Vernalee needs a little more time but don't worry, you'll see her soon enough."

So we go back to waiting again, though this time the atmosphere in the room has completely changed. Finally, after hours and hours, another nurse comes out, the one they call nosy Beth, and I'm shown toward his room.

I look back over my shoulder at Hank and everyone else. "Hank, Fox, aren't you coming?"

"Take your time," Fox says. "We'll be right behind you."

I give them a grateful look, knowing how many things are bubbling up inside my heart, wanting to come out. There was so much I wanted to tell Shane even before he went inside that burning house and this just made me realize the longer I keep it in, the more damage it will do. He has to know how I feel, he has to know everything.

But when the nurse opens the door to his room and I see him lying there in the hospital bed, I don't even think I have any words at all.

Shane. My beautiful Shane.

He's attached to an IV, his arms and legs sticking out of his hospital gown, rigid. His shoulder is red and blackened in some spots, his legs pink and white. The burns look painful and there's a strange, unsettling smell in the air.

But he's looking at me, head back, unable to lift it. And he smiles.

God, that smile. It's everything good and pure and true in this world.

That smile is love.

"Shane," I whisper, inching closer to him.

He licks his lips. "I don't bite." His voice is raspy, like his throat and lungs are singed.

"How are you feeling?" I ask him even though I'm sure it's a stupid question.

"I feel fine now that you're here." He raises his hand and I slip mine inside. His arms aren't too badly burned but even so, I don't want him moving much.

"What have the doctors told you?" I ask him.

"That I'll live," he says, so soft that I have to lean in to hear him. His smile is crooked as he stares at me. "They said I'm lucky. Real lucky. Only my shoulder is pretty bad. Might have to get a skin graft on it. Might not. My legs will heal up. I'll have scars but all the best cowboys have scars."

I shake my head, biting down my grin. "Even after all this, you're still optimistic."

"Because you're here." He pauses. "I heard your mother is going to be fine."

"Only because of you."

"You tried to do the same. I couldn't let that happen. I would have lost you both."

I exhale steadily. "I wasn't thinking, obviously."

"You were beyond brave, Rachel."

"She would have done the same for me. I know that now. I didn't know that before, but I know that now."

I give his hand a gentle squeeze, aware of the nurse lingering out in the hallway, talking to the rest of the group. "Listen," I tell him. "I won't keep you too long—"

"You don't mean that," he says, wheezing. "Please, keep me long. Keep me forever."

God, I'm melting. How is he still able to bring me to my knees, time and time again?

"Shane," I tell him. "I'm not going anywhere. I'm staying here in North Ridge. With you."

"These pain meds are sure fucking good," he says. "I could have sworn you said you were staying in North Ridge."

"You might be high but I mean every word I say. I'm not leaving you."

He frowns, looking at me with apprehension. "Don't stay out of pity..."

"It's not pity, Shane. It's love. I love you. I never stopped. I only stopped believing that I deserved love, your love. I want to spend my days with you, I want to live my life here. I want to start over, fresh, from scratch, and get things right. I know now what really matters and that fear...well, fuck fear. I'll use it, I won't cower from it."

He swallows hard, his gorgeous eyes growing misty. "I don't even know what to say."

"Say nothing. You've said so much and I've been nothing but lucky to hear it. It's my turn now to give. I love you Shane Nelson and I love you wild. You're my heart and my home and my whole damn life. I promise."

I bend over and kiss his forehead, his nose, his lips. Softly, sweetly, but trying to tell him all that he is to me, all that he will be.

"I love you," he whispers back.

"Are you two done having your heart-to-heart?" Dick's voice booms from behind us. "You don't want to get him too excited, Rachel, though I guess this is the hospital and if he has a heart attack he's in pretty good hands."

Shane and I smirk at each other before I turn around.

Dick is at the door with Hank and everyone else.

"He's all yours," I tell them, stepping back and making a flourishing gesture.

"And it sounds like you're all ours too," Hank says, giving my shoulder a squeeze. "I'm glad you decided to stay."

I grin at him, my heart feeling so impossibly full at all of this, all of them.

My family.

Turns out you can go home again.

CHAPTER 24

SHANE

Two weeks.

It's been two whole weeks since Rachel left me and went back to Toronto.

If it were any longer, I'm pretty sure my heart would call it quits on me. I know two weeks is nothing compared to six years but I swore to God she'd never be out of my sight again.

Thankfully, she is coming back.

Today.

I'm currently parking my Tacoma at Kelowna's airport, counting down the minutes until her plane lands.

When Rachel told me she wanted to move back to North Ridge and live her life with me at the ranch, I thought I couldn't be that lucky. And even though that's all I ever wanted, I didn't want to make her seem like she had to. I didn't want her to feel pressured.

But she was adamant that it was what she wanted.

So I told her she was free to live with me in the guest house and then we'd figure out what to do next. I stood back and watched, wondering if she was really going to do this.

And she did. She stayed in North Ridge until I got better, until her mother got better, then she left.

In those two weeks, she's put her condo up for sale. She's quit her job at the ad agency. She's done all she can so she can have closure with that city and create another fresh start here.

The truth is, if she loved that city and wanted to stay, I would have followed her. I should have done that years ago, I should have tracked her down, I should have gone wherever she went. And if that was the way it had to be now, I wouldn't hesitate. I would leave North Ridge and the ranch behind. I would do what needed to be done in order to be with her.

It wasn't in the cards.

This hand didn't play out like I expected.

And *she's* my wild card.

When it's time to get her, I go inside the airport with a bouquet full of roses, gathered along with the other people waiting at Arrivals.

I watch the passengers exit. People are hugged, cheeks are kissed, tears are shed.

And still no Rachel.

My heart falls.

The last I heard from her was when she called me, the day before yesterday. Cell reception is spotty at the ranch, as usual. I thought maybe her texts weren't coming through but now that I'm in Kelowna with full bars, I don't see anything from her.

Maybe she changed her mind.

Maybe she decided it was too hard.

Maybe she decided to stay.

Shit.

Maybe it was too much, too soon, and it scared her. I know she's been here for me but maybe it was only because I was recovering from the burns, maybe she just couldn't tell me the truth.

Rachel...

And then, like a mirage floating in the distance, I see her.

She's dragging a carry-on suitcase behind her, looking wide-eyed and hopeful as she searches the crowd.

Then she sees me.

Runs to me.

I grab her in front of everyone.

I don't care.

I kiss her.

Hard.

It's completely different from how we last kissed before she left. That was soft and tentative.

This one is hunger.

I am *starved* for her.

I've been starved for her for the past two weeks. I've done nothing but dream about her, about all the things I want to do. All the promises we've made, the promises we'll keep.

Now she's here, in my arms, and I'm slowly unraveling.

"I didn't think you were coming," I tell her breathlessly.

She grabs my face, peering deep into my eyes. "I'm here."

I pull back and hand her the flowers which are now a little crushed. "Sorry. These are for you."

"They're gorgeous, Shane. You shouldn't have." Her cheeks flush and she looks so damn adorable I want to pick her up all over again.

And I do. I pick her up, twirl her around, reveling in the fact that she's here and she's mine.

"I booked us a hotel," I tell her later as we get her two massive bags from baggage claim and bring them to the truck. "We aren't driving back to North Ridge tonight."

The hotel is a massive, fancy one along the shores of Lake Okanagan. Since her flight landed in the afternoon, we have time to relax on the beach if we want to. It may be October now but the temperature is still holding strong here and the numerous vineyards in the area are in full swing, though give it a few more days and things will start to get cold.

But we aren't here to explore or make a vacation out of it.

The only place I want Rachel right now is lying in that plush hotel bed.

We get up to the room and I take her flowers, plucking off the petals and scattering them all over the floor and the bed. Well, they were crushed anyway.

Then I'm on her.

I unleash myself on her neck, licking and sucking until she's starting to weaken at the knees, soft moans falling from her mouth. Honey on my tongue. Music to my ears.

I get undressed to my briefs in a flash, she's ripping her shirt over her head and I drop to my knees to help her out of her skirt and underwear. I pull the skirt down first and peer up at her as my hands slowly work their way back up her thighs.

She grabs a hold of my hair instead for balance.

My fingers find her underwear, the thin material damp with her desire.

"God, you're so wet for me," I murmur, staring up at her. "Can I make you wetter?" I move her panties to the side and slip my finger along her, the sensation making me delirious with lust. She lets out a lengthy moan, her hands tighter in my hair. "I want my cock to slide into you, just like this." I add an extra finger and move them in together. "Just like this," I whisper as my fingers go along. "You want it deeper?"

She groans and I look up to see her arch back, her breasts pointed forward, her sweet, pink nipples tight and hard.

My beautiful raven girl.

"Do you want my cock?" I ask softly, knowing she loves it

when I'm bold. "My tongue? How would you like me to fuck you?"

"Any way," she says through another moan as I drive my fingers even deeper. "Shane..."

She trails off into a moan as I press my face in, my tongue snaking out and licking up to her clit. "You taste so good," I murmur into her and she shudders from the vibrations. "Like you belong on my mouth, your taste made for my tongue." I pause and look up at her. "You were made for me, you know that?"

I suck her clit into my mouth, wet, warm, and she gives a sharp cry, calling out my name in such a way that it will be my undoing if she keeps this up.

I pull away and stand up. Her eyes are half-closed, dazed, mouth open.

Gorgeous.

Even though it's just a few steps to the bed I pick her up and carry her over, laying her down on her stomach on top of the strewn petals.

She pulls herself forward so that she's in the middle of the bed and I climb on top of her, my thighs on either side of hers, tanned skin against pale, straddling her just below her ass. The burns that run down my thighs are horrible to look at but when they're contrasted with her beauty, they only remind me how lucky I really am.

I grab my cock at the base and steadily push it in between her legs, into her as deep as I can go. She feels like a tight velvet fist. So damn soft. So real.

With a shuddering breath, I press my hand down on her shoulder, slowly pulling myself out, then back in, trying to find the rhythm. My thighs are doing most of the work, shaking slightly, the muscles popping as I move faster and faster, my cock disappearing entirely inside her.

My hips circle and I shorten my thrusts so I don't slip out.

She's wet down to the middle of her thighs and I want to stay inside her deep like this, firmly packed. It's such a fucking squeeze that a sweat is breaking out at my temples, my muscles wound too tense.

I know I won't last much longer, but it doesn't matter.

We have all night.

And we have all the nights after.

I move one hand down to her waist and grip her while the other squeezes in between her hips and the mattress until I reach her clit. It's soaked and my finger slides over it with ease.

That's all it takes.

Her body tenses and then starts to quake beneath me. She pulses around my cock, her clit throbbing under my finger. A sharp cry leaves her lips, then fades off into breathless little moans that bounce off the walls.

I come immediately after. There's a rush along my spine until something at the base of me explodes. I grunt like an animal, thrusting deeper and deeper, the bed shaking. The neighboring rooms are getting quite the show.

I exhale loudly, trying to find my breath again, my heart thudding to a marching beat inside my head. I lean back on my thighs, absently run my hands over her ass while I remember how to breathe. Then, when it doesn't feel like I'm having a heart attack, when the sweat stops rolling off my brow, I gently pull out.

Leaning forward, I put my lips to her ear. "Did you miss that?"

She turns her head, her eyes closed and makes a sweet murmur of agreement.

I brush the hair off her face and kiss her cheek. Then place tiny, soft kisses on her neck, shoulder, down her spine.

"Welcome home," I whisper.

EPILOGUE
RACHEL

A waft of cigarette smoke hits my nostrils seconds before Delilah cries out, "Damn it Joe! What in God's name did I tell you about smoking?"

I bite back a laugh as she leaps over the bar like some kind of superhero and stalks across the peanut-shell covered floor to where Old Joe is sitting in his usual booth. I've seen this scene play out weekly over the last four months I've been living in North Ridge and the only difference in tonight is that Joe isn't sitting alone. In fact, he's got a lady friend sitting with him, who I'm pretty sure is Suzy Richardson who used to be the cafeteria lady in high school.

I watch as Del gets to his table, about to rip the cigarette from his lips, then pauses once she notices he has company.

"Oh, sorry," she says, looking between the two of them. With a hand on her hip she puts on her most pleasant voice. "Joe, you know the rules. You can't smoke in here. Besides, it's not exactly the best manners to be smoking in front of your gal."

At that Joe's old face turns beet red, all the way to his white hair and he gives Suzy an apologetic shrug.

Del turns around and heads back to the bar, exchanging an exasperated smile with me and rolling her eyes.

"Well that's a first," she says to me as she begins to wipe down the bar. "All my years here and I've never seen Old Joe with a woman."

"It does get pretty cold in the winter," I tell her. I'm not kidding either. It's early March and the snow has been falling steadily for weeks now. I guess it's a good sign since the snow packs the ski hills and glaciers and ensures that next summer we aren't so low on water, but I'm not used to the temperature. Sure, it got extremely cold in Toronto but that was a city. You were usually inside a building and the city was a maze of lights. In North Ridge it gets black as sin, which makes everything seem even colder.

"Right," Del says, "I guess when you get older you're more likely to settle for anyone."

I glance over my shoulder at them. Joe has the cigarette stubbed out and is chatting away to Suzy, who is leaning forward on her elbows and listening to everything he's saying. It doesn't seem like either of them are settling but I can't blame Del for being cynical. I'm acutely aware of how badly she has it for Fox and how oblivious Fox is.

The bar is pretty empty tonight. A lot of the skiers and snowboarders who come into town are young and are usually at the more obnoxious establishments in town. The Bear Trap is pretty even keel, which is great. It's really become like a second home to me (again).

I thought at first that it would take a bit to get back into the small-town, everyone knows everything, North Ridge, swing of things, but it's like I never left at all. Actually, that's not true. The town isn't the same as it was when I used to live here. My father is gone, put away for good, my mother and I finally have a good and honest relationship, and I'm making new friends. Sure, none of them stay for long but ever since we rebuilt the worker's cottage and added an additional structure, we've been able to turn it into an Air B&B.

It's perfect, actually. Not only does it bring us extra income, which is always needed on that damn ranch, but I finally feel like my skills are being used for the best. I'm able to create amazing advertisements and copy and make sure the place is consistently booked. In fact, I've heard from a few guests already that it's one of the best places to stay in the area, which is pretty amazing because it's only been going for a few months now.

So maybe the reason the town is better is because I'm better. I'm finally doing something I love and really love. Not something I thought I had to do because it was different, because I had something to prove. I never loved advertising, I just liked that I could do something that was hard. But there are plenty of things that challenge you because they are a labor of love.

Running the B&B is definitely that.

Shane, on the other hand, is not a challenge at all. Being with him, loving him, is the easiest thing in the world.

I know they say that you can't go home again and in some ways, I think that's true. Because when you leave, you change. But that doesn't mean a place can't be a home to you again, it just means it becomes a new one. We all carry this yearning in our hearts for a place for us to truly belong. Somewhere where we can be ourselves and give love and receive love and never have to worry about the cost.

North Ridge is that place to me. And I've made a home for myself right inside Shane's heart. I know now that I never have to be afraid or feel alone again, not while we're together.

A cold blast of air hits me as the door to the pub opens and I swing my head around to see a familiar sight. Not just Shane, shaking off snowflakes from his jacket, but Hank and my mother.

Hand in hand.

You think it would be weird to have my mother dating my boyfriend's father but the truth is, it feels right. Like it always should have been this way. My mother took a few wrong turns in life, fell for the wrong man, but even though what he did to us both was horrific, she was still able to find the man she always should have been with.

And Hank, wonderfully grumpy Hank, he turns into a smitten kitten when he's around her. It's adorable to see, especially since Dick has told me on more than a few occasions that he hasn't seen his son that happy since before Emily died. Both Hank and my mother have had to overcome loss of love in different forms and managed to find each other. They were broken but they loved with all their broken pieces until they were made whole.

When my mother and I decided to press charges against my father, we really weren't sure what the outcome would be. In fact, the first lawyer that we hired had advised against it, telling us there was no point, since my father wasn't going to be coming out of prison anytime soon.

Needless to say, we got another lawyer, one who completely agreed with our need for closure and for the correct justice to be served. It takes a long time for things to go through the courts here, but it's been set in motion now and every day I'm more and more grateful that my mother decided to take a stand and proud that I had the courage to stand with her.

My mother waves at me cheerfully and comes over, gesturing to the empty bar stools beside me.

"Are these taken?" she asks me.

I roll my eyes. "Even if they were, I'm sure Del could get them to move in a second."

At that, Del flexes her biceps. They're actually pretty impressive.

"Sorry I'm late," Shane says, coming over to give me a kiss on the head before sitting down on the other side of me. "We had some trouble in the snow."

"Think it's about time to get a new truck," Hank grumbles. "Lord knows how you'll be able to afford it."

"Technically," I say to Hank as he sits beside my mother, "Dick promised Shane a truck for Christmas."

"And how would Dick afford a new truck?"

Hank grumbles again. "He has his ways. I wouldn't be surprised if he had a treasure chest hidden somewhere on the property. He told me when he was young he used to save every single penny his mother would give him for candy until he was finally able to buy his own damn pony."

"We'll see," Shane says as he gestures to the keg, nodding at Del. "I'm pretty sentimental about the old girl. I won't give up on her until she's truly done with me."

I can't help but smile. It sounds a lot like Shane's attitude toward me. And thank God he didn't give up. He was resilient in his love for me and didn't stop trying until I was finally brave enough to see the truth.

He loves me beyond reason, just as I love him. And love either makes you afraid or brave. I chose to be brave.

Del pours Shane a pint, gets Hank a glass of whisky and my mother a cider. I get another beer and lean against Shane, feeling all my worries slip away. There might be a snowstorm raging outside but beside Shane I feel as safe as can be.

Another cold blast comes in, a few snowflakes floating across the bar.

Everyone turns to look because that's what you do in a place like this, but instead of seeing Fox, who was supposed to come by tonight, or maybe even Maverick if he's off-duty, it's someone I've never seen before.

And she's fucking gorgeous. Fairly tall, slender and pale with long blonde hair, pouty lips and sweet green eyes. I mean, it's pretty rare you see a babe like that in North Ridge, let alone the Bear Trap pub.

Del doesn't seem to miss a beat though and smiles at the newcomer.

"What can I get for you tonight?" she asks.

"A glass of white wine, please," the girl says. Her accent sounds American.

I know none of us should be staring but we all watch as she goes and sits in a booth, takes out a paperback from her leather knapsack and starts reading. I guess she doesn't know that Del's not exactly a waitress.

"Do you know her?" I ask Del as she pours her wine.

"Not really," she says, keeping her voice low. "She came in the other night. Ordered a wine, read a book. Her name is Riley, that's about all I know."

"Oh," Shane says slowly as Del goes over and drops off the drink at Riley's table. I hope she's happy with the house wine because that's all this place has.

"What?" I ask.

He looks over his shoulder at her and then back at me, nodding. "She's the new hire at the Search and Rescue."

"You mean with Maverick?"

"Yeah. Mav said they hired a woman from Colorado called Riley. He says he hasn't met her yet..." Shane trails off and starts grinning. "Man, he is going to hate this so much."

"Hate having to work around a hot piece of ass?"

"Rachel," my mother admonishes.

"What? She's got a good ass."

"I haven't noticed," Shane says, totally straight faced. "And anyway. Yes. Maverick is the head of the crew, he can't go around screwing the people he works with and believe me...he's going to fall head over heels for her."

I can't help but smirk. "Good. It's about time he can only look at something and not touch it."

"You're right about that. Oh man. If only I could be a fly on the wall."

I look back at Riley who seems to be totally engrossed in a book. "She's reading something with an Oprah Book Club sticker on it. She might even be smart enough to stay away from Maverick in the first place."

"Let's hope," Shane says.

We spend the next couple hours at the pub drinking, though Shane just has a glass or two because he's driving. The Riley chick stays for almost the whole time, giving us all a shy smile as she leaves and steps out into the cold.

"We should probably head back too," Shane says to me.

"We're going to stay for a bit longer," my mother suddenly says.

"Really?" My mom is not the type to stay long at a pub, in fact I'm kind of surprised she and Hank decided to come tonight to begin with.

"You two go ahead," Hank says and I swear to God he winks at me.

I glance at Shane, eyebrows raised. "Okay?"

"I'll give them a ride home later," Del speaks up.

"Suit yourself," I tell them as I get off the stool. "Don't do anything I wouldn't do."

"Don't worry about us," Hank says. "Just go and enjoy yourself."

Go and enjoy ourselves? It's a Saturday night, nothing unusual about it at all. Usually we just go to the bar, then come back home, drink some whisky by the fire and have crazy sex and I'm pretty sure that's not what he meant. If he did...well, maybe we've all gotten a little *too* close.

We open the door and step outside, the winter air hitting me right in the face. I shiver, pulling my toque down until it covers my eyebrows, tucking my scarf into the collar of my parka. Shane grabs my arm and helps me down the snowy steps to the parking lot where cars sit amongst snows drifts. Under the streetlamps, the snow dances with an orange glow, swirling together in time with the howling wind.

"Fuck it's cold," I say.

Shane doesn't say anything and when we reach the truck, he reaches out and pulls me to a stop.

"Rachel," he says and there's a strange nervousness about him, the way his eyes are both hopeful and cagey, the way he's pressing his lips together. Snowflakes gather in his brows, pile up on the shoulders of his coat.

"What?"

He's either about to say something amazing to me or something totally horrible and I honestly can't tell. I've never seen him this anxious before.

He closes his eyes, breathes in deep through his nose and gives his head a little shake.

"I'm going to make this short and sweet," he eventually says.

Uh oh.

He goes on, managing a smile. "Mainly because it's cold as fuck and when I originally had this all planned in my head it was the end of summer and everything was still sweltering hot. But anyway. Rachel, I know that this is just a parking lot to most but it's more than a parking lot to us."

I raise my brow, looking around. Looks like just a parking lot to me.

"This," he says, grabbing my left hand and slowly pulling off my glove. "This is the place where we came apart, a distance that could have lasted forever had you not come back to North Ridge, had we both not found each other again. Had we not been brave enough to try again. I don't want this parking lot to stand for that. I want it to be the place where we finally came together."

Part of me wants to point out that he's waxing poetic

about a parking lot and the other part, well that part is yelling SHUT UP RACHEL AND LET HIM TALK!

"Rachel Waters," he says, his voice shaking. He drops to one knee in the snow and looks up at me with so much love that I've got a universe expanding in my chest.

I can't believe this is happening.

Is this even happening?

"I've loved you since forever and you have my whole heart for my whole life. Will you do me the honor of becoming my wife?"

He holds out a rose gold ring that glows amongst the snow.

Oh my god.

It's so beautiful.

This is so beautiful and it's going so fast and I need to hold onto this forever and—

"Are you going to say yes?" Shane asks. "Because I can't feel my fingers anymore."

I burst out laughing.

"Yes!" I cry out. "Yes, of course, yes. I will be your wife. I will marry the hell out of you."

I expect him to slide the ring on my finger but he just holds it out to me. "Read the inscription."

I peer inside the ring.

It's engraved: *This was what I wished for.*

And the tiny symbol of a wishbone.

I glance at Shane and now the tears are coming, though they're freezing on my cheeks. "That's what you wished for all those years ago, when we were nine?"

He nods. "I wished I'd marry you one day," he says earnestly. "And I spent a long time holding out for it to be true. I still have that half a wishbone saved, tucked away in my closet. I don't need it anymore."

"No, you don't," I say, wiping away my tears while he slides the ring on. A perfect fit. "My mother gave me a wishbone before her surgery and I saved it, too afraid to wish on it. Now I don't need to. Shane, I'm yours forever."

"My wish come true."

Suddenly applause and hoots and hollers fill the air and Shane gets to his feet as we turn and see everyone crowded at the entrance to the pub. Hank, Vernalee, Del, even Old Joe.

"Way to go, cowboy!" Del yells.

"We're so happy for you!" shouts my mother.

"Beers are on me," says Old Joe, attempting to light a cigarette that Del snatches out of his fingers and tosses into the snow.

"Now will you two get back inside here before you get frostbite and we can celebrate?" Hank mutters, shaking his head. "Sheesh. Young kids these days, you know?"

"Oh I know," Vernalee says, kissing him happily before they go back inside.

"Come with me, future Mrs. Shane Nelson," Shane says, taking my hand in his and holding tight.

"Whatever you wish," I tell him and let him lead me home.

THE END

THANK YOU SO MUCH FOR READING WILD CARD! THE NEXT book in the series—the super spicy and thrilling Maverick—is available HERE!

ACKNOWLEDGMENTS

This book first published in August 2017 and as I am updating the content for these new covers (in this messed up year that is 2025), I realize I never wrote any acknowledgements for this book!

I could tell you why, though. It's not that I didn't have a ton of people to thank, but more than I was finishing up this book on the road. Literally. I was supposed to be done before our camping trip and of course that didn't happen. I finished up the book by a crackling fire during the first few days of our trip (and what an amazing trip that was...we took our "Egg"— the trailer we used to have—down south because the forest fires in BC were so bad that year, and we had to go as far as Florence, Oregon before the skies were clear. We just played it by ear and eventually ended up as far south as Donner Lake, California, where we watched the solar eclipse...also, if you've read Death Valley, you'll know the significance of that place).

Where was I? Oh yeah.

Anyway, I remember Aestas, a book blogger at the time who was super influential but hard to win over, actually took a chance on the book and LOVED it! That in turn helped me sell enough copies to get me on the USA Today Bestsellers list (as did the rest of the books in the North Ridge Series). I celebrated at Lake Tahoe with a bottle of champagne.

Suffice to say, being on the road, rushing to get the book uploaded before Amazon shut me out, etc is probably why I didn't write any acknowledgements for this book but let's see if I can come up with some...8 years later (*cries at the passage of time*)

Definitely have to thank my husband Scott for putting up with me writing on yet ANOTHER one of our vacations. My dog Boo-Boo Pants who was the best doggo ever! Aestas, who definitely helped make this book POP, as well as all my wonderful readers who heard I was doing a small-town cowboy book BEFORE small-town cowboy romances were popular and said YES PLEASE, I WANT THAT.

So thank you! And if you're new to this series, thanks for taking a chance on a contemporary of mine and I hope you enjoy Maverick (super spicy!) and Hot Shot (angsty AF with the most fucked up hero ever).

Karina Halle is a producer, screenwriter, a former music & travel journalist, and the New York Times, Wall Street Journal, and USA Today bestselling author of River of Shadows, The Royals Next Door, and Black Sunshine, as well as 80 other wild and romantic reads, ranging from light & sexy rom coms to horror/paranormal romance and dark fantasy. Needless to say, whatever genre you're into, she has probably written a romance for it.

When she's not traveling, she, her husband Scott, and their pup Perry, split their time between a possibly haunted 120-year-old house in Victoria, BC, their sailboat the Norfinn, and some sunny destination elsewhere in the world. For more information, visit www.authorkarinahalle.com

Find her on Facebook, Instagram, Pinterest, BookBub, Amazon, and Tik Tok.

ALSO BY KARINA HALLE

<u>*DARK FANTASY, GOTHIC & HORROR ROMANCE*</u>

River of Shadows (Underworld Gods #1)

Crown of Crimson (Underworld Gods #2)

City of Darkness (Underworld Gods #3)

Goddess of Light (Underworld Gods #4)

Black Sunshine (Dark Eyes Duet #1)

The Blood is Love (Dark Eyes Duet #2)

Nightwolf

Blood Orange (The Dracula Duet #1)

Black Rose (The Dracula Duet #2)

A Ship of Bones and Teeth

Ocean of Sin and Starlight

Hollow (A Gothic Shade of Romance #1)

Legend (A Gothic Shade of Romance #2)

Grave Matter

Darkhouse (EIT #1)

Red Fox (EIT #2)

The Benson (EIT #2.5)

Dead Sky Morning (EIT #3)

Lying Season (EIT #4)

On Demon Wings (EIT #5)

Old Blood (EIT #5.5)

The Dex-Files (EIT #5.7)

Into the Hollow (EIT #6)

And With Madness Comes the Light (EIT #6.5)

Come Alive (EIT #7)

Ashes to Ashes (EIT #8)

Dust to Dust (EIT #9)

Ghosted (EIT #9.5)

Came Back Haunted (EIT #10)

The Devil's Metal (The Devil's Duology #1)

The Devil's Reprise (The Devil's Duology #2)

Veiled (Ada Palomino #1)

Song For the Dead (Ada Palomino #2)

Demon Dust (2026)

Nocturne

Realm of Thieves

CONTEMPORARY ROMANCE

Love, in English/Love, in Spanish

Where Sea Meets Sky

Racing the Sun

The Pact

The Offer

The Play

Winter Wishes

The Lie

The Debt

Smut

Heat Wave

Before I Ever Met You

After All

Rocked Up

Wild Card

Maverick

Hot Shot

Bad at Love

The Swedish Prince

The Wild Heir

A Nordic King

The Royal Rogue

Nothing Personal

My Life in Shambles

The Royal Rogue

The Forbidden Man

The One That Got Away

Lovewrecked

One Hot Italian Summer

All the Love in the World (Anthology)

The Royals Next Door

The Royals Upstairs

9 781068 953675